# EARTHSHINE

## CHAD T. DOUGLAS

**EARTHSHINE**
by
Chad T. Douglas

Copyright © Chad T. Douglas 2015
Cover Illustration Copyright © 2015 Andraya Avery
Published by Mythos Press
(An Imprint of Ravenswood Publishing)

Ravenswood Publishing
6296 Philippi Church Rd.
Raeford, NC 28376
http://www.gmtapublishing.com

Printed in the U.S.A.

ISBN-13: 978-1507540152
ISBN-10: 1507540159

# TABLE OF CONTENTS

CHAD T. DOUGLAS

# 0.0
# BETΛ

*"What is lonelier, to be the last of your kind, or to be the first?"*
—Aldemund Ehrkindt, "father" of the Galatea Model 1

Accidents never happened at Tika Incorporated's product development facility. An underwhelming and inconspicuous structure with no windows or first floor entrances, it was intentionally hidden away in the lower districts of Genesia, Mars. Almost as old as the city itself, it was the birthplace of true artificial intelligence, private vehicular transport automation and the popular Tika brand personal neural assistant module.

Accidents never happened, at least not until the early morning of April 3, 2499 CE, and for just that reason, the scientists, security and other staff hugged the walls in chilled fear and anticipation as Geralt Schenck, head of software development, entered the facility's largest test atrium in the company of twenty armed police officers. His steady footsteps echoed as though they were two stones falling down an empty well, and even on the fourth floor the programmers peering over the railing could hear his administrator's white and black bodysuit crease when he sat down at a table in the center of the test floor. Schenck's receding and naturally silver and spiky rooster-crest head of hair attempted to undercut his severe demeanor, but the strict professional's long, jackal gaze hid his sleeplessness and curbed his outward anxiety.

"Ahem, stand 'round us in a hemispheric formation and concentrate your aim over my head at an imaginary point about half a meter in front of the subject's torso," he said clearly to the score of police officers escorting him. "If she acts out, you'll want to dispel the excess kinetic and thermal energy away from us so that no one is injured or killed by the blast cone."

The officers exchanged uneasy glances and followed Schenck's instructions without argument or debate. Schenck turned to face away from them and tried not to snicker. He knew they were already afraid, and perhaps it was mean spirited to prey on it for kicks, but every now and again it satisfied him to be able to yank back on the strings that yanked on Tika Incorporated every day, never allowing him to ask for anyone's pardon.

"Good morning, Mr. Schenck," said the woman across the table from Schenck. The robotic operating board underneath her rotated itself automatically to allow her to assume a standing position, and she struggled to turn her wrists in her restraints to wave to Schenck and the police officers.

"Good morning, Beta," Schenck answered her, folding his hands in his lap and sitting back in his chair.

"Why are all these men here?" she asked, turning her head with the slow acceleration of a wind-up toy, a glistening of digital images and words appearing briefly across her irises as she gathered data on each one of the men aiming their EMP and directed kinetic energy rifles at her. Her perfect, polished and bald head shone like a mirror, and her fair skin made her thin, dark eyebrows pop, complimenting her royal blue eyes.

"Don't pay them any mind, Beta. You experienced a lapse two days ago. At two hours, two minutes and seven seconds after midnight, you published anti-corporate, anarchist propaganda on more than thirty-thousand public, electronic sites and crashed a number of commercial shopping hubs. It caused these men a lot of grief, and I've invited them here to demonstrate that the problem has been resolved."

Schenck lifted a leg and calmly rested it across the other, cutting his eyes at a corner of the room where Ana Cassini, the chief of the State Investigation Bureau, stood behind two walls of shockproof glass. Her dark eyes probed Schenck and his android in vexation, her arms crossed as high and tight as her short, straight, black hair. Next to her, with a burly escort on each handcuffed arm, stood Andrew Rumford, the neural software engineer responsible for Beta's previously-assumed "behavioral glitches." Shrugging his shoulders and smirking through twenty-three days of unkempt stubble-going-on-beard, he rocked on his heels and shook his hair out of his eyes.

"Go ahead and have her prance for them, boss!" the smug young software designer shouted from behind the noise-resistant glass, "Beta's a good girl, now! Right, Beta?"

"Eyes on me, Beta," said Schenck, taking a small cube from his pocket and placing it on the table, "Now, recite *La Vie en Rose* for

7

me. Begin in French."

"Yes, Mr. Schenck," the woman replied with a cheerful smile. She did as she was told, the tone and pitch of her voice changing instantaneously as she began to sing in perfect French: "*Des yeux qui font baisser les miens, un rire qui se perd sur sa bouche, voilá le portrait sans retouche…*"

"Good, now in German?" Schenck fiddled with the little cube on the desk as Beta's sweet, soothing voice filled the test atrium and more scientists and staff gathered around the upper balconies and listened in.

"*… von dem Mann zu dem ich gehöre. Wenn er mich in den Arm nimmt …*" she continued on, changing tones without missing a beat.

"Korean!" someone in the climate control mezzanine shouted.

"Sure," Schenck agreed, turning around and cracking a relaxed smile as the police and Chief Cassini shared a chuckle as Beta continued her performance in a higher pitched Korean. "All right, all right, Beta. Say, I'm hungry for pad thai. How long will that take to make and what will we need to make it?"

"Pad thai? Easy!" she immediately stopped singing and began listing ingredients with the pep of a cooking show host, "Rice noodles, cornstarch, soy sauce, garlic, bean sprouts, onions, cilantro…"

"Who's hungry?" Schenck joked over a shoulder. "All right, Beta, I've changed my mind. I'm not hungry, but I could use some conversation. Tell me, what's your favorite story and why?"

"Oh! I've seen and read so many. It's hard to choose!" she exclaimed. "Have you ever read *Dracula*?"

"For the sake of demonstration, assume I haven't," replied Schenck.

"Oh, where do I begin ..." Beta then proceeded to briefly outline the plot before elaborating on every conceivable critical interpretation of the work, digressing every now and then and excitedly recalling her own, personal reaction to every twist and turn.

"The Galatea Model 10, ladies and gentlemen!" Schenck held out his arms like a proud parent. The scientists and police smiled and the room collectively began to exhale. "Okay, Beta, that's good. All right, now let's show them what your incredible brain can really do." Schenck looked across the room at Chief Cassini. *That's what you really came for, isn't it*, he thought to himself snidely. *You came here to spy on me for your superiors because they think everyone at Tika is a bleeding-heart quack like Rumford.* "All right," Beta, without using your hands, pick up the cube," he said, setting the little block down on the table once more.

"Yes, Mr. Schenck." Turning her head down, the woman on the robotic operating table fixed her gaze on the cube. *Wuum ...* A powerful vibration buzzed the chamber. *Wuum ... Wuuuum ...* The space between Beta and the cube shuddered like air over the hot asphalt of a desert road. The neural activity monitors on the hologram displays in the mezzanine began to report spikes unthinkable for a human being, but of course Beta wasn't human.

All eyes turned from the monitors to the woman on the test floor as the cube on the table in front of her rose up into the air and sat on a cushion of focused, controlled kinetic energy, and then came back to rest on the table once more.

A round of cheers erupted from the second and third floors and even a few of the skeptical police officers shook out some half-hearted claps.

"Ladies and gentlemen," Schenck said, standing with a confident smile, "The Galatea 10 is easily the most sophisticated re-creation of our accomplished species to date. Its cognitive and emotive capabilities almost fool one into thinking there's a real woman standing there against that operating board, and cutting-edge neural augmentations will soon render exoskeleton technology and who knows what else obsolete. Imagine, if you will, being able to lift fifty pounds ... or a *thousand* ... without the aid of prosthetics, using only your mind ..." Dramatically he touched his forehead and swept his gaze along the upper floors. "Imagine being able to survive a fall from a mile off the ground or flying without a vehicle."

"Tell them the other good news!" Beta chimed in.

"Ah! Thank you, Beta. How could I forget?" Schenck smiled. "We at Tika believe that within the decade, android safety and reliability will rate highly enough with AISA standards to abolish rights-restrictive practices preventing androids from becoming registered caregivers, both private and public." Slowly, his speech thawed a few more frowns.

"You build gods and what do you have them do?" shouted Drew Rumford as he momentarily pulled away from his police escorts and threw himself against the shockproof glass, "Have them clean bedpans and babysit and be obedient mistresses for your rich clients? Have them pick things up and put them down again with psychokinetic parlor tricks? You're a monster! She's not a tool! They're going to decommission you, Beta!" He turned his attention away from Schenck and began shouting at Beta. The android became noticeably alarmed.

"Shut up! Shut him up!" demanded Schenck, getting to his feet the second he caught a glimpse of something amiss in Beta's eyes.

"Resistance is not a glitch! Free will isn't something you can patch! They are gods! They could make us all better and you package them and market them like— agh!" Rumford buckled over as one of his escorts put an elbow in his diaphragm and began to remove him from the room.

"Pick things up … put them down," Beta mumbled to herself, her eyes growing wide and panicked.

"Beta?" Schenck turned to the android and walked around the table, taking out a flashlight and shining it in her left eye. A small, discreet red light blinked on the contour of her retina—a warning diode, tripped by a malfunction associated with her neural processing drives and, of most concern, the partitions dedicated to her kinetic energy projection centers.

"Pick things up … put them down," she said again. Looking up slowly from the table, she began to hum *La Vie en Rose* again and fixed her gaze on one of the police officers.

"Beta? Beta!" Schenck snapped his fingers in front of the android's nose and didn't receive even as much as a blink in response, "Beta! Begin sleep cycle one! Enter resting state!"

"*Hold me close and hold me fast ...*" the android's nostrils flared as she sang, and the police officer she stared at leapt into the air and froze, dangling on a cloud of humming kinetic energy.

"Beta, stop!" Schenck moved himself directly in front of the android to protect her from the officers as they fumbled their rifles and took aim at her as they backpedaled away from the table.

"*... The magic spell you cast ...*" Beta ignored Schenck, her eyes locked on the officer in the air as she manipulated the energy beneath him and whipped him across the room and into the shockproof glass in front of Chief Cassini.

"Neutralize her with EMP!" the Chief shouted, bursting from the room and into the atrium, drawing her sidearm.

"No! Just wait!" Schenck held out his arms and pleaded with Beta, putting his lips to her cheek and repeating every failsafe command he could think of.

"Get that man away from her!" The chief shouted as two bold officers tackled Schenck to the ground. They hit the floor as a pulse of invisible energy exploded from Beta and blew the remaining seventeen armed men off of their feet, breaking legs and arms and wrists.

"What did you do? What did you do?" Schenck clawed at the floor as he tried to pull himself out from under the two officers, jabbing a finger and swearing at Drew Rumford as his escorts wrestled him out of the atrium. The detained programmer slapped his knees and wheezed in pained laughter until he was out of sight. The next instant, several loud bangs rang out through the atrium, and the screams of frightened staff hushed as all hands covered their heads; several debilitating DKE rifle rounds beat Beta in the chest as the robotic operating table keeled backward and dumped her shivering body on the cold floor.

"Beta! Beta!" Schenck threw himself on the floor by the android's side and scooped his arms underneath her, trembling as he watched years of development and a handful of private fortunes vanish before his eyes.

"Please don't ... don't decommission me ... There's nothing wrong with ..."

Beta shook like a hypothermic infant. With every passing second another warning diode in the dark recesses of her eyes began to blink silently.

"That product," Chief Cassini huffed, holstering her weapon and clutching her knees, "is hereby ordered by the State Investigation Bureau to be..." she wiped a palm across her forehead and caught her breath.

"I know! Don't worry about it! Get the hell out of my facility!" Schenck turned and barked at the chief and all her wounded officers.

"You're lucky I don't make more trouble for you, and tell the SIB that your whole company is in league with that nutcase,

13

Rumford! Just for that, I'm ordering you all to begin this project again from the very start—project proposals and all! Everything from scratch, and every step had better be accompanied by a compulsory report to the Office of Private and Public Development Affairs! You hear me, Mr. Schenck? Don't you dare pull any more stunts as you showed us here, today! Who are you kidding? That thing isn't safe for a battlefield, let alone a babysitting job!" The Chief tied back her hair and ruffled her armored bodysuit at the shoulders, "And make sure the next freakish thing you build actually works before you name it!" With that, the chief activated her Tika module, a small, neural augmentation implanted in her head just above her eyes, and called for immediate medical assistance.

"Beta isn't a *name*," Schenck muttered under his breath. As he raised a hand to touch Beta behind her left ear and access her manual shutdown and neural wipe failsafe components, he stopped. Beta moved and looked Schenck in the eye. A drove of laboratory staff stormed the test floor, lugging heavy disassembly equipment in their arms, swarming Beta like a pit crew and ushering Schenck out of the way.

"Please, don't!" Beta pleaded. Her arms were too weak to hold back the staff and their instruments. Her bottom lip trembled and her mouth hung agape as she watched her lower right arm unclasped and unbolted at the elbow and pulled away in the hands of a man in a white lab coat. With the left arm, she reached out as the bottom of her right leg was dismantled and tossed aside like an

14

old tire.

Schenck brought one of his injured hands to his mouth. As much as he may have wanted, he could not look away. Summoning every bit of his will, he bit down on his cheek and clenched his teeth to keep the words behind them from slipping out in front of his colleagues and superiors. Beta said nothing more, her eyes searching his in fear and confusion for a moment longer before she shut them tight, turning her head and wincing as the staff opened her skull and began the manual override routines that would turn off her conscious mind.

"*And though I close my eyes …*" she began to sing again. Her blue eyes fluttered open and dribbled tears, "*I see la vie en rose…*" Staring off across the test floor, synthetic blood substitute and coolant trickling from the corner of her lips, Beta sang herself to sleep.

# 1.0
# SPHERES OF TOMORROW

*"Wherever humankind should venture, human nature will certainly follow."*
—Jane Lillian Ashley, founder of the Church of the Filii Solis, 2402 CE

Nearly fifty years after the Beta incident, Ian and Jamila LaKay—a young, native New York graduate student of journalism, and a younger, recently immigrated Lebanese ballet student—boarded a crowded ARC shuttle at Ellis International Aerospace Center and left America for a better life on Mars. Like everyone else on board, many other young couples included, Ian and Jamila hoped to soon see a spiny patchwork of white freckles on the face of the Red Planet, a city-state owned and governed by the Genesis MTI Corporation, aptly named Genesia.

Following the turn of the 25$^{th}$ century, Genesia had replaced all other human nations as the paradigmatic land of opportunity—the city of cities for the young, the old, the wealthy, the poor, the dreaming and the desperate. Like all other immigrants to Genesia, Ian and Jamila passed through Hawking Bay, the largest receiving center for interplanetary flights in the city, and one of only three built above ground—a shimmering, ovine complex buzzing with aerospace traffic, Hawking Bay appeared to grow in size as the ARC shuttle approached for landing. As it received the shuttle, its broad, sweeping canopy cast a great shadow upon the shuttle, and all the passengers hushed in anticipation. A pleasant, soothing voice came over the sound system, announcing their arrival had been successful and ahead of schedule.

When the boarding platforms extended and lowered, emptying the ARC shuttle's passengers into Hawking Bay's central civilian traffic atrium, Ian, Jamila and hundreds of others stopped to shield their eyes and gaze upward, mouths agape. For the first time they looked at the great monuments—statues of Genesia's founders that adorned the soaring glass walls, which buttressed the pressurized airways containing the landing platforms outside of Hawking Bay. A wild, orange desert and a fiery sky surrounded them in all directions. Mighty, transparent windows and ceilings protected them from blasting winds and solar radiation, while the outstretched rhodium arms of two-hundred foot tall likenesses of the famous android Piers Pelops and shipping empire mogul Siyang Chen welcomed all through the gateway to the Red Planet. Between them hung a great banner that read, "From ideal hearts and minds is born an ideal city." Fear and excitement gripping their spirits, Ian and Jamila held hands and staid their breath, wondering what great possibilities awaited them just inside… Genesia's crystal doors.

\* \* \* \*

For twenty-two years, three months and seven days, Ian and Jamila's great-grandson Caan had woken up each day to a Martian sunrise. On an ordinary morning in the year 2622 CE it rose to heat the edges of the white blinds of his bedroom window a bright orange like hot steel ingots and stained the soft white walls with sienna stripes just as it did every day. Instead of walking outside and looking up past the clouds and seeing blue, Caan and all Genesians were an audience to alien orange. The megalopolis outside his bedroom window was monumental, sleek, soft, clean and strong, a geometric statement of human authority over the xenographic desert. Skyscrapers on Earth couldn't hold a candle to Mars's shortest human artifices. Even some mountains didn't come close. Martian architecture epitomized use of vertical space. Many Genesians lived more than a few thousand feet from the ground, and that was where Caan was most comfortable. Almost a mile from the ground, he gazed outside as he dressed and could see the farthest reaches of the city, the forests, farms and other spheres of wilderness carefully packaged and segregated from inner civilization. The harsh atmosphere outside his windows changed suddenly, affecting the air between his interior window and the reinforced pane outside. The inside window fogged momentarily, and he wrote a message in the perspiration for Benni, his girlfriend, who lived across the way in the west tower of Nioua Point, a super residential complex fo average to average-high income Genesian families.

* * * *

Benni Dublanc woke up that day about ten minutes after Caan. Just as always, she opened her eyes to the message: "Tika Personal Assistant—we're always with you," in semi-transparent font stamped across her field of view. As her Tika module exited sleep mode, a digital desktop overlay replaced the message and another appeared: "Good morning, Benni." Benni swiped the greeting away with nothing more than a thought and closed the applications she'd left running when she'd fallen asleep the previous night. Once the clutter vanished from her sight, she got out of bed.

Looking out her bedroom window, she saw the words "good morning" written on Caan's. Tika always beat him to it. As she watched the small early morning sun outside her window, she lost sight of it through a burst of misty clouds emanating from a nearby greenhouse gas production plant. The moisture sparkled, refracted the morning sunlight and cast rainbows across the sky, then was quickly sucked up and blown away by a passing ARC shuttle. The great space ship crept past Nioua Point and darkened Benni's bedroom, its powerful engines barely vibrating the walls and floor such that it tickled her feet and she danced around in surprise and leapt back onto her bed. After the shuttle passed by Benni walked back to her window and looked at the rising sun again. It did not hurt her eyes because a dark, circular shadow in the sky followed it up from the horizon—a special space station named Newet. It was one of five that was programmed to continually cast a protective umbra on the city, always hovering overhead in geosynchronous orbit, screening the city from radiation. When Benni was six or seven years old, her favorite children's story was *The Sun's Many Shadows*, a book about the space stations. Now twenty-two years old, Benni belonged to the tenth generation of Dublancs who had lived under the protection of massive space stations like Newet.

As the air conditioning came on, Benni imagined she could smell trees. The air filling her apartment and the rest of the tower that morning came from vast farms outside the city, one of only a few places civilians were not allowed to go. In truth, trees were mostly for show. The city's natural, supplemental oxygen mainly came from large quantities of less romantic sources that were easier to grow and more space efficient—algae and the like. Although the farms grew real plants in real soil with real water and everything else one would expect, there was, in a sense, no such thing as "outside" in Genesia. Its original designers even took to calling the outermost structure the "chrysalis"; Genesia's skeleton had been designed to protect and contain a masterpiece within. Every street, every park, every airway and every building was sealed up tight and safe, typically behind atmosphere-proof glass— hundreds and hundreds of billions of square feet of the stuff contributed to Genesia's topical appearance. Benni liked to think that Genesia was not unlike a bunch of jars of different shapes and sizes, some arranged inside of others but all ultimately arranged inside of one big jar that never opened. It was like New York or Tokyo, only flipped inside-out, or rather, outside-*in*.

Benni closed her eyes and breathed deeply again. She had been to almost all of the city's parks and seen, touched and, once—just because she was dared to—licked a tree. When she went to the parks, it wasn't always for the trees. Benni liked to sit on a bench and create digital artwork from time to time, as long as she didn't already have a project due for one of her classes at Academy Aeraea, the state-funded institute of the arts for privileged students.

Benni was late for class that particular morning, which was not at all unusual. Her daydreams were always her scapegoat, and she refused to leave her apartment without looking her best.

"Beauty isn't everything," Benni always told Caan and her friends and peers, "but appearances are!" Always thinking in terms of design, Benni prioritized quality of expression over technical perfection, whether she was sculpting a masterpiece, applying makeup or downloading a new fashion design into her digital wardrobe.

After getting dressed she promptly scooted a little tomato plant on her dresser into the warm, filtered rays of the sun. The pot it grew in bore the ARC logo, which stood for Allied Response Convoy. Everything was brought to Mars on ARC shuttles at one time or another. Food, clothing, machinery, building materials— the people owed everything to the allied nations on Earth who originally drew up the blueprints for Genesia and came sailing the void to land on Mars and affix humanity to the orange dust.

\* \* \* \*

Genesis MTI, a leading multinational corporation and cutting-edge research and development giant, advocated for the entire project. The first global company to ever achieve "extramarket" status, Genesis MTI was also the first corporation-state. Genesis MTI transcended corporate status in 2203 CE, having no specific national loyalties and no official base of operations. It began to seek recognition as a cyber-sovereign, since it had no geographic claims or physical base, other than colossal offices and a network of headquarters in all corners of Earth.

As a cyber-sovereign, the company was met with mixed reactions, criticism and much controversy. The solution proposed by Genesis MTI, with the agreement and cooperation of many major world powers, including much of Europe, the Americas, China, Saudi Arabia and India, was to pool resources to establish the first extraterrestrial human colony on Mars.

The Dandelion Initiative, as the project would be called later, was passed. Genesis MTI officially settled Genesia in 2349 and began to repay its investors on Earth with startling and amazing new technologies that had become possible only because of the collective sums of wealth carried by the superpowers back home. The rest of its debts were assumed to be paid back by way of the newly established export of minerals and other resources garnered from Martian mining operations—copper, for example, among the more urgent, and ice among the list of limited needs.

\* \* \* \*

The lazy way Benni showered every morning made light of the fresh water ration policies on Mars. In less than a minute, a Martian shower could have her spotless as the face of an egg, but efficiency and comfort were not terms Benni used together.

Two other things she didn't do at the same time were sitting down and eating. No modern, active person, especially an academy-level student like Benni, had sat down to eat since a time no one could recall. Benni's mouth was full of delayed-digest energy snacks from the moment she boarded the big maglev elevator down the hall from her apartment, to the second she stepped aboard a vacuum tunnel train at the base of the tower, to the minute she snuck into Professor Fox's art studio at Academy Aeraea and sat down. Benni's Tika module—the little implant in her head just above and behind her right eye—displayed the time "08:03" in the upper right hand corner of her field of view. Class had begun thirty-three minutes before she'd arrived. Using the module's direct neural and, most importantly, *silent* interface, she accessed the professor's class notes for the day and skimmed them quickly. Out of the small hip pocket of her one-piece, Octattire bodysuit, she took a pair of rings and put them on her left index finger and thumb. Making an "L" shape with the two fingers, she produced a holographic canvas in her lap, then fished a stylus pen from out of the same pocket and pretended to have been sketching something before Professor Fox turned and saw her.

# 1.1

One particular week, halfway through Caan's first year as a graduate student at Academy Aquaea—the academy for liberal arts and sciences, religious studies and language—had been kind to him. His mother had begun to make breakfast every morning, and it was *real* breakfast, not the unappetizing, concentrated, "smart food" Benni and the other art students with the bloodshot eyes ate. The deal that had been struck involved Caan's coming by his parents' apartment to pick up his little sister, Jobi, and taking her to school. In exchange, Caan got a hot, fresh meal.

Because her profession, like many, allowed it, Caan's mother, Kolianne, worked at home, instructing the automaton chefs in her restaurant via direct Tika module communication, assuming control of their android bodies directly if necessary. Whatever Caan was eating for breakfast was what the customers at *Kolianne's*, a small but successful establishment up in the First Mile, were going to get from sunrise to midday every day from then on. The First Mile was home to the Genesian elite—the latter term was an expressional taboo in Caan's grandparents' day.

After cleaning the maple syrup off of Jobi's face, Caan left his parents' apartment with her, saying goodbye to his mother in the kitchen and to his father, Isaak, who was pacing circles in the living room, a holographic contact screen orbiting his head, projected by a Tika module public display lens located to the upper right of his right eyebrow. He was an architect for the ARC Company and sometimes lived, in the most literal sense, in his office, or rather the virtual atmosphere around his head, through which he constantly communicated with contractors or even remotely operated automaton carpenters on-site with a few lines of command garbled through a mouthful of buttered toast and black Honduran coffee.

Because of Isaak's tendency to forget the tangible world around him, especially his ankles, Kolianne had invested in omniform furniture long ago, which was almost infinitely malleable and storable, and which, like modern, top-dollar fashion, could adapt to an infinite number of shapes and styles that the owner could simply download and install through a digital catalog. When his parents first moved into their current home, Caan was used to seeing new designs and arrangements each time he visited. Kolianne had loved to display and discuss these new designs, but within the past five or six years, following an economic recession, it had devolved to a largely empty white space full of finance or work-related holograms. Jobi's bedroom remained something of a last bastion of old-time Genesian spirit—colorful, expressive and imaginative, and cluttered with the happy odds and ends and other musings of a child. Caan often imagined Jobi living on an island in the middle of their parents' much paler reality, which began a mere step into the hallway and throughout the rest of the apartment.

Caan walked with Jobi out of the apartment and to a maglift, a high-capacity, vacuum tunnel elevator that carried scores of people night and day up and down the core of Convoy Court apartments, the colossal residential building where a number of ARC employees and their families lived. Once inside the maglift, they both moved toward the windows and waited for the cabin to fill. Jobi planted her little hands on the glass and bounced excitedly, ready for the exhilarating ride down to the levbus terminal. Genesia was a world of windows, and Jobi wasn't the only person to cling to them as she did. The smooth glass that defined the boundary between Mars and every Martian kept folks from succumbing to capsule fever, the restless torment suffered by people locked up in spacecraft or space settlements for the long-term with no view of the outside. That word, what a misnomer! But "home" didn't quite cut it, either.

For people like Caan, who needed a strong, therapeutic illusion, Genesian architects had long ago constructed many public parks, wonderfully beautiful and spacious spheres of Earthlike lawns and ponds, complete with real weather, enhanced solar warmth and even simulated blue skies and pleasant breezes. Dispersed generously throughout the city, the parks effectively dissolved the cool and clean aesthetic of the white, urban geometry and helped blend two favorite Genesian design flavors: organic and Agoric. One of Caan's fondest memories was ascending a maglift at night once, when he was five or six years old, watching the silent blooming of fireworks through the diamond cranium of nearby Hermphrey Park. He had imagined himself as a deep-sea diver,

26

rising through the dark and passing a giant, bioluminescent jellyfish.

When the maglift slowed to a stop and the soft white doors split apart, everyone exited to the busy levbus terminal and general market district outside. Pedestrian traffic swarmed the ground-level streets, and air traffic buzzed between forty-five and eighty feet overhead. For fast or long-distance travel, vacuum tunnel maglev trains were an option. Several of them made continuous looping circuits around the city at varying heights, usually one vactrain every hundred feet from ground level.

"What a fine lady," Caan said to Jobi, straightening her prim outfit as he led her to the levbus stop by her hand.

"Where?" she asked, missing his meaning and whipping her head this way and that, looking for the beautiful woman he had mentioned, flipping her curly brown hair into her eyes.

"Never mind. Go get the seat that Alka saved for you before someone else does," he urged her, pushing her by her oversize coral-pink backpack toward her grinning best friend in the seat right behind the driver.

Alka was the only daughter of some family friends. She had uncannily straight, fiery red hair, evenly toned skin and honey hazel eyes—traits her parents chose from a palette of legally sanctioned genetic options before she was born. Alterations to certain characteristics such as intelligence and personality traits, which generally were felt to be best developed by the nurture half of the nature-nurture recipe, had long been established as ethically taboo.

Sitting next to the two girls, Caan watched as, from stop to stop, graduates, undergraduates, professors, dockies and every other variety of industrious and, for the most part, content Genesians boarded the levbus and began their days. The vehicle they shared was large and long, able to hover just a few feet from the road surface while picking up passengers before lifting off to a cruising height of about seventy-five feet via a magnetic field on-ramp, and buzzing through the major airspace between Convoy Court and the Academic District. The ride was always smooth and quiet, meditative. Quantum levitation had been merely a physicist's dream on Earth. On Mars it had become a reality—a feat of magic in a new age of scientific understanding.

After arriving at the greater State Academy Terminal, Caan herded Jobi past Academy Terraea, the institute for legal studies and military training. He wondered which of the academies Jobi was destined for, and if it should be Academy Terraea, how the educational system would transform a little girl whose optical desktop was always full of adventure stories into a soldier or state employee. Jobi ran off ahead of him. Benni, who had just gotten out of class and had been doing some overdue sketches, snatched up the little girl and tickled her. Benni had always treated Jobi like a younger sister, and Jobi couldn't get enough of it. She wanted to be everything that Benni was, down to the hair, so she was always asking her and Caan's mother if she could cut her hair short. That's how Benni kept hers, even though it was thin, straight and blond—

everything that Jobi's wasn't.

Caan had first met Benni while going out for drinks with some of his guy friends down in the docks, the commercial and shipping district underneath the city, two years earlier. He thought she was fascinating, and the feeling was, to his surprise, mutual. Benni was as much a work of art as any of her kinetic light sculptures, most of which were abstractions of cityscapes or animals or other non-Martian things. Something the two had in common from the start was a fascination with a place they'd never been: a phantom limb called Earth.

Jobi wrestled away from Benni and ran off to class squealing with laughter. Benni turned to Caan and winked, flashing him a smile and waving with her fingers. She came up close to him, running her fingers through his short, dark brown hair, messing it up and scolding him for not letting it "be itself" as she did every day. Out of time, they both silently agreed to meet up after school. She mouthed, "I love you" and he mouthed, "I know." Benni's eyes narrowed in teased amusement as she blew him a kiss.

# 1.2

An underground world known only as "Dark Town" made up the innards of the city. Dark Town was coarse, humid and steeped in the perpetual roar of whining aerofreighter engines, screaming gearworks and all manner of small, humming aerial vehicles. ARC shuttles flew in by way of massive tunnels, a network miles long that opened up to the unprotected Martian surface outside the city. A series of atmosphere-controlled canals and locks kept them in line as they made their way in, and the sound of changing air pressure blasted the cavernous docks all hours of the day. Additionally, the drone of industrial size generators producing artificial "gravity", or directed kinetic energy, pushed the industrial cacophony in the docks to unsettling levels.

Oskar "Wolfie" Weisser would awake every morning to these tunes. No warm, orange sky swirled overhead; no bright, pleasant sun would grace the apertures of his apartment. When he opened his eyes, the same, weird cocktail of LED glows that blazed through the long, tall and narrow series of windows next to his bed would still be striping the walls with vertical bars when morning came, surrounding him on two sides. The tireless roar of ARC shuttles moving in and out of Edwin Wharf and the greater bay would vibrate the walls and floors like bass drums, commanding him to rise and get to work.

The great ships that stirred the shadowy docks beneath Genesia could be seen in the night sky by those living topside, by the light reflecting off of their solar sails, the mechanisms used to perpetuate the longest legs of their flights between Earth and Mars. As they approached Genesia, the sails would collapse and traditional thrusters, burning a highly efficient yet expensive and limited biofuel called ichorol, would take over. Dockworkers, or "dockies," like Wolfie Weisser met with unloading ARC crews, tallied inventory, moved goods, provided maintenance for ships before re-launch and paid for shipments in "reds," electronic Martian currency.

Neither Wolfie nor his brother, Reese, nor any of their friends made a great amount of money working in the docks, not nearly as much as young people their age going to school topside, and not a fraction of a *fraction* of what the wealthier Genesians living in the First Mile or higher made. The pittance that appeared on the screen of his Tika PDA when Wolfie checked his credit account that morning made the bags under his eyes rise in ire, even against the weight of complacency that kept him from caring to complain. At least he was paid in reds, he thought, and not in any standard Earth currency, as most of the topsiders.

The value of reds came with a unique advantage to spenders from Earth. With reds, anyone could purchase cutting-edge tech and materials which could only be produced in Genesian manufacturing facilities. Genesians could do the same, but what was important was that tech exchange kept the reds circulating back to Mars, giving Martian currency legitimacy. Anyone could come to Genesia and buy food or clothes or whatever else, but if they wanted a personal vehicle like a levbike or levcar, or if they wanted transhuman medical tech, stocks with Genesis MTI or any of its corporate offspring, they needed reds. Wolfie was particularly interested in reds because they gave him the power to buy medical equipment and pay for otherwise impossible hospital expenses his mother had accrued over the years.

That morning, like every morning, after throwing on his pilot's bodysuit and climbing into the cockpit of his aerofreighter, Wolfie reached into his pocket, taking out his PDA and making sure all his credit accounts were balanced and his paycheck wasn't late. Luckily everything was in order and he wouldn't have to make an unnecessary trip across Dark Town to have a shouting match with one of Topside Express's payroll officers. Stepping into his tiny apartment's closet, he opened a safe and took out his Danziger DKE pistol, a small sidearm he carried against company policy— and federal law—and tucked it into a pocket in the waist of his bodysuit. Arming his apartment's security systems, he stepped outside, climbed aboard a company aerofreighter parked in his back lot, and warmed up the engines.

"There's no such thing as a perfect day in the docks," Wolfie grumbled aloud as he piloted his large aerofreighter out of the neighborhood and into the warehouse district in between home and work. It was noon; his shift had begun in the worst part of the day and already the air traffic looked like overlapping ribbons checkering the docks, so thick Wolfie couldn't tell the front of one aerofreighter from the back end of the next. High above, the airspace vanished into blackness. Great, hazy halos of light mottled the darkness and large, structural supports jutted down like the shiny, jagged bottoms of metallic-amber clouds in a sky that didn't really exist.

"Hey, Wolfie," said a friendly voice through the PDA in Wolfie's pocket. He'd been sitting on the thing and had barely heard it at all. Tika-brand PDAs were so outmoded they may have well been rocks with buttons. Most dockies berated the things all day long, wishing they could afford the more expensive neural modules that most topsiders owned by the time they started school. Wolfie didn't care too much. He didn't like the idea of having a computer implanted in his brain anyway, no matter how "unnoticeable" and "convenient" they were supposed to be.

"Hey," said Wolfie, "is that you, Fae?"

"How many other pretty little girls do you know that fly aerofreighters?" she replied.

"If I knew any at all, I'd keep that information to myself," Wolfie answered back, getting a laugh out of Faela. The two had been friends for some time, ever since Faela had moved to Dark Town.

"You think it's hard to *find* pretty girls down here," said Faela, "Try *being* one." Faela merged out of her lane of traffic and pulled up beside Wolfie. Her big aerofreighter, notable for the custom-painted tropical flowers and waves on the side, rolled to the right, and she braced herself. A little gyroscopic fishbowl on her cockpit's console swiveled and lurched, the little beta fish swimming inside not acting a bit upset. "My dad found the exact model of levbike you've been looking for," she told Wolfie.

"Are you serious?" Wolfie burst, running a calloused hand through his long, dirty-blond hair, "That's great! How much do I owe him?"

"You don't," said Faela, "I told him that if not for you, I wouldn't have a job. So the bike is a gift, and don't tell me no because I won't accept a refusal."

"Fae! You shouldn't have!" Wolfie's day had been made. He didn't care why or how the levbike was free. In the docks, that's just how some "transactions" happened now and then. Now Reese wouldn't be able to give him grief about being the only guy without a ride when they all went to get drinks at *The Shoe* on the weekends. Maybe he would race a couple of the guys, too, and shut them up for good.

"It's no trouble, really," said Faela, "We've got to watch out for one another down here, right?"

"Isn't that the truth," Wolfie mumbled, glancing at the bulge at his waist where his Danziger rested against his skin.

"Speaking of which, I need to get moving," said Faela. "Dad won't be home until late tonight, and Nati is all by herself at my apartment. I need to finish up my shift so I can get home and make dinner for her."

Nati, Faela's little sister, was nine years old and spent most of the day by herself in the tiny apartment in which Faela lived. ARC had supplied Faela with the humble accommodations through her first employer, Viking Delivery. It wasn't much, but it was home, and after all, it was the best deal she could hope to get in Dark Town. Things could have been better, she knew, but how could her parents have known? When Faela's father first talked about moving to Genesia, his automotive repair business on Earth was not doing well, and going to live anywhere else would have been an improvement. Faela had been twenty-three at the time and was finished with school, but the minute she became a Genesian, her credentials were no longer valid; in fact, degrees from the most prestigious schools on Earth were considered inferior at best and irrelevant at worst. Her younger sister Nati had to leave traditional school behind to begin taking subject lessons through a computer-based system at home with an android tutor who was slowly helping her catch up to Martian standards.

"All right. Yeah, I need to go too," Wolfie spoke into the PDA. "I've got to pick up some friends after work, and I don't want to be late."

"All right. Take care, Wolfie," said Faela, pulling out of traffic and turning down another airway.

"You too, Fae, and thanks again."

* * * *

"After this if you want, Danae asked us to go out tonight," said Benni, touching Caan on the arm as they got off a levbus in Heinze Square. They were across the city from the Academic District and above the commercial lifts that moved vehicles, people and goods into the metropolis from the docks below. Caan led Benni onto one of the lifts, giant platforms situated on slanted rails a few thousand yards long that climbed up to the surface of Genesia loaded with aerofreighters, like ski gondolas full of people. Several of Caan's friends, who attended Academy Aeraea, were performing a show at *Fretz's Bar* that afternoon, and he and Benni were going to see them.

"Danae? Have I met her? Where is she going?" Caan asked Benni, waving to a pilot in one of the large aerofreighters parked in the lift. The driver was a guy nicknamed Wolfie, a friend of Caan's. Wolfie was twenty-four and had left Academy life early, losing interest in the career set forth for him by the Academic Council. A comical, outspoken, though perhaps too often volatile former student of theater, Wolfie flew aerofreighters—long and sleek ships that could be driven along magnetic field tracks or flown through Genesian airspace. Aerofreighters had a distinctive, swooping, fat belly on one end that made Caan think of a frigate bird.

"She and Jules are going to the *Blue Morpho*," Benni said, adding "this place, here," as a little sea foam green point of light above Benni's left eyebrow blinked on, projecting a holographic screen about a foot in front of her face. A browser loaded up and the words "Blue Morpho" appeared to type themselves into a search field, but of course they weren't; Benni commanded the text to be typed by direct neural interface. The module implanted just above her eye required no verbal or physical interaction. Like two dark little beauty marks, it was easy to forget the module's projector, camera and external sensor were there. Caan had a set as well. He and Benni, both privileged graduate students, were afforded the modules as part of their graduate studies amenities.

Wolfie hadn't stayed in school long enough to get his. As Wolfie brushed back his long, wavy, dirty blond hair, Caan noticed the strange, blank quality of his friend's grease-stained, sweaty forehead. Not all Genesians had or could afford transhuman tech, especially dockies, though dockies generally made fun of people with Tika modules. Wolfie called them vampire bites. "Might want to get those looked at, man! Sure they're not cancerous?" Wolfie shouted as he eased his aerofreighter to ground level, making it bow like a flamingo. The hot engines blasted the ground and hot air swept across Caan's ankles as he climbed up into the cabin and offered Benni a hand.

"Yeah, right." Caan laughed it off as always. It wasn't a big deal, and he wasn't the type to make the point that if Wolfie hadn't dropped out, he could have had a Tika module, maybe even his own levcar.

"I know what you're thinking," said Wolfie, smiling and shaking his hair as his fingers worked their sorcery on the holographic control console of the aerofreighter, "You're thinking I'm just sore about it because I dropped out."

"Oh, here we go," teased Benni, pressing her palm to her face.

"No, no, let me speak," said Wolfie, holding out a hand and

begging for an audience. "Your little Tika beauty marks are stylish and helpful and everything, and I'm sure you feel special because the Academic Council chose you two for graduate programs, when they could've chosen anybody else ... me not least of all ... and it's fortunate you didn't have to compete with *this*," he added jerking a thumb at himself.

"They could have," Caan repeated, smirking at Wolfie, who held up a finger and demanded to be allowed to finish.

"But what?" Benni pressed, folding her arms and waiting for Wolfie to speak. "Let's hear it."

"I'm just saying," said Wolfie, moving his arms about the air of the cabin and steering the aerofreighter out of the lift as it reached the docks and the traffic began to move, "The day they switch on autopilot and smart people like you turn into their vampire army, don't say I didn't warn you." Caan shook his head and Benni groaned. "Of course," Wolfie continued, "I could always be wrong. Maybe you all will transcend the modern age, and I and every other remnant member of the human species will get left behind like diesel engines or paper...or the dodo!" "I don't think you're a dodo, Wolf," Caan replied facetiously, offering Wolfie a sympathetic pat on the shoulder, "You fly much better than that."

"Hey, you know one great thing about what I do?" said Wolfie, "Being a dockie means you're so unimportant, no one can blame you for anything!"

"Aw, that's a terrible thing to say!" Benni burst, laughing as

Wolfie feigned a clownish frown.

As the aerofreighter lurched forward and pulled out of the lift, Wolfie turned the conversation to work. It wasn't the usual set of tall tales about dock accidents, some poor guy losing an arm to a DKE generator he thought was disengaged or a hovercart driver getting sucked out into the canals, but instead, uncharacteristic concerns about ARC shipments.

"Seems they're getting more and more irregular," Wolfie said, rubbing his cheek and dialing something into the aerofreighter's console. "Sure, I mean, we're getting all the right amounts of supplies coming in, but I've never seen or heard of ships coming in as late as they have these last two weeks.

"Could be because we're almost in the back forty-five?" What Caan meant was that Mars was currently in an imaginary forty-five degree arc on the other side of the sun from Earth, where it was notoriously difficult to reach with ARC ships. In fact, when Caan's great-grandparents were still young, ARC ships didn't fly at all when Mars was in the back forty-five.

"No," said Wolfie quietly, "I think things aren't so good on Earth and they just don't want to say anything and upset everyone here. The recession is going on and ... I don't know, I think something worse is brewing. We solved all those back-forty-five issues decades ago, way before I started piloting. I wouldn't be worried about it if my boss weren't acting strange. He threatened to fire us if we tell anyone about it. So you guys—"

"Oh, no, we won't say anything," Caan assured him. "When are you gonna start leaving that at home?" he asked, noticing the Danziger DKE pistol jutting from the waist of Wolfie's bodysuit. "The day they assign an actual police force to patrol the docks," Wolfie responded grimly, "I know you guys don't condone it, but it's already kept me from getting robbed twice. Plus, I don't know if you've heard, but they're saying some more transhumans went haywire recently and—"

"Oh, you don't believe that nonsense, do you?" Benni scolded him.

"I've got a buddy that says he saw one of them kill seven cops in the docks about a year ago!" he argued.

"I thought there were no cops down there." Benni cocked an eyebrow.

"They came down there looking for him because he owed the hospital a ton of money," Wolfie explained, "I mean … you know how many of those types end up in the docks, right? Well, they came after him and he went crazy or something and my buddy says he saw some eye witness videos of the guy doing impossible stuff, like throwing levcars and—"

"All right, all right, keep your gun if it really makes you feel better." Caan resigned, deciding not to let Benni upset Wolfie anymore.

Wolfie shook his hair, looking out the window to his left and putting his palm to the console, making circles with it and rotating the aerofreighter ninety degrees. Dragging his index finger down a vertical bar dial, he adjusted the vehicle's altitude and brought it close to the ground. "Honored passengers and guests," he began in a stately tone, "thank you for flying with us today. We have arrived at *Fretz's*, here in the lovely Dark Town shipping district." He didn't have to say any more to tease amused smiles out of Caan and Benni as they climbed out of the cabin. "Oh, hey," he called after them before lifting off again. "I'm going to get that levbike I talked to you about. You'll get to see it soon!" Wolfie nodded a heads up as the aerofreighter lifted off the ground and its engines drowned out his voice. "It's going to make me look real sharp! Like a celebrity!"

"A levbike?" Caan propped his hands on his hips and laughed. "Damn, I never thought he'd save up that money as he said he would. I'd like to see it." Caan wondered if Wolfie was really paying for the levbike, or if someone he knew was helping him get it under the table somewhere in the docks. Ashamed of thinking of his friend that way, Caan dismissed the thought.

Wolfie had been Caan's best and closest pal as long as he could remember. Their fathers worked together for ARC, in the same architectural branch. Their mothers used to take them to the parks every day after school and let them run free and wrestle and chase their carefree childhood imaginations all afternoon. Caan and Wolfie had spent almost all their time in school together as well, were notoriously mischievous but also clever high-achievers. They and everyone that knew them thought of them as brothers, even called them twins.

They were first separated when it came time to begin academy life, though it came as no surprise. Caan had been selected for privileged placement in Academy Aquaea for a long time prior; Wolfie, Academy Aeraea, as he had always been a talented actor and aspired to perform professionally. Wolfie began working in the docks when his father died on an interplanetary trip. The accident, the catastrophic failure of the *Sunspanner*, an ARC shuttle headed from Mars to Earth, was famous, and even after several years had passed, ARC continued to lose money in the transportation sector. People opted just to stay home after hearing of the disaster. Wolfie had been in school and performing his way to certain stardom, but after his father's death, the subsequent weakening of ARC and the Genesian economy—along with the persistence of the high cost of academic life—he couldn't summon the will to continue caring. Instead, he got a job in the docks so he could help his mother pay for his younger brother Reese's education.

Reese hadn't stayed in school for long, either, because their mother was hospitalized for an uncommon condition known as genetic modification regression. The daughter of a wealthy couple, she'd been given artificially selected traits at birth. Nearly ninety-nine percent of genetic modifications were successful even when Wolfie's grandparents were children, but rare cases like his mother would suddenly experience rapid DNA degeneration and accelerated aging around the age of forty. Her condition, along with her inability to reconcile her husband's death, was complicated further when she decided to begin camouflaging both problems with a third: regular, unprescribed use of expensive painkilling medications. When the hospital began to refuse her the meds, she discovered they could be bought in quiet corners of Dark Town. Wolfie and Reese had worked in the docks to support themselves and their mother ever since.

As Wolfie lifted off and waved goodbye, Jimmy, one of Caan's friends, walked out of *Fretz's* and shook his hand, introducing himself to Benni afterward. Jimmy had chosen to study twentieth century rock and roll music for his graduate thesis and insisted his friends play some songs with him. Begrudgingly, they agreed, though they didn't understand why he obliged them to play at *Fretz's* and not in the modern music concert hall at Academy Aeraea. Jimmy explained to Caan as they went inside that ancient rock and roll wasn't allowed to be played in the same venues as orchestral music. It had something to do with social and religious codes, as far as Jimmy understood, and he wanted the show to be historically accurate. He even went as far as to employ some theater students to dress in period clothing, like denim jeans and leather, with which Academy Aquaea's Museum of History had been willing to part.

The band began with the song *All You Need Is Love*. During the intro, one of the theater students punched the other in the nose, because Jimmy had told them that brawling was commonplace and in fact encouraged during a rock and roll performance. Caan thoroughly enjoyed the show, but Benni had crossed her arms and begun to look miserable before the band had gotten through five songs. He didn't blame her. The music was centuries old; one of those inexplicably weird things their ancestors may have been fascinated by, thinking the electric guitar was some sort of sorcery or something. Before long Benni left, after telling Caan she'd call for a ride back to the lifts and wait for him out front.

A song or two later, a girl Caan had never seen before wandered into the bar and made quite a face upon hearing the racket, silently raising both eyebrows and looking generally uncomfortable because of the number of visiting, academic patrons. Recognizing her as a dockie, Caan noticed she was young and uncommonly pretty—for an aerofreighter pilot, anyway. Everything about her was dark—hair, eyes, skin and all. Caan watched as she ordered a drink and carried it over to a corner of the bar where all the other outnumbered pilots and greasy dockies were huddled. After a moment, they all left through the back.

Caan stood up and curiously ducked out the back of the bar after them. Outside, they'd all gathered around a bunch of levbikes, aerofreighters and empty shipping junk—cargo crates and mechanical parts. As he lingered in the back doorway, hidden and unassuming, Caan felt a great distance between himself and the strangers who chattered and laughed and drank and wore the grit of their daily work on their faces, their oily cheeks and arms shining when the pressurized docks in the distance opened up and let the wild Martian sunlight in. In the dramatic light of the sun they looked ancient, scarred and vigorous. Caan imagined Wolfie among them, tattooed and with a bushy beard, dancing and chanting around a blazing fire with a spear or mysterious fetish in hand, reciting some old poetry he was always going on about. Pictures of the founding of Genesia came to mind, and the old-timers, the pioneers in their funny bodysuits looking up from their work to smile at a camera or point at something they'd accomplished or believed they were accomplishing. For a moment Caan, a student of anthropology, also felt very far from himself, as if he were watching from somewhere else, and the twenty-two-year old hiding in the back doorway of the bar was some unimportant observer, and not Caan; someone without a fire to dance around and without anything vital or primal to celebrate or claim—a shadow in the mouth of a dark cave, a bland, timid shape cast by something brighter and more ferocious outside.

The girl with the dark features cut her eyes at Caan, looking him up and down, then smiled and gave him a strange look before turning back to someone who was teasing her and taking a drink of his beer. Caan looked away bashfully, his discomfort returning as he shied away back inside, paid the tab and left through the front of the bar. After congratulating his friends on their show and saying goodbye, he found Benni out front and left with her.

# 1.3

Seated high on the Genesian skyline, the top of the *Blue Morpho*—a slowly rotating crystalline sphere of soft blue fluttering lights—mesmerized Benni as she and Caan waited for the levbus to gently bank around the next corner and drop them off about a block from the club. Her small nose nearly touching the window of the levbus, Benni turned and smiled at Caan, the little freckles high on her cheeks crowding up beneath her eyes.

"What do you think?" she asked him as they got off of the levbus, taking two steps ahead of him and turning to face him directly. The Tika module above her eye came to life and emitted a little sea foam green light. In Benni's field of view, a menu appeared and from it she selected a style of clothing more form-fitting than what she wore presently. Making a selection, the smart bands on her sleeves, waist, bust and legs shifted place and drew up the fabric of her loose-fitting attire and took on a sleeker, more curvaceous and alluring shape.

"I like that," said Caan, touching a finger to his lips and studying her with his eyes. In his field of vision he brought up four cursors and took a discreet picture of her as she whirled around and modeled her new look for him.

"Did you just take a picture of me?" Benni's jaw dropped and she laughed nervously, giving Caan a good smack on the chest.

"You don't blame me, do you?" Caan pulled up another menu and adjusted his own clothing to match hers, making sure it emphasized his shoulders and chest. "There, now we're perfect."

"Not yet," she corrected him. "What color?"

"Hm, you're sure you don't like the white?" The outfits, a technology developed by Octattire, named for an octopus's brilliant camouflage skills, were quite stylish without much customization, thought Caan, even in their default white and gray color scheme.

"No!" insisted Benni. "It's my birthday, and I want to be colorful tonight! How about dark purple?" Selecting a complex set of colors and textures, Benni stood still and watched as her body and limbs took on the deep sheen of midnight plum, the belt around her waist as well as her jewelry turning onyx. Her sleeves disappeared at the shoulder and her pant legs fused and retracted, becoming a mini dress, while a keyhole cut opened at her cleavage and her collar grew tall and modestly lacey—a look made popular during a recent neo-Victorian revival.

"Gorgeous," Caan approved.

"Now, for you. Dial these numbers in for your outfit," she said, taking his arm as they began to walk down the street. Her module sent the details of his outfit directly to a communications screen in his field of view. Promptly, Caan directed them to the software in his Octattire bodysuit and soon his clothing adopted charcoal gray, maroon and white detailing. "You look handsome," she cooed, kissing him on the cheek.

Benni's friends, Danae and Jules, were waiting for them outside of the *Blue Morpho*. Jules, like Caan, had dressed a bit more conservatively. Students of higher academia often did, even when outside of school. Danae, Benni's best friend of seven years, true to Aeraea style, had opted for a loose top and oppositely inclined leg wear, all shining in tones of opal, somehow dodging gaudiness.

While the girls stood ahead of them in line, Caan and Jules began to chat, discovering they worked in the same laboratories after school, assisting the Circle in different shifts. The Circle was originally a small academic organization comprised of the forerunners in the fields of science belonging to Academy Ignaea. Since its inception, it had come to be known as the paragon of learning, research and discovery in Genesia, a club for intellectual superstars, some might say. To gain acceptance into programs leading to potential membership was the goal of essentially everyone attending any of the four state academies, although less than three percent of all students would ever reach that goal, and less than one percent would earn a place among the Circle Board themselves. Jules was a student of Academy Terraea, bound for the legal field, perhaps a political seat in Genesis MTI if he worked hard enough. Caan respected Jules in the sense that he respected anything sentient enough to do more than the bare minimum to survive and reproduce. He wasn't interested in politics and business, and grew bored of Jules's list of accomplishments, or rather, Jules's *father*'s accomplishments, the glory of which Jules spoke of as if they were his own. After no more than several minutes, Caan's marginal respect waned to disinterest, and he imagined Jules was the type of businessman who sat in a corner office all day only because of his fraternal legacy networking and then assumed greater success would surely follow if he could stare at his Bachelor's degree long and hard enough.

Caan pretended to listen as he activated his Tika module and called up an acquaintance dossier program called MetaMeet. Silently, the Tika module snapped a photo of Jules, a rather unflattering one in which his eyes were frozen in mid-blink and his mouth hung agape, and placed it in a formerly empty rectangular box in the upper left of Caan's field of view. The application took a few seconds to search countless social media databases and compiled a series of ratings that evaluated Jules according to what anyone had ever said about him publicly online, as well as any information Jules had provided about himself—everything from his hobbies to his political stances to his favorite alcoholic drinks to his love for people's humorous pictures of their cats.

In a matter of moments Caan was able to decide he and Jules would never be more than indifferent acquaintances by virtue of whom they happened to currently date. Caan then began manually filling in some text fields with info about Jules, closing the program the next moment and committing Jules to the Tika's digital memory with the meta tags, "boring," "bad hair" and "nepotism." Luckily, Benni yanked on Caan's arm and pulled him inside the club before Jules could go on about himself anymore.

"Wow, I told you I've never been here, before, right?" Danae gasped, coming through the doors just behind Caan and Benni.

"Oh, my…" Benni was just as awestruck.

"Happy birthday," Caan whispered, planting a kiss on her as her head turned this way and that. "What do you want to do? Do you all want drinks?" Caan asked everyone. "It's her birthday and I'm paying."

"Thanks, but I've got us covered," said Jules blandly. "You know, my father composed all the building contracts for this place, back before he started working on…"

"Oh, yes, yes, you already said, sweetie," Danae interrupted him.

"I want to dance!" said Benni, tugging on Caan and pointing up toward the ceiling. The low-lit, multi-stage lounge they stood in was not the main attraction at the *Blue Morpho*. Rather, Benni aspired to reach the rotating globular atrium high atop the club.

"We'll join you in a bit," said Danae, as she and Jules headed toward the bar.

Benni and Caan started off through the crowd, both as excited as little children, skirting past islands of young, single people schmoozing with drinks in hand, some they recognized from the Academy. Stepping into a maglift with several other couples, they ascended the club to the Butterfly Room, exiting at the top to behold a visual and musical wonder. A club usher got up from a desk and held up the crowd so he could instruct all to keep their hands on the railings as the walls around them peeled back to mere windows. Outside the lift, the Butterfly Room thundered with ambient melodies and energetic beats. People literally moved around the globe in all directions, through the air and up the walls, their feet striking the infinite dance floor and producing pulses of blue light that looked like the fluttering wings of butterflies to club-goers in the lounge below, hence the name *Blue Morpho*.

"When the walls come down, a DKE generator suspended in the center of the dance hall will create an artificial change in gravity, meaning you can dance anywhere in the Butterfly Room, even on the walls and ceilings if you have footwear with variable-surface-attraction soles and proper strength and balance correction Octattire or augmented limb prosthetics with at least class-B muscular exertion thresholds. If you do not, you must remain within the safe, clearly marked bottom levels…"

"Blah, blah, blah," Benni muttered to herself, "I came here to dance, not for Physics 101."

"Welcome to the heart of the *Blue Morpho*. Tonight's featured musical artist is Hileah Al-Messer. Enjoy the show!" said the usher.

"Oh my God," Benni exclaimed, "Hileah's the best! Did you know she's performing tonight?" she asked Caan, clutching his hands tight.

"I may have." Caan nearly fell over as Benni threw her arms around his neck and kissed him again.

The usher fired some more information with the verbal agility of an auctioneer and the enthusiasm of a sedated slug and then flipped a switch behind a desk as he took a seat. When the walls came down, his stoic, professional hair began to rise in a humorous way as the gravity in the maglift dropped. All the couples clung to each other and laughed nervously, pointing at one another's clothing, hair and jewelry as it began to swim freely in the air.

"Sir," the usher said as everyone exited. "Sir, you two will have to stay here and go back to the lounge." He struggled with a disgruntled, drunk man whose date cursed at the top of her lungs. "We can't allow you to use this room, sir. I'm sorry, it's for the safety of our other customers."

"I paid to get in! You can't throw me out! I'll buy the whole place out and fire you! Get your damn hands off me!" the man shouted. "Yeah, you throw me out and I'll be right back, you better believe it!" The agitator, an apparently wealthy man in a sharp, black Octattire club suit, drew everyone's attention as he was roughly escorted away.

Benni noticed that his bald head was partially comprised of casings with Tika brand neural prosthetics inside—devices used to supplant brain tissue and augment mental functions following emergency cranial trauma surgeries. He was a transhuman.

"Wow, did you see that guy?" Benni asked Caan as they moved into the Butterfly Room. "That kinda makes me nervous."

"He's just drunk. They'll kick him out," Caan assured her. "Are you worried about what Wolfie said earlier?" He laughed and couldn't believe she'd been spooked by the story. "Come on, don't let that ruin the mood. Let's dance, huh?"

"Yeah, all right. Come on, we're going straight to the top!"

Benni led Caan up the walls, through the dreamlike droves of moving bodies, the strobing silhouettes of arms, legs and heads. Benni hurried along, smiling and watching as her feet left a trail of electric blue prints on the surface beneath her. As they ascended, their shoes and outfits adjusted accordingly, aligning their feet with the floor—or rather the walls—and managing the changing burden of standing upright and keeping their heads pointed toward the center of the spherical room.

When they cleared the crowd, reaching the top of the room, the effect was surreal. Hileah Al-Messer hovered overhead—or rather, *under*head—dancing on the main stage centered on the floor of the Butterfly Room, surrounded by sound machines that drove patterns of beautiful light through the floor with each beat and tempo change. Dancing bodies covered every foot of the inside of the spherical, luminous wonderland. The spectacle distracted Caan for the longest moment, and when he looked at Benni again, she was dancing. Through the blasts of light and music he followed her pretty blue eyes and purple curves, moving with her as she smiled and twisted. Her short hair flew on the fluffy light air. Unopposed by gravity, they touched, turned, kissed and laughed, over and over—two fireflies in a glade of light and sound. Beneath their colliding forms, their feet felt the pulse of life beating from far below, the heart of the *Blue Morpho* channeling music through their veins as they turned in the Genesian sky.

Benni had a way of reaching into Caan and extracting things he didn't know about himself. As she danced, she watched him come to life on his own for the first time since they started dating. The truth was they'd never danced together. Caan had expressed great interest in the theory of dancing, but never the practice. He knew of hundreds of dances and their complex sets of moves, he could name their origins and understood their deeper cultural purposes and interpretative qualities, but he himself had never danced. He was self-conscious about the entire idea, and so Benni never bothered him with it after the one time she'd brought it up. However, for her birthday, as she'd already found out, he had asked Danae to suggest going out to the club for him. His way of going about new experiences were often silly, she thought, and she was unable to guess why he didn't take any outward pride in his guarded but honest adventurousness. There was greatness and modesty about him that she had fallen in love with. She thought of him as an unfinished sculpture, bound to be something brilliant despite some unchiseled dimensions yet to be described.

After nearly half an hour, Caan moved entirely on his own, no longer needing to follow Benni's moves exactly. His reservations about dancing melted away and he realized that he wasn't half bad. Something about seeing the approval on Benni's face made everything else irrelevant. If he looked like a fool, swinging his head and swaying fluidly as he did, he didn't care. Not caring was refreshing, because as long as he had lived, his life had been an ongoing performance, mostly in the Academy, where he was held to a high standard, expected to expend his talents to any one of a few specific ends. He was expected to understand things from a distance. He was supposed to know why people danced, but knowing how to was optional. If he'd been an Aeraea student, dancing would still have only been a calculated art, a performance, to be observed by others.

"You ever get tired of this city?" he suddenly asked over the music. "Do you ever want to travel, to see what Earth is like?"

"Not a day goes by, my love." She smiled and pulled him closer.

"Genesia is like a great big—"

"Bubble?" she finished for him. "I know. We all live outside-in. That's why we're here, so we can let our insides out, for once!"

"Can we go to the outside of the city sometime and see the farms and gardens?" he asked her.

"Yeah, of course. You've never been?" Benni asked, cocking her head in surprise.

"No, I mean, I used to go a lot, when I was young. I miss it."

"Sounds wonderful," she agreed, her white teeth blooming into another pretty smile. "We've been at it for a while," she realized, releasing a breath of exhaustion. "You wanna go downstairs and see—" A violent crash erupted over the music.

"What the hell was that?" Caan's brow furrowed as he and Benni, as well as all the other dancers looked around through the strobing haze for the source of the noise. The music even slowed, as Hileah, on the stage below, was asked to stop her performance. Confusion buzzed in the air as shouts came from several club ushers on the main floor, and bursts of light shone through the maglift shaft leading to the Butterfly Room. The sound system buzzed loudly and everyone clapped their hands over their ears as the sound levels rose, popped and whined. The floor lights malfunctioned, humming deeply and strobing irregularly. *Wuum...*

"Something's going on downstairs," whispered Benni, hanging on to Caan. Low-pitched crackles and pops were coming from just outside the Butterfly Room, the kind of sounds issued by disruptive, electromagnetic pulse weapons. The police were inside the club.

In the next moment, a terrible screech followed by another crash rocked the Butterfly Room, causing the sound systems to hiss and buzz. The crowd burst into panic and began to push and shove, creating a nauseating and disorienting effect as the floor lights continued to strobe brightly, making the room hot and bright. The artificial gravity vanished suddenly and dozens began to fall, slip and slide down the curved walls into awkward piles, struggling to stand as legs and arms beat against each other.

Caan swore as he grabbed hold of Benni and tried to move through the crowd. Feeling the natural gravity in the room returning, and guessing the emergency regulators were restoring the room to its former state, he tried to lead the way to the outside of the mob of fleeing bodies, so they would not be buried under the other clubbers as they fell and tumbled awkwardly over one another.

"Caan!" Benni stopped him and pointed to the large windows by the maglift, where a levcar had come crashing through into the

Butterfly Room and was spinning circles across the floor. Shoving through the bodies next to her, she pulled Caan toward the main stage, taking cover from the runaway vehicle with several other frightened people. This was an unfortunate choice, for the rogue levcar came sliding across the floor toward the stage. Caan followed Benni around the other side of it as ushers urged everyone to evacuate the room. However, Benni stopped short. "Caan, she's stuck!" The night's performer, Hileah Al-Messer, had become trapped under the collapsed sound machines after the levcar struck the stage the first time. Benni pulled away as rushing bodies broke her grip on Caan's hand. Wasting no time, she told him to wait for her and climbed up on stage, taking hold of Hileah and helping her to her feet.

"Benni! Benni!" Caan shouted over the crowd, giving a swift elbow to anyone in his way. "Get back down here!" Over and over he pleaded with her until his face was crimson. Knocked off his feet by a sudden churn of the crowd, he lost sight of her. In the next moment, several cries rose as the levcar smashed into the stage again, wedging itself underneath, auxiliary engines screaming and wobbling, dangerously loosened by severe damage.

Amid the pandemonium, a tall, bald man in a sharp, black Octattire suit calmly walked onto the dance floor and stood, still and calm, as the police began to file into the Butterfly Room and aim their weapons at him. Benni caught sight of the man and broke out in goosebumps as she watched his feet rise from the ground until he hung weightless in the air. A little red light blinked somewhere in the darkness of his pupils, so faint that she saw it only when he turned his eyes to look right at her. *Wuuuum* ... A haunting vibration shook the room as the police opened fire on the man. A powerful pulse gathered around him and burst outward, knocking the crowd off their feet and rocking the maglifts off their rails. The bald man fell to the floor, and the police opened fire again.

Benni jumped down off the stage before Hileah, who tried to stop her. The levcar wedged into the stage began to strain against itself and one of its auxiliary engines pried itself off the vehicle and came skipping across the dance floor, followed by a flash of electrical fire and explosion of chassis metal. The blast licked and pelted the crowd, and the belligerent, roaring engine cut a path through the place where Benni stood, slinging her to one side like a little purple spark off the teeth of a buzzsaw. The ringing in Caan's ears made him think the entire world had gone mute. Something heavy struck him in the face, and when his head stopped spinning he tasted blood. A muffled, drumming sound thumped against his head. Adrenaline sped up the world around him then slowed it down again. An usher grabbed Caan's arm and then slipped away. He caught sight of Benni through the crowd. Her eyes were shut. *Wuuuum* ...The police fired their weapons again, and the nearby maglift screamed as it came off its guide rails and plummeted to the first floor. Caan couldn't hear himself screaming Benni's name as he ran for her.

# 2.0
# THOSE WHO WILL GO AFTER

*"The word 'unnatural' is synonymous with 'impossible.' If God demanded a rigid natural process, he would not have afforded intelligent species the means to augment natural processes, or the natural body. The circumstances of creation could have just as easily marked rocks, minerals and metals as the vessels of life. The approach of the literal physical unity of humans and knowledge entails closeness to God himself."*

—Ismaan Al-Messer, public advocate for transhumanism, from his speech, *The Advent of the Postcestor*, 2599 CE

"Hello, I'm Dr. Sadie Iverforth. I'm the hospital's chief neurosurgeon." The curt utterance, soaked in a Scottish accent, came unexpectedly from above Caan's right shoulder. A tall, tawny-haired woman of thirty-eight, dressed in a long, white medical suit stuck out her hand and shook his. Her fingers were chilled like the air of the emergency ward. "Normally I prepare my words beforehand but we haven't any time for softness and subtlety. Benni is dying, and she is dying quickly. The measures we've taken have only slowed the process—"

"Dying? What do you mean? That's it?" Caan jumped up from his seat and drew the eyes of every startled and already anxious stranger in the waiting room.

"Please," Dr. Iverforth interrupted, raising a hand to silence him. "I was about to say we are prepared to operate, but we must

59

acquire very important legal permissions before we do a thing."

"Are you kidding?" Caan shouted. "She's dying! Worry about that later!"

"Caan, please," his mother, Kolianne, said as she touched him on the shoulder. "Please, just calm down, and we'll do whatever they need."

"Listen to your mother and hush," his father added, pointing an authoritative finger between Caan's eyes. "Please continue, Doctor. What's to be done? I agree with my son. It's unusual to take such caution before proceeding with an urgent operation."

"I'll be brief, then," said Dr. Iverforth. "We can save Benni, but only if we operate now and we have permission to use transhuman technological implants on a number of damaged body and brain tissues. The Al-Messer family has offered to pay for all medical expenses, and they ask for nothing in return. A few of the operations we'll need to perform are lengthy and only sanctioned as of two years ago. We can guarantee a full recovery, but law requires us to acquire permission from someone with power of attorney. Benni has no family within our reach. Her parents are listed on record as living on Earth, and because she is entirely incapable of speaking for herself, the only option is for one of you to assume power of attorney. We'll operate if we have a signature of someone close to Benni who is willing to take on full legal responsibility for these procedures. I urge you to decide quickly."

"How soon?" Caan asked, his eyes wide and alarmed, the color drained from his cheeks. What was being asked of his family was not a matter of triviality or something to be mulled over in a moment or two. Benni's life was at stake, but the operations necessary to save her would change her life permanently, and in ways Caan could not quickly or easily foresee. He and his parents believed the doctor when she guaranteed successful recovery, but successful transhumans were few and far between. Stories of patients' long recovery times, exhausting therapy and arduous social readjustments had left a bad taste in the mouth of most anyone in Genesia who kept up with the news reports.

"I am terribly sorry, but I'll need your decision in three minutes. If you'll all follow me, please, I need to prepare for surgery should you decide to proceed. You may wait outside of the operating room." Dr. Iverforth's green eyes swept over Caan's and his parents' faces once and then twice with a mixture of sympathy and suspense. Then, with a simple gesture and a "Follow me, please, right away," she led them to the operating room. Calling up a holographic chart for a nurse, she spoke to him in foreign, medical jargon. Another nurse programmed the doctor's white coat for her, commanding it to reform into an operating smock, and tied back her wavy, tawny hair.

"I don't know … I don't know her parents. How long has she been independent?" Caan's father said, shoulders pinched up in anxiety as his mother rattled on.

"What are you two talking about?" Caan butted in, knocking his elbow into an empty, passing gurney. It spun and slid away from him, bumping into a nurse who nearly dropped a small bottle of pills.

"Caan, dear, we don't entirely understand this kind of situation. We … we want to help her, but your father and I can't afford …" his mother tried to hurriedly explain.

"But the doctor said the Al-Messer family is paying for everything!" Caan argued, a hot anger rising inside him. In the moment, he refused to believe his parents wouldn't agree to save Benni's life, and in his panic he began to shout again.

"Quiet!" his father barked. "Son, listen, we understand, but there will be enormous costs after the operation. We don't know how long Benni will need therapy, how often she'll need doctor visits—"

"Dad, she's dying!" Caan shouted over him.

"Caan!" his father barked back. "If we can't afford to pay for these things and Benni can't pay for them either, what will she do when she needs therapy six months from now and can't get it? What kind of life will she have then?" As his father pulled the dark curtain of reality over the situation, a short man with a balding head scurried up and interrupted him.

"Hello, sorry but I need everyone's attention," he began. "I am Mr. Habel. I'm a social worker, and I have the documents we'll need to sign power of attorney to one of you. I understand the girl in the operating room is in need of immediate surgery." His short, stubby fingers shaking, he pulled up a holographic tablet.

A cry of pain came from a room nearby, but it wasn't Benni's. Three nurses hurried by, splitting up Caan and his parents.

"Let me know what you've decided. If everything is in order I'll tell Dr. Iverforth and she can begin right away." Just as he mentioned her name, the doctor came over, wiping her forehead with a cloth and speaking through a white operating face shield and sanitary respirator.

"Has a decision been made? We have only moments." Her green eyes snapped back and forth across their faces, lingering on Caan's, as if she had an idea who he was and why his red, swollen eyes kept looking at the girl buckled down to the robotic operating platform in the next room.

"Caan," Kolianne said softly to her son, touching his cheek. "I don't know how we'll afford everything, or how we'll be able to help Benni after the expenses today, but we can try. She means a lot to your father and me, too, sweetheart." Kolianne wiped her eyes and contorted her face in anguish.

"Kol, what are we doing?" Caan's father asked.

"Mr. and Mrs. LaKay, the Al-Messers have offered to pay for all expenses, and I mean everything. Surgery, therapy, anything involving today's procedure," Dr. Iverforth quickly explained. "I'm sorry I didn't make that perfectly clear before."

"Everything?" Caan's father turned quickly and his face lightened, as if suddenly a weight had been lifted. "That's wonderful. That changes everything."

"I can sign for her," offered Kolianne, extending a hand, "We'll explain to her parents if it ever becomes an issue. I don't know how long it's been since she's seen them or if they ever visit, but…" She looked to Caan's father and received a nod of approval.

"No!" Caan stopped her. "I'll sign it. I can sign it. I know it might not be comfortable for either of you."

"Caan, dear, it's perfectly all right. Your father and I …" his mother started.

"I know, I know! I appreciate it. But if anything … if anything happens, I'll be responsible. I can't know for sure what Benni will think, but I don't believe she'd be ready to die right now. She'd want another chance." Before his parents could argue, Caan moved his fingers and palm across the transparent, light blue holographic screen hovering in front of their faces where the social worker directed him. A laser field scanned an image of his fingerprints and affixed them to the waiver.

"Excellent. Doctor, you may proceed," Mr. Habel said with a quick nod.

"I won't waste another moment," said Dr. Iverforth, "If you'll excuse me." In a blink she left them and hurried into the operating room, followed by two more surgeons and a dozen nurses. A woman in a white uniform approached Caan and his parents and asked them to wait away from the busy doors or outside the surgery wing. The operation would take longer than any of them could afford to stay anyway. Jobi had been left with her friend Alka and her family and needed to be picked up and reassured everything was all right. Caan told his parents to go on, that he would stay overnight with the consent of the hospital and go out that night if only to eat dinner and return.

From outside the operating room windows, Caan struggled to determine what was going on. Dr. Iverforth and the two other head surgeons were seated at consoles, surrounded by holographic monitors and other virtual interfaces, their eyes obscured by apparatuses providing them assisted visual feeds of Benni's body and tissues while they issued commands to numerous artificial intelligences. Pale, skeletal, robotic hands appeared from out of the dark, casting shadows of their dexterous fingers across the operating table and the contours of Benni's shrouded form, making laser incisions; stripping off blackened, burnt skin; sucking up blood, severing, suturing, stapling, removing, reassigning, reassembling.

Next to Dr. Iverforth's head there appeared an image of Benni's brain, various parts highlighted red or yellow or light blue, contained in an x-ray image of a grinning, toothy skull with wide open sockets. Another surgeon's monitors displayed an arm, a shoulder, a spine, hips and two legs. A third provided a real-time image of Benni's circulatory system, a network of little red lines and twigs, so numerous they seemed to take the form of a red ghost. Pairs of dots appeared where the robotic suction drew or diverted blood flow. As the surgeons talked to their consoles, the operating table, enclosed in a sterile, glass, interior chamber, turned this way and that as needed while the robotic hands worked. Figures dressed in white, nurses, moved to and fro on the other side of the window. Occasionally they entered the interior chamber to change the instruments the automated hands were using, or to assist the surgeon working on Benni's circulatory system.

After some time, Caan caught a glimpse of Benni's colorless skin beneath the shroud and looked away when suddenly several new bright monitors came to life. His eyes were tired; his heart, even more so. On his way out of the surgery wing he met Hileah Al-Messer. She was speaking with a nurse and greeted Caan with a great deal of concern as soon as she recognized him. Hileah stood out from everyone and everything else in the hospital. She sported more elective genetic flair than anyone he'd ever seen. Her hair, shaved on one side and long and straightened on the other, was white and shone with iridescence. Her eyes looked silver from a distance but glistened with the same sparkle as her hair up close. A professional dancer as well as a singer, both her legs were cutting-edge, Tika-sponsored prosthetics, most likely custom-made, judging by their abnormal, glassy, highly abstract and artistic design. They were provocative and alien, smooth and feminine like real human legs, but seamless and elongated, and the shins and ankles transitioned seamlessly to two dainty feet with stiletto heels built right in.

"You were with the girl, weren't you? Is she all right? Did my father's message get through to the doctors?" she asked, her arms folded in discomfort.

"Yes, I'm Caan, and she's in surgery right now. I can't thank you and your family enough for what you've done for Benni," Caan replied, suddenly noticing the weak, hours-after saltiness of his tear-stung eyes. "They said she'll be all right."

"My father has absolute faith she will be, too," Hileah reassured him. "He is the CEO and public spokesperson for the top biotechnology developer in the city."

"Ismaan Al-Messer, yes, I've heard of him," said Caan. "But now I know him a little better, and he is obviously a man with a good heart."

"He wanted me to apologize for him, because he was not able to come with me to visit, but I will tell him that," said Hileah, smiling. "He knows that if Benni was not in that operating room, I would have been, and he was more than happy to help you both."

# 2.1

Once outside the hospital, Caan realized he hadn't eaten in eight hours. Leaving, he looked right, left and up, quickly noticing lights were out in most of the district, except the hospital. The Tika module in his forehead informed him it was early morning. Most of the city would be shut up for the night, but there were still places serving food. Walking two or three blocks didn't turn up anything, though. Caan could have looked up a place on the module but didn't choose to. He'd planned to return to the hospital, but he knew Benni would be moved in the next hour or so to a more permanent operating room, and the doctors would continue to work the next day. She wouldn't be awake any time soon, and the best thing he could do was leave her in the hands of those who could help her and make sure he was well-rested when the first opportunity came to visit. His thoughts hung on the Al-Messer family and their kindness.

Benni would soon carry a special civilian status—"transhuman"—a person whose body consisted of both human flesh and the paragon of human biotechnology. In his famous speech, Ismaan Al-Messer called this kind of person a "postcestor." He and other transhumanists raised them up on a philosophical pedestal, calling them the future of humanity realized in the present. In theory, postcestors were capable of being the humans of tomorrow, today. They would learn and understand things in ways unaugmented people couldn't, and not just simple things—they would understand themselves, others and everything around them differently, and by thinking as multiple individuals at once, not just one. They would age slower, perhaps not at all. They would be physically and mentally superior to their ancestors in every way.

In his head Caan imagined Benni jumping forty feet into the air, running faster than a levcar and solving advanced mathematical equations in less than a fraction of a second. For the first time since the accident he laughed a little. But the silly ideas retreated as he began to wonder, not what the surgeons were doing to save Benni, but what they would do to change her. Most of the great questions of his day buzzed around transhumanism. For the first time in history, certain death could not only be fought with intervention, but significant improvement. After all, becoming a postcestor wasn't everyone's inherent right. Just like any expensive procedure, it would save someone's life as long as money wasn't an object. If not for the Al-Messers, Benni's death would have been a financial inevitability. But now, because of the circumstances, Benni had fallen into the clutches of death only to rise again as someone better, and in all aspects.

At one point or another, while he was waiting outside the operating room, a nurse had been kind enough to detail the numerous procedures being performed on Benni. Caan had made notes in his Tika module and began to research them as he quietly walked several blocks toward nowhere particular. In about fifteen minutes of digging around Academy Ignaea's online medical journal database, Caan had collected a wealth of knowledge to fill in the details of the operations. Benni was receiving a great deal of implants and transplants, the most costly and complicated of which were meant to replace or repair damaged brain tissue. After the operation her emotions and thoughts would remain organic, but they would be processed in part by augmented brain tissues—a synthetic, superconductive substitute for missing or damaged neural networks. Her lost bones and joints would be reinforced or replaced entirely with miraculous alloys; her blood, with smart cells, so that even if the calcium, marrow or t-cells failed her, her body and limbs would drive like machinery, and her veins and arteries would fire liquid life through her like self-cleaning industrial pipelines. These nanomachines would live inside her every bodily tissue, always on the lookout for infection or disease. They would be able to detect and eradicate anything from a virus to a cancerous cell before symptoms ever began to show. *What if the procedure radically changes her?* he wondered. *Will she have lost memories? What if she doesn't remember me? What if she doesn't remember anything at all? How much of Benni will be coming back, and how much will have been lost, if anything?*

A late-night levbus turned the corner ahead of him. Caan caught sight of it lighting up the off-ramp and hurried to the nearest stop. Gathered around it were a few dockies, and when the levbus touched down, Caan decided he'd ride to the commercial lifts with the others. Maybe there were aerofreighter hubs open for breakfast down below. He thought about finding out if Wolfie was working, just to have someone to eat with. Caan wasn't even sure he wanted to talk about Benni, but if he planned to see Wolfie there was something of a responsibility to let him know about her; he was just as much a friend of Benni's as anyone else. After spending all day in the hospital, Caan had worn himself out on the matter, but he knew it wouldn't be leaving his mind anytime soon. Who was he fooling? He didn't expect to just ignore it and feel better while occupying himself with something else.

Caan opened the TikaTalk application in his field of view and searched for Wolfie's name in a list of contacts. A little light next to Wolfie's name told Caan that Wolfie was awake and available. Caan would have opened an audio feed, but he'd have felt awkward talking to himself in a quiet levbus with only a few other people, so he sent a message in text form to Wolfie and waited for a reply. After about twenty minutes, Wolfie's name went dark and Caan figured he was busy or going to work. He closed the TikaTalk application and stared out the levbus window as it pulled into one of the commercial lifts. Bright white lights appeared every twenty-five or so feet as the lift descended, casting a powerful, passing glow as if they were scanning his and the dockies' faces to get every detail. A short, avian trill of gears sounded and the lift doors pulled apart, every vehicle departing in turn. Caan used his Tika module to access the levbus's public interface and signaled the driver to stop when a little place called *Yao's Dockside* came into view. Opening a credit application with his Tika module, Caan paid his fare instantly. Thanking the weary, cordial driver, he stepped off the levbus and squinted, covering his face as it lifted off again and brushed him with the warm breeze of its engines.

Sliding into *Yao's* like a shadow, Caan planted himself at a table and ordered breakfast and some coffee. Again, he opened up his credit application and the little diner's digital menu came into view next to it. A waiter approached Caan from behind but then saw him staring into space and realized he was looking over a menu.

"A Tika man, huh?" the waiter joked, turning to go back to the kitchen. On the surface, restaurants were accustomed to having customers come in, seat themselves, order, eat and pay all without ever needing any assistance, but such a sight was uncommon in the Dark Town docks.

Caan made some selections that went straight to the kitchen and got his food quickly. He was alone, save for perhaps two dockies half-eating, half-snoozing by the bar. The coffee he'd chosen was a bit expensive, but Caan rested assured that the Giffen good incentive would reward him for his choice to pay a little extra.

Special applications kept a record of Tika module users' spending—what they bought, where and how often they spent more money than they had to—and Genesis MTI would eventually make returns on these purchases in the form of special credit. It was a simple system that encouraged people who had the money to spend it, either on more expensive brands of food, personal items and especially charitable donations. Keeping independent companies and manufacturers from charging too much was a special variable tax curve. The more money companies or individuals made, the more they were taxed, and this greatly discouraged price gouging.

*Utopia doesn't nickel-and-dime you* ... the words of one of Caan's economics professors came to mind. When he'd first heard the saying, he didn't know what a nickel or a dime was, and had been embarrassed to ask. Caan began to think about the intricacies of the little purchases he'd made since leaving the hospital. He thought about the dockies, who watched him interestedly as the machine in his head issued faint sounds and lights. How much more streamlined things would be if everyone had access to the Tika module, thought Caan. He began to try to wrap his head around the economics of Genesia, but economics wasn't his forte. The whole subject gave him a headache.

Instead he looked up and over the servers' bar at an old fashioned wireless monitor rattling off the news of the day. One story kept his attention for a bit: Jose Juan-Bautista, a twenty-four-year old former baseball player for Academy Aeraea who had been drafted by Flexis Tech, was being released from Genesia General Hospital following his highly televised contract scandal. Juan-Bautista, who'd been a pitcher for Flexis Tech for less than two years, violated the terms of his contract when he traveled to see his fiancé in a private levcar a half year prior to his contract's two-year renegotiation. As a professional sports performer, he'd broken a caveat not to travel in a flying vehicle that wasn't supervised or approved by a Flexis Tech team chauffeur or manager. All this, Caan knew, was to say that Juan-Bautista risked damaging the incredibly expensive muscle, joint and ligament augmentations in his limbs which belonged to Flexis Tech. On screen, the pitcher talked about his recovery and his enthusiasm to have been drafted by a new team owned by People Plus with the same nonchalance that an old pistolero would talk about shooting a hole in the side of a barn. Incredulity cast Caan's face in cement as he listened to the interview—the young athlete didn't appear to have been concerned about the prior six months he'd spent in a hospital bed as a quadruple amputee after Flexis Tech repossessed his augmented arms and legs. But Juan-Bautista's situation was normative, and most contemporary athletes were more like ancient stock cars than anything else. Athletes had to perform and succeed, of course. Out-of-shape bodies were known to reject athletic transhuman implants in almost eighty-five percent of attempted procedures. But once drafted to a professional team, if an athlete didn't accept standard augmentation surgeries, they could expect to be a career bench-warmer. Those on the playing field became stars, but of course they owed most of their physical talents to top-of-the-line transhuman tech, which their team owner always provided. And in cases like Juan-Bautista's, when a contract was terminated or a player was traded, the proverbial vehicle would be dismantled, the chassis would be hospitalized, a new team would pick it up and stick new tires and an engine in it, and *voilà*—a star athlete was reborn. The only thing that changed was the sponsorship decals.

As the news digressed to another topic—celebrities—Caan's mind crept back to the hospital, to Benni. His vision was still full of minimized digital windows plastered with medical journals. He closed them all. Although the Tika module itself was always online and he couldn't do anything about that, he'd rather have a clear field of view for the moment, and a clear head.

# 3.0
# KINTSUGI

*"Suppose you lose a finger to a common, household accident. Biotechnology replaces the lost finger with an identical, albeit synthetic one. Is your body still the same body? Most, including myself, would say of course it is. Now, suppose something similar happens to the bottom half of your right leg. Perhaps disease or something of the sort demanded amputation, but again, biotechnology is able to replace your leg with an identical one. You would likely continue thinking of your body as being the same body. But consider if the pattern were to continue, and your entire body were slowly replaced, part for part, including every distinct part of your brain—memories, personality and all—until you consisted entirely of replaced parts without a single original one still in place. Is it the same body, the same mind, the same individual that it was before? And what if our entire species were to be replaced in the same manner, part by part over some span of time? How would we address the question then?"*

—Jude Chai, author, *Grandfather's Axioms*, 2071 CE

In the beginning, brightness engulfed everything intensely, though not painfully. Benni could look straight into the light but sometimes it would run from her, and her eyes would chase it. When she blinked, red, blue and purple broken spider webs flashed in her vision. A blue orb hovered up in the corner, shaking and bouncing around, leaving a spectral tail behind it like a stylus pen writing on her retinas. The inside of her head felt empty and light; her eyes, swollen and fuzzy, compelled her to blink because the light tickled them. Minutes passed—one, two, three, four, five, six—but Benni did not know this. Several passed before any of the hands noticed her watching them. The hands flew all around above her, paying her no mind. Benni couldn't move her head enough to chase them as she chased the light. Shadowy fingers appeared over the horizon, streaking across her field of vision and vanishing beneath white waves covering her arms and legs. They stirred up the soft landscape, pushed the white waves around and scurried about this way and that, over hill and dale. One of them paused. It had a great big face and one eye that studied her closely. She wasn't supposed to be awake yet, but no matter. A hand came down over her nose and mouth and Benni became sleepy. A tunnel formed around her vision and slowly she retreated into it as the hands worked. Another minute passed and Benni was gone again. Two minutes, three minutes, four minutes passed. Not much left to do. Five and six minutes passed, and by the seventh, the hands paused to rest.

* * * *

"Benni! Benni, dear, please stop!" A dark-haired nurse stooped over Benni's bed, holding tight to her shoulders and calling for assistance. "Benni! Benni, listen to me! You're all right!"

"Where am I?" Benni cried hoarsely. She hadn't used her vocal chords in three weeks. That, and the fact she still had a cluster of little tubes down her throat made her weak voice sound even more pitiful. Gagging on the tubes and choking on fluids she surrendered, falling back into bed and curling up in a fit of coughs.

"Benni, you're all right. You're in the hospital. I need you to be still, okay?" The nurse wiped Benni's hair out of her face and straightened the bed. Calling a holographic display up, the nurse opened Benni's monitors and looked over them automatically before ordering the IV system to administer more fluids.

"Why am I here?" Benni managed to say as she began to look around her. Warm, artificial sunlight spread across the room. Almost everything else was white or light blue and clean.

"You were in an accident, dear," the nurse said sympathetically. "You almost died, and you needed a lot of surgery. You've been under or asleep for three weeks now. That's why I need you to rest. Your blood pressure won't stand for that kind of energetic burst. I'm glad to see you've got a lot of life in you, though! Just promise me you'll save it for Dr. Emerich, okay?"

"Who?" Benni blinked, felt her eyelids stick a little and saw a vase of flowers on a table nearby. Their petals looked unreal, like nothing she'd seen in electronic journals, videos or even in the Genesian Hybrids and New Species Botanical Gardens. Its petals were five in number, all curling outward into little fiery rolls of orange to blue to white, surrounding a plume of soft yellow and white stamen, the middlemost of which was tipped bright green.

"Dr. Emerich is your physical and psychological therapist," said the nurse, her voice bringing Benni's attention back to the woman's smiling face. Gently, she touched Benni's forehead. It made Benni think of her mother, whom she'd not seen in several years. How terribly she missed her, and her father. Where were

78

they now? They couldn't possibly know what had happened.

"What happened?" asked Benni.

"You were hit by a levcar, at the *Blue Morpho*," replied the nurse. She assumed Benni meant to ask what had happened to put her in the hospital.

"No. Where are Mom and Dad?" asked Benni. The drugs in her system cared more about the past than the present.

"Oh, I'm not sure, dear. Your parents are on Earth, I believe?" The nurse touched the holographic monitor again. Benni was beginning to show signs of pain, though she wasn't verbally acknowledging it. The monitor quietly alerted the nurse to the source: the leg that had been operated on. It was a simple thing to fix, though. Dr. Iverforth had prescribed the best and safest pain medicine available, a substance created from rare cone snail toxin, more than one thousand times the potency of archaic alternatives like morphine. It couldn't be rendered ineffective by any kind of developed tolerance, didn't cause addictive dependence, and left no damage behind after use. Benni settled as the nurse administered a tiny amount.

"Those are so pretty," said Benni, looking again at the flowers.

"Would you like to see them?" The nurse asked, bringing them to her and holding them up for her.

"*Mane virens*," she said, reading the botanical card.

"Mhm, they're fiery greendawn flowers. These are a new species," said the nurse.

"Caan …Where is Caan?" asked Benni, suddenly upset. She

had seen his name on the card, disregarding the endearing poem he'd composed for her.

"Benni, lie down and relax, please. Is Caan your boyfriend? He came to see you. He left the flowers. I've told him you're all right."

"Caan? Caan is here? Tell him … I'm …" Benni quieted down as her medications got the better of her. Every part of her felt soft, as if she'd become part of the bed sheets, and light, like the cool hospital air. Raising her right arm, she pointed to something, or someone, for a reason she couldn't have articulated. That was the first time she saw part of her new body, a clean white and light blue casing with little lights. She couldn't feel it, or at least, the medicine told her she couldn't feel it. As she forgot that it was her arm moving back and forth in front of her eyes, Benni began to think some alien being was looking back at her; some other girl's arm, some other Benni.

After three months of physical therapy, Benni was walking, jogging, writing, typing, eating, lifting, talking, thinking and generally doing everything she used to do. She had begun to improve around week four, mostly because she'd gotten used to seeing herself in the mirror. She'd stopped compulsively touching and tinkering with her right arm and its new prosthetic parts the way one would prod a dead mouse in the corner of the room with a broom handle to see if it were alive. Technically beautiful as it was, the dull shine of the blue electronics beneath white casing were something that had come to reside in a place that used to be her skin and flesh. Benni felt like half a person and half a brand new levcar. Embarrassingly, she'd had something of a fit the first time she came back to full consciousness. No one was around to explain to her where she was and where a good portion of her two right limbs had gone, as well as what had even happened to put her in that bed. The only message she'd received was the same one she had always received upon waking: "Tika Personal Assistant—we're always with you."

Caan came by the hospital to visit every single day, usually during a time when he and Benni could eat something together and talk, or sit outside in the therapeutic gardens. It was, without question, Benni's favorite time of the day. Caan was the only person who didn't seem to notice all the changes that had taken place on and in her body since the surgery. At least, he didn't say anything or stare at her new parts as much as anyone else. He held her hand when they walked—the real one—and hugged her and kissed her the same way he always did. Other people, strangers, would ask about the places where her skin became solid and cool; the stares—even of the nurses and other hospital patients—at the little blue lights on the side of her head behind her Tika module, were difficult to ignore, especially since the little hair she had was entirely gone, and still trying to grow back following the surgery to her skull and brain.

In the afternoons after physical therapy, f Caan weren't around to visit, Benni would draw models with her digital studio kit. Caan had been thoughtful enough to retrieve it for her from her apartment. Without understanding why or stopping to wonder, she'd been vastly more inspired of late. Her surgery had little to no effect on her creative spirit; in fact it was stronger than ever. Ideas came to her by the scores, and she passed much of her free time in her own world, fascinated with parts of her work she'd never stopped to notice before. When Caan wasn't around, she'd freely wander the numerous hospital complexes, particularly the many therapeutic rooms: the indoor gardens, recreational gymnasiums, immersive digital reality entertainment theaters and patient art galleries. The hospital could be an uncanny place. Some days it was peaceful, a solitary sanctuary, and all the faces Benni saw were much like her own, friendly and content to be on their way to recovery. Other days, such as when a major traffic accident had occurred, the complex was filled with tension and noise, tears and pain and frowns.

* * * *

One day Caan came to visit with a gift, a little handmade, jade pot with fresh flowers for Benni to plant in it.

"I know I'm a little late," he apologized to her, handing her the beautiful little pot, "But I remembered on the way here that you needed new flowers, and I thought they would last longer in one of these."

"Oh, yes! Thank you," she happily accepted. "I'll have you help me plant them, and I'll put them in the window of my dormitory. What is this, here?" Benni turned the polished pot in her hands, tracing the strange pattern in its surface with her finger. Long, irregular and uneven streaks of shiny gold interrupted the smooth jade in several places like thin clusters of tree roots growing through soil.

"That," Caan explained, pointing to the streaks, "is gold."

"*Real* gold?" Benni burst, her eyes wide in disbelief. "But that … doesn't make sense," she said, turning it over and over, "Why and how would someone make a pot like that?"

"They wouldn't," said Caan, smiling the way he did when he knew something Benni didn't and was preparing a history lesson, "That's a broken pot … er, it *was* a broken pot. The woman I bought it from repaired it by pouring lacquer resin into the break lines, brushing powdered gold into it and letting it sit and assume its original shape once again. It's a Japanese art, believe it or not, and almost twelve-hundred years old if I remember correctly."

"It's gorgeous," Benni replied, her lips still parted in awe as she inspected and touched the delicate gift.

"It was different, so I just knew you'd like it," said Caan, putting an arm around her shoulders.

"It's wonderful." Benni smiled at him and gave him a kiss. "How did you afford it?"

"I sold some old software licenses I don't need anymore, and agreed to a few extra teaching jobs. I'll be back again in the morning," said Caan, getting up and stretching. "You have psychological therapy in, what … five or ten minutes?"

"Yeah, it's that time again. Dr. Emerich will be here soon, I'm sure," Benni said, smiling as Caan leaned over and kissed her.

"How has it been?"

"The therapy? Dr. Emerich is very nice, even if a little unusual. She's well-spoken, and her general knowledge is amazing. She's full of stories and ideas, and never boring, but … I don't know, she seems a little strange. Her expressions are quirky. She *lingers* on them. I don't know if that makes sense? Do you know what I mean? Any of those brains you hang out with act like that?" Benni made a face as she tried to explain.

"The Circle? Yeah, they're a bunch of machines. How weird," Caan agreed, eyebrows jumping up as he laughed along with her and shook his head and gathered his things. "Well let me know how it goes. You aren't in any pain, are you?"

"No, no I'm not," she answered softly, managing a smile.

"Let me know if you ever are, or need me to do anything."

"I will."

"Love you."

"I love you, too."

* * * *

"Good afternoon, Benni," said Dr. Bellafonia Emerich.

"Hey, Dr. Emerich," said Benni, waving nervously as she opened the doctor's office door and gently shut it behind her. Dr. Emerich made Benni self-conscious without having to say or do anything outright to warrant it. When she first met the doctor, Benni had opened her Tika module and used the MetaMeet application to instantly learn everything she could about her. The doctor's education was decorated with some of the highest honors

84

and awards in Genesian academic realms. She'd spoken out against Proposition 4 and a number of other anti-android rights bills in the past five years. She loved minimalist art and early 24$^{th}$ century heliogenicist poetry. In fact, the doctor was an entirely amiable and warm woman, but Bennie felt intimidated nonetheless. Perhaps this feeling was due to the way Emerich carried herself, or it could have been her immaculate, short black hair, royal blue eyes, pretty face and her stylish manner of dress that communicated an intimidating degree of intelligence, insight, eloquence and professionalism. Benni fancied the thought of looking and acting like Dr. Emerich in ten years, as a thirty-or-so-old woman. Where the doctor was from, or how old she was, Benni wasn't sure. She had an accent to some effect, but it was subtle—idiosyncratic rather than regional.

*C'est toi pour moi, Moi pour toi dans la vie…*

The doctor had her music on, as usual. She glanced at a hologram orbiting her desk to turn down the song that had been playing.

"You've been doing so well, I hear," said Emerich, seated behind her desk and finishing up some other business on a holographic screen. "I saw the artwork you sent me last night. Forgive me for not replying as I would have liked. Other matters came up with another patient."

"Oh, no, it's all right. Shirro again?" asked Benni. Shirro was a young man, a few years her senior, who'd had surgery similar to hers about a year previously. She'd met him during group physical therapy when it was being held in the in-house aquatic gardens, a peaceful little gathering place enclosed floor-to-ceiling by an aquarium, specifically, a marvelous coral reef system.

"Yes, the poor young man. I suppose you know him well enough to guess what's been going on. But no matter, we're here for your session, and I mustn't speak of other patients," said Emerich. Collapsing the holographic display, she relaxed in her chair, folded her arms in a way that made her breasts pop out. "As I was about to say, your light sculptures are beautiful. I don't have to be clever to guess you're an Aeraea student?"

"Yes, I am," said Benni, nodding and beaming.

"You're quite creative. I shouldn't mind asking if I might have some of your work to display in my office, once we're all through with your therapy and you're free to have fun and be young again."

"Of course!" Benni agreed.

"I'd be ever so grateful," said the doctor. "Now, about today's session … I really don't see any reason we need to continue. I've watched you recover over these past weeks with the greatest of ease, and, I've thought about your artistic inclinations. If you would like, we can move on to the next step and have you spend some time in the somniscope. Do you know what that is?"

"No, I don't think so."

"Well," Emerich explained, leaning forward in her chair and gesticulating with her long fingers, "It's essentially a device that allows patients undergoing psychological therapy to freely control and manipulate their dreams. Overnight, you would sleep in the somniscope as opposed to your normal bed, and your brain activity will be monitored. You'll be free to generate and manipulate vivid, lucid dreams all you like, all night long … Oh! And the technicians can't see what you're actually dreaming about during private sessions, so take advantage." Dr. Emerich leaned forward and winked with a charming smirk on her lips—something strangely outside her normal character.

Benni burst into laughter.

"I'm terrible with jokes," the doctor said, "but the machine really is fun for all my patients. What do you say?"

"That sounds great," agreed Benni.

"Superb! Well, unless you have any other concerns this afternoon, I can let you go early." Dr. Emerich's desk made a soft tone, and she pulled up her holographic display again. "Ah, I see a handsome young man has returned with chocolate for you out in the lobby. Oh! I apologize. I hope that wasn't supposed to be a surprise!"

"I'll do my best to pretend I don't know." Benni began to stand to leave and then paused for a moment. "Actually, Doctor, I have a question. I wasn't sure if the hospital was able to contact my parents about the surgery yet. I checked with my nurse last week and she couldn't say."

"Ah, yes, let me see …" Emerich waved her fingers and began to search around the display in front of her face. For the first time, Benni consciously noticed that the display made little tones when the doctor's fingers touched it, which is to say they touched the *air* occupied by the clever optical illusion. Why was it necessary that the display talked back and made sounds as if to appear to be a solid object? What was it really saying, other than reaffirming that contact had been made?

"I see here that you separated from your biological parents nearly twenty years ago." Dr. Emerich was speaking again, her thumb rested on her lip and a thoughtful expression seemed to weigh down her brow.

"What?"

Benni hadn't quite heard the doctor, uncharacteristically lost in deep thought.

"It says here your original parents' custody of you was overturned in a legal ruling when you were two years old. Your adoptive parents declared you independent five years ago and are now resident aliens living in Turkey. No wonder we haven't been able to contact anyone." Dr. Emerich showed Benni the records confirming that indeed, a young couple, Nicolai and Sara Reading, had been her parents before Hugh and Pauline Dublanc, the only parents she was ever aware of.

"I … I wasn't aware I was adopted. Is that true?" Benni asked, a constrictive feeling developing in her chest.

"I …" Dr. Emerich shook her head in a way that revealed she'd exposed Benni to information she didn't know was supposed to be forgotten. Nevertheless, she didn't attempt to take part in whatever façade Benni's original parents had built around the early part of her life. When Benni asked her to find out why the Readings had given her up, the doctor didn't object. It was an understandable request and relevant to Benni's predicament. "I see here that you were born in this hospital ..." Emerich's eyes swept back and forth as she read "... at the request of your parents. Your biological mother and father were having difficulty conceiving, and they chose to have an alternative birth."

"I'm a synth, then? Is that what you're telling me?" Benni sat down, feeling weak in the legs.

"That isn't a proper term," said Dr. Emerich, raising her eyes in disapproval, "And no, you aren't an android, Benni. You were an *alternative birth.* The differences are many, but the main distinction is that you are the result of the combining of your parents' reproductive cells. You were just born from an artificial womb rather than your mother's."

"Well I might as well be a s— ... *android* now, considering ..." Benni raised her augmented arm and pointed to the polished white and blue quarter of her head, frowning sourly.

"I apologize for this news, Benni. I wasn't aware your adoptive parents never told you about all of this. Your original parents apparently could not pay back a loan they used to fund your birth, and—"

"And *returned* me?" Benni interrupted, crossing her arms and looking down at the floor.

"Let's give them the benefit of the doubt," said Dr. Emerich calmly. "I expect, as with most people in their situation, they decided you would be in better hands with parents who were not in a great deal of debt. Both your original parents were dockworkers. Alternative birth is not something so easily affordable on those kinds of salaries. Also consider that their action ensured that you now do not have to work in the docks. Before you were born, you were ensured accelerated learning skills. Any genetic diseases would have been removed from your DNA structures as well. You're an advantaged young lady."

Benni didn't say anything. She wouldn't have known what to say anyway.

"You're a human being, Benni," Dr. Emerich reiterated. "I promise you."

"How can you be sure?" Benni demanded to know.

"You have organic tissues. You were conceived and not built. You grow, you dream and you create. You eat foods and drink fluids—"

"How do you know my insides are real at all? You can't see them without opening me up. You weren't there during surgery, were you?"

"In fact I can see them without having to know you personally," Dr. Emerich corrected her, folding her hands and resting them on her desk. "I didn't have a natural birth, either, and I can sense these things."

"What do you mean?" Benni sat up straight and felt uncomfortable. She wondered if she'd offended the doctor and only then realized it. "Oh … Oh, I'm so sorry! Were you … were you an alternative birth, too?

90

"It's all right," said Dr. Emerich, "and no. Actually, I am an android, an entirely artificial human being."

"Oh." Benni was shocked. She kept herself from expressing it verbally, suddenly unable to decide what to do. Dr. Emerich noticed anyway. Benni's eyes had widened only momentarily and her jaw was shut tight, the muscles up near her ears twitching in discomfort.

"I'll schedule you for your first somniscope session tonight, if you like," said Dr. Emerich, deciding to relieve the tension by returning to business. "The sooner you get started, the sooner you'll be through with all of this prodding and testing. That's good, right? I'll start you off in group therapy, so you won't be all alone. The machine can make you a little claustrophobic, even if you are asleep in it."

"All right," Benni agreed.

Dr. Emerich wrote a reminder for Benni using a stylus, scribbling away at the display hanging in the air over her desk. Benni rarely saw anyone outside of art classes using a manual stylus to do anything. She opened the TikaNotes program with her own module and quickly downloaded the reminder.

*Somniscope, 21:30 group, 301st floor, Yellow Wing*, it said. The doctor had drawn a little happy face beneath. Something she'd normally overlook, Benni thought it was an odd thing for the doctor to include, considering …

"Stay positive," said Dr. Emerich, snapping Benni out of her forlorn trance. "There is a time to put things down and a time to pick things up, and I want to see you healthy and uplifted again," she added, smiling.

# 4.0
# AS WE MAY THINK

*"Because it is inseparable from us, and we are inseparable from the universal gearworks, language, like all the great cosmic cycles we understand, will, over time, fall into a pattern of expansion and collapse. We and our understanding of ourselves do simplify and complicate just as a pendulum swings in the belly of a ticking clock."*

—Bellafonia Emerich, anthrotect and doctor of psychology and medicine, from her seminal work, *A Natural History of Synthesis and Symbolism*

When the maglift began its ascent to the 301$^{st}$ floor of the hospital, Benni felt as though she were rocketing straight into space. The research and development towers were some of the tallest high rises in Genesia. Indeed the upper wings of the megalithic compound were purposed to the task of discovery, not recovery. Emergencies, surgeries and the everyday were dealt with far below, closer to the ground, while high in the Martian sky above, inquisitive minds picked at the leaves and fibers of family trees; they unraveled strands of DNA and spooled them back together; they built microscopic robots to send into the dark unknowns of the human brain and circulatory tissues, to cross deep neural crevasses and swim rivers of cells, making greater leaps with smaller steps than humankind ever could before.

The Norwegians, as a matter of fact, opened up their seed vault and used nanomachines to give corn a borrowed brain. Quite some time earlier, smart vegetables in Scandinavia nearly ruined the American GMO-based market overnight. As it would seem, upon the approach of the 21st century, the macroscopic world had been thoroughly combed over enough to suit the purposes of human beings. Following the Information Age, the dreams of science and technology appeared to be buried not in the great masses of things, but in smaller and smaller vessels—"things" became "micro-things" became "nano-things." The answers to demands for convenience, sustainability, availability, portability and consumability were found in compaction, not expansion—sophisticated simplification, not organized complexity. The telephone became the cell phone became the smart phone became a pair of smart glasses became a smart screen embedded in the arm—all precursors to the Tika module, the electronic "omni-device," simplified and expedited until the moment it became a next-to-naturally occurring human organ.

About the time that happened, the Filii Solis and a number of other Post-Nano Age religions sprung up and from that point on, the steeples of hospitals outgrew those of churches. The literal search for the soul began. No longer was the spirit thought to be a glowing ball of light that would spring from the chest of the dying and fly off into the cosmos to some eternal afterlife. Rather, it was certain that the human mind, not outer space, was the final frontier, the new wilderness through which scientists pursued clues as to the whereabouts of personality and God. By the turning of the 23rd century, everyone was certain that everything they'd ever looked for was masterfully hidden in plain sight. Copernicus was correct about the arrangement of the celestial bodies, but the most telling spheres of all had always been sitting atop the necks of men and women.

* * * *

Benni stared through her Tika desktop and out the window of the maglift. The little black eye in her head recorded the ascent, snapping pictures when Benni commanded it and committing them to digital memory. With a Martian sense of natural longing she placed her left hand against the window. For no conscious reason, she had chosen that one and not her new, transhuman arm. As though she were a mannequin, she stood quietly, absorbing the view from the maglift, wondering so much. Her mind raced in a way it had never before. She was not anxious or upset or preoccupied, but rather terribly intrigued by things she normally overlooked—the rush of the maglift, the stars in the night sky, the public parks scattered about the city below, condensation on the glass, her far-off heartbeat. Colors and lights and little sounds suddenly fascinated her. Small, seemingly unimportant or mundane details were captivating and seemed to tease universal truths.

Suddenly the maglift slowed and Benni wobbled, unprepared for the effects of the changing momentum on her legs and knees. The maglift issued a soft tone, and a genderless voice announced that Benni had arrived at the 301st floor. The great white doors pulled apart and the maglift sat silent and still, as if impatiently waiting for Benni to exit into the hall. Benni did not immediately exit, instead lingering by the window for another long moment. She wished she could have the view all to herself any time she wanted, or even more, to share it with Caan. She wondered how the experience of elevation would feel without the window, and with fresh air and wind. The genderless voice spoke again and repeated its announcement, then politely asked all passengers, Benni being the only, to exit and to mind their step.

* * * *

The Yellow Wing took some effort to find. Other than being named the Yellow Wing, nothing about it was colorful. In fact it was as steeped in white and soft blues and greens as any other place in the hospital. Despite the disagreement between reality and the naming convention, Benni did feel as though there were something yellow about the hall. Just to make sure she never lost her way again, she commanded her Tika module to commit the hall to digital memory using an application called Saintly, which remembered and highlighted familiar places, words or objects particularly in respect to their physical and spatial orientation. It made finding lost items and especially scarcely visited places easy to locate. Its desktop icon depicted a logoized St. Anthony giving a reassuring thumbs-up.

In the upper right hand corner of her field of view, a set of digits counted out "21:24," reminding Benni that her therapy group would be beginning soon. Luckily all she had to do was walk a bit faster; before long she came upon the correct room, the somniscope laboratory.

It was hard to miss. More like a large resort bedroom than a laboratory, it housed eight somniscopes, machines that looked like full sized beds with lids, too inviting and cozy to be compared to caskets. The lids of the somniscopes were windowed for monitoring purposes, and their concave undersides were speckled with what looked like little black camera lenses—thousands of them, all arranged around the head of the bed. Across the room, in a corner by itself was an administration hub, where a number of researchers were already conducting their work on other patients.

If it were any less conspicuous, Benni would have taken the lab for an eight-person luxury suite. After a moment she was approached by a portly young man in a white coat who introduced himself as Gary so-and-so, a doctor's assistant who would be monitoring Benni's sleep patterns overnight. Benni's Tika module automatically made notes on Gary as he yammered away about the components of the somniscope and how it worked, none of which meant anything to Benni. She nodded her head as if she understood, although she was distracted and making silent observations about Gary, namely that his hair stood up in the front and his nose was crooked in a peculiar way. So many doctors, nurses and aides had introduced themselves to Benni since she was admitted that she could never have kept track of them all without her Tika module. Sometimes, she thought to herself, the intermediate reality the module created between her and her surroundings was the most organized and least stressful world she knew—a nice filter between reality and her tired brain where only basic images and labels told her all she needed to know, sparing her the grimy, heavy work of sorting through details.

Gary directed Benni to an empty somniscope and invited her to climb in when she was ready. Benni hovered over the device for a moment, touching the sides and mattress and fiddling with the pillows. She felt awkward standing next to the humming machine in her pajamas. Gary had already gone back to the administration hub and waved a hand to signal Benni that he was ready. Benni looked all around at the other somniscopes, their patients shut inside, surrounded by robotics and electronics and emanating bright colors that reminded her of pictures she'd seen of fireflies in glass jars. Climbing into the machine, she lay on the sheets and uncomfortably folded her arms across her chest. She wondered if it would be hard to breathe when the lid shut.

Not until the top closed down around her did she feel any sense of privacy. The transparent lid became opaque; a number of little lights appeared briefly and vanished as the machine went through a number of startup routines, its many components powering on. In the next moment a menu appeared before her, and a disembodied voice prompted her to select a scene from a list of several hundred. Benni raised a finger and selected one at random. The miniature thumbnail of the scene expanded to occupy all the visible surface area of the somniscope lid. A series of still images played one after another, all beautiful and varied landscapes from Earth. Benni had selected a vibrant rainforest. The disembodied voice asked Benni to confirm her selection, but Benni wanted to see more. Closing the window, she reached out and touched another image, one of a Saharan desert vista. The miniature expanded, and replaced the misty green rainforest with an expanse of smooth yellow-orange hills, tinted a glittering peach and pink by the setting sun piercing the clouds in the endless distance. Benni collapsed the stills and selected another set. When they expanded, they showed her a great expanse of North American wilderness, pine forests in the throes of late summer and cool black lakes, dark and shining in early evening light.

"That's where most of the group is, if you'd prefer to join them." Gary's voice suddenly came through the somniscope's voice channel.

"So I just pick this one?" Benni's fingers hovered over the pretty stills.

The somniscope asked Benni to confirm her selection, and this time she did, wondering what all the images and scenes were for. The menu above her face disappeared and the somniscope darkened. Benni heard faint beeps and whirs coming from somewhere. Little yellow lights flashed and ran across the surface of the now opaque glass around her.

Suddenly, a cool breeze blew across her skin and she lifted her arm, the real one. The little hairs on it stood up and fell as the cool sensation passed. Benni sat up and to her surprise, she found herself to be lying on the ground by the edge of a pine forest, the pink and purple sky above her beginning to show the first sign of stars. At first a persistent tone Benni mistook for mechanical beeps was the only sound breaking the overwhelming and tranquil silence. But there was no artificial source. Benni had never heard the chirping of crickets before, and the mystery of their omnipresent singing bewildered her. No amount of trying could help her remember how she'd gotten where she was or how long she'd been in the forest. Never before had she seen pine trees, nor the little brown needles they shed, covering the ground underneath her. Benni grabbed up a handful of them. They gave off a sharp and fresh smell. Standing, she looked all around her and watched as another breeze blew the branches of the trees, made ripples in a nearby pond and combed her hair with its crisp airy fingers. Benni drew in several breaths and felt a rush of excitement. The air was so clean and light. She caught the odor of something else on the wind, a heavy and woody smell—smoke—coming from somewhere nearby.

Walking softly through the trees, Benni caught sight of the hazy trail of ash rising from a fire just up the next hill from where she was. Stricken with curiosity, she moved toward it, often getting distracted along the way. In the air above her, little dark bodies leapt from branches and flapped their little wings as they flew like darts from one tree to another. Their chitterings and squeaks harkened the approach of the night, only two or so hours away. A great antlered creature drank from the pond in the distance. Benni stopped to watch it. The mere shifting of her weight was enough to crack a twig underfoot. The sudden pop alerted the animal, and its head rose to look directly at her. Its two big, black marble eyes glistened, and fresh water dripped from the little beard of fur on its chin. Another breeze swept the clearing, and the animal turned slowly to walk away, its short tail flicking this way and that, head swinging back and forth and antlers rocking.

Benni continued to climb the slope toward the source of the smoke, stopping to pick up and inspect a prickly pinecone, a thing she was hesitant to interact with, presuming it to be some sort of animal. She collected fourteen different rocks along the way, fascinated by each and every one, their rough texture and multicolored mottling sparkling when she held them to the weak sunlight.

Her hands full of woodland treasures, Benni reached the crest of the hill. It opened to a treeless, rocky outcropping that hung out over a sheer drop into the forested valley beyond. Several paces away, a bright fire popped and hissed, throwing its warm light against the strange faces of five people, all seated around it and wearing colorful dyed blankets and painted masks that concealed their faces. Each of their blankets displayed unique symbols and patterns. One of the people sitting by the fire noticed her and beckoned for her to join them. Several people pointed to a yellow blanket draped over a wooden drying rack. Benni took this to mean it was meant for her, and she retrieved it and wrapped it around her shoulders.

With each pass of the breeze, the temperature was becoming

more brisk. As she meandered over to the fire and took a seat, her blanket changed. Symbols that did not exist before began to appear, providing a pleasant decorative pattern to her blanket. The same person who had noticed her before sat up straight and gestured for everyone to look. Some of the people spoke sounds Benni did not recognize as language, or even human tones. When they spoke to one another and moved their hands, symbols like the ones on the blankets would briefly appear in the air like ghostly writing and then vanish again. Benni didn't understand a word, but she somehow knew that everyone was excited she had come to join them, and that they were happy to meet her. One stranger, whose mask was shaped like an old welder's visor and painted with little stars, reached out and laid a friendly hand on Benni's shoulder. Benni turned to the person and smiled, not realizing her face was also hidden behind a mask.

After some time the group got up and moved to a clearing by the edge of the cliffs, and Benni got up to follow them. Their blankets began to shine with rows upon rows of symbolic language, not one identical to another. One of the strangers beckoned to a conspicuous pile of stone cubes on the ground, and with the help of a few others, began to arrange them into orderly shapes—a pyramid, a tower, an arch—all without ever touching them! Benni watched in amazement as the strangers simply held out their hands and directed the blocks to do as they commanded, like magicians.

"The others wanted to show off a little, since you're new,"

Gary's voice echoed over the cliffs from some place unseen. "This is where our patients can safely practice controlling the kinetic direction centers of their neural prosthetics."

"This is incredible," said Benni, her words coming from her mouth as foreign noise. The others stepped back as she approached the blocks and began to imagine what she wanted them to do. A sloppy first try, she did manage to make a few of the stones wobble and scoot across the ground.

"Fifteen minutes to sunrise," came Gary's voice again. It was a standard announcement he made before the group was to be woken. Even after the rest had returned to the fire, Benni stayed by the cliffs, trying to manipulate the stone blocks until her brain felt like fluff, and when she awoke in her somniscope she smiled like a teenager who'd just earned her driver's license.

# 4.1

Although she'd slept all night, Benni was still groggy and tired. In fact, her left leg felt sore, as if she'd actually hiked through the forest she'd dreamt about. The ghost of exhaustion haunted her right leg, too, until she placed her hands on her thighs to rub them and no report of feeling came from the artificial limb or the specter trying to massage it. Benni's prosthetics were designed to emulate the sensitivity of her lost arm and leg, but being able to truly feel pressure, pain, texture and temperature again would be a long shot, depending on her body's ultimate acceptance of the technology, and even then, she was prone to "sensory blackouts" as the doctors called it.

The smell of pine needles, earth and smoke lingered on her mind, and for a moment, as she got up out of the machine, she thought she still smelled them. What excitement she'd had, seeing the Earth for the first time! Of course, it hadn't really been Earth, only a simulation, but there was no true difference to Benni or the other patients. And what a thrill it had been learning about the new things her brain could do! Could she move things like the stone blocks in real life, with nothing more than her imagination? She eagerly wanted to know. If so, goodness, did she have a lot to tell Caan!

None of the other patients were in their somniscopes when

Benni left hers. Only a few of the medical aides and technicians sat at the desks behind the monitoring station across the room, running analyses and drinking coffee. Benni left the lab and headed to the 45th floor, one of many that housed long-term patients in single dormitory-style bedrooms. Benni had decorated hers with her art, and she knew exactly what she wanted to model next—the forest and lake from the dream. As she changed out of her pajamas and stepped into the shower, she tried to imagine it all again. The cylindrical glass doors of the shower closed around her and fogged. Automated water jets aligned by her feet, soaking her ankles and toes in pleasant, warm water. In synchronization they rose and rotated, spiraling up to her head and then back down. Benni shut her eyes and wondered how it would feel to swim in a real river or lake or ocean. The water jets continued to spiral up and down, adding soap to the water and then repeated their cycle a third time to rinse.

Fixing her gaze on her toothbrush, she whipped out her arms like a dancer and squinted and bit her lip, willing the brush leap up from its holster. Nothing happened. Trying again, she poised and shook her hands, making an even stupider expression and holding her breath. The brush moved! Then she realized it had simply slumped down into its holster on its own. Exhaling and slacking her shoulders, she let it go and finished washing.

Not wanting to eat breakfast in her cramped little dormitory, Benni went down a few floors to one of the hospital's restaurants. She enjoyed it because she could sit at her own table by the great big windows and see the city as the day began. Powering on her Tika module, she saw "09:17," earlier than she was used to being awake. The restaurant's greeting application popped up into her view and offered her a breakfast menu. The moment Benni saw images of food her stomach cramped, and she realized she'd neglected a mounting hunger. Ordering several dishes, Benni closed the menu application and turned to look outside. How differently she felt about what she saw that morning, the mile-high superstructures, the airspace full of hovering crafts, the greenhouse gas plants— all standing in great contrast to the orange Martian desert beyond. None of it was comparable what she'd seen, heard, touched and smelled in the forest. Strange how little she knew of Earth and how badly she wanted to return to a place she'd never actually been.

"Hi there." Standing by her table, a young man with short black hair, a few days of stubble and smooth, dark brown eyes waved to her and smiled. He shifted his weight from leg to leg and touched his face anxiously.

"Oh, hello, Shirro," Benni replied.

"Were you in dream therapy last night? I think you joined the other five of us in Gary's program, the one with the forest and whatnot. He's conducting an interesting experiment with language with several of us. I guess you're going to be taking part in kinetic manipulation training, too, from now on." Shirro laughed and put his hands in his pocket.

"I guess so. I just wonder why I was never told before," said

Benni, "I thought all the rumors about transhuman superpowers were science fiction nonsense."

"Well it is, in a sense. We can only do that stuff in the somniscopes because the simulation allows it. Gary is testing to see whether it's even valid in theory, let alone practical to develop for real-world use," explained Shirro.

"Oh." Benni deflated into her seat.

"Mind if I join you?" Shirro nodded at the empty seat across from her.

"Oh, no, please. I always have to eat alone like some nutcase." Benni offered him the seat.

"Ah, that's no good." Shirro laughed again. "And yeah, the somniscopes are addictive. Did you know they're illegal for private use or ownership? They're like narcotics, I've read. Before much study was done on them, dockies would sometimes sell them off to buyers on Earth through the black market."

"Oh, my! You're kidding?" Benni exclaimed in surprise, suddenly feeling awkward about the previous night's therapy. "Are they safe?"

"Well they're safe enough for the hospital's purposes. The people upstairs are professionals, and we're not free to use the machines the way addicts do. Gary had us locked into a fixed dream, with limits and rules we can't break. For instance, we can't use spoken language. We also can't change the landscape or the outfits we wear. It's all part of his experiment, but you get the idea. People who go crazy are the ones who use the dream machines to escape into their own personal fantasy worlds, that kind of thing. But I'll admit, it sounds like a fun way to pass the time." Shirro looked as though he were staring off into space as he said all this, but then Benni realized he was ordering breakfast with his Tika module.

"Ah, I thought as much. That's comforting to know. But about Gary's experiment. What's he doing?" Benni thanked the hospital aide who brought her food and turned back to listen to Shirro.

"It's really interesting," Shirro repeated. "He's a pre-doctoral psychology student from Academy Ignaea with a cross degree from Academy Aquaea in linguistics. I'm not sure what he's doing just yet, but it involves removing spoken language from social settings. As I said, we aren't allowed to speak any known meaningful language to each other in group therapy, and we've all had to try and work around it. I actually came up with the solution the group uses currently," Shirro said, a tinge of pride in his tone, "but it's still kind of frustrating sometimes when you want to say something specific and don't know how. You see, all we use are simple tones of color and sound. Transhumans are thought to be able to learn how to broadcast their thoughts to one another directly."

"Oh, wow! So, telepathy, you mean?"

"Yes, that one *isn't* science fiction," Shirro affirmed, chuckling.

"Oh, no, now I'll have to guard my thoughts," she thought aloud. "Suddenly this all sounds awful."

"Oh, don't worry, it's a lot like wireless communication,"

Shirro reassured her. "Your mind is protected by a number of digital encryptions and even more resilient, conscious allowances. To share thoughts directly, you literally have to want to, and it's a two-way street."

"Thank goodness. If you don't mind my asking," Benni interrupted, "Are you a student? You sound so interested in all this."

She wasn't half as interested in technical details as Shirro, but his enthusiasm was cute. It reminded her of Caan.

"Oh, well yes," Shirro said, laughing. "I should've explained. I attend Academy Ignaea. I'm a student of astronomy. That's how I came up with the color and sound language. You see, I'm always learning things about stars by their colors, their brightness—"

"… the noises they make," Benni joked.

"Well yeah, seriously," Shirro continued, "they're too far away to go and prod with instruments, so astronomers have to learn about them with the only available details, which aren't a lot to work with."

"So Gary's experiment is a familiar problem for you," Benni concluded for him.

"Exactly!" Shirro smiled in his quirky way. "I enjoy trying to solve puzzles, though they can be maddening." He held his head and Benni nodded, smiling and taking a bite of the fruit in front of her. "Anyway, I'll have to help you get caught up on the language. That is, if you'll be joining the group again."

"That's very nice of you," said Benni, accepting his offer. "And yes, Dr. Emerich has me scheduled for a few more weeks."

"Dr. Emerich?" Shirro said it as if the name bothered him for some reason, but then he smiled and continued on. "Okay, well I'm usually free all day unless I have physical therapy." Shirro brushed back the hair on the back of his head and turned so Benni could see the white casing that covered the skin. "I used to play sports at the academy, as you can guess," he said, holding up his arms, which had both been replaced numerous times with athletic prosthetics, "but not since my accident. I'm still working on my coordination."

"Ah, I have some of those too," said Benni, tapping on her head and waggling her new arm. "I've had a Tika module all my life but this has been difficult to get used to."

"I know what you mean. Mine's not been as quick to fix up the damaged brain tissue as the doctors estimated. Who knows how much longer I'll be here?" Shirro frowned and gave Benni a shrug. "Oh, I just got a message from Dr. Emerich. I have to go, but I'll see you later." Shirro got up just before his food arrived.

Benni couldn't help but wonder about the young man. Dr. Emerich had mentioned him briefly to her before for being a troublesome patient. Shirro certainly seemed to be an amiable guy, smart, too. Benni guessed he must have been the stranger in the dream who had worn the mask with the stars on it. He was an astronomer, after all; handsome too, when she really thought about it. As he turned to leave, Benni's sight lingered on his smooth dark brown eyes once more, and the way he left his Octattire carelessly open at the collar, subtly exposing an athletic chest.

A message appeared in the upper right of her field of view as she got up to leave the restaurant. It was from Caan, waiting for her on the 23$^{rd}$ floor outpatient landing jetty. Benni opened her voice chat channel.

"Hey, sweetheart!" Caan's voice filled her head.

"Hey!" Benni felt as though she hadn't seen him in so long. It was the first day she was allowed to leave the hospital for a while, and she and Caan had planned on going out for the morning and afternoon. She couldn't wait to see him and tell him about the somniscopes.

"Hurry up!"

"All right, all right," she answered, smiling and hurrying out of the restaurant.

Back in her dormitory, Benni dressed herself nicely, putting on her good Octattire and setting it to take on a sunny yellow color. Turning this way and that, she looked at herself in the mirror and frowned. It would be the first time she'd be going out after her surgery. She wondered if people would notice her head, arm or leg. Caan had told her it didn't bother him, and he meant it, but she knew he had to notice. It wasn't as though a lot of transhumans walked around Genesia every day. For good measure, she wore jewelry on her other arm and around her neck and worked quickly to apply some makeup to her eyes. Benni hadn't developed any good way to style her hair around the casing on her head yet, and as she fought with it, another message from Caan popped up in her view. Frustrated, she gave her head a few tosses and let her hair do

111

whatever was natural while trying to hide the smooth, artificial shell casing on the left side of her head, and hurried down to the $23^{rd}$ floor. She found Caan out on the outpatient jetty. He handed her a pretty little blue flower and took her hand, the real one, in his as they both hopped into a levbus.

# ५.੨

Caan and Benni repeated their routine for several months, making time to fit romantic rendezvous between therapy and counseling. Benni didn't speak, laugh or smile often in public. She couldn't eat when she was being watched, and the two couldn't go anywhere without receiving stares. Caan caught on quickly and soon planned more nighttime dates, more private and cozy atmospheres. After some time, though, Benni sensed that the limited and monotonous routine grated on him a bit. He expressed his discomfort in always feeling as though the two held their dates in confined and lonely spaces. They didn't go out to the clubs and parks as they used to do. Dancing was out of the question simply because Benni needed more physical therapy before her leg could bear it.

Benni slept in the somniscope at least every other night. She and Shirro were the only two patients who didn't miss a session, and as a result, Benni became increasingly involved in Gary Von Monne's social experiment, nicknamed "Tribe." Shirro's enthusiasm for the machines was contagious and difficult to resist. It was easy to understand why. In dreams, Benni and Shirro could do things they never could in real life. Amazing things weren't even the real lure, either. Sure, being able to visit Earth, swim, fly, or skip stones with their minds was thrilling, but "sim life," as Shirro called it, was not about being superhuman.

Shirro's obsessive interest in the Tribe program was partly the result of what Genesian psychologists called classic familiar bond crisis. Shirro was a good friend, intelligent and kind, but some days Benni worried that he struggled to differentiate simulated reality and true reality. Enhanced mental processing seemed to drive a wedge through him, as was common for transhuman patients. Biotechnology could, in theory, produce a better human being, but life as a transhuman quickly taught Benni that Genesia was not full of "better" human beings. There were androids, of course, artificial people created to perform physical and mental tasks more efficiently than humans, but they were not *human beings* at all.

On certain nights, the somniscope groups met for sessions to which Benni particularly looked forward—the flying sessions. Everyone, the doctors and administrators included, shared an enthusiasm for them. The only participant who did not, and in fact harbored a crippling fear of them, was Shirro.

As the glass lids on the observation beds came down on one of those nights, Benni lay with her hands on her stomach, fingers laced, and the corner of her bottom lip pinched in her teeth as she awaited the familiar sounds of the machines' startup routines. As the administrators' voices came over the communication systems, reviewing safety protocol and other information she'd heard a thousand times, Benni turned her head and caught sight of Shirro lying in his somniscope chamber just a few paces away. His eyes cut this way and that, his mind clearly racing and his face drained of color. Benni frowned, sighed and wondered if this time Shirro

114

would make the leap.

Opening her eyes to a vast, bright and time-sculpted desert, Benni took a deep breath. The somniscope told her the breeze was arid and baked, still more refreshing than the air piped into her hospital dormitory each morning, afternoon and night. She wiggled her toes and felt the presence of sticky grains of silicates rubbing her skin until it turned pink and irritated. The blanket wrapped around her shoulders whipped in the wind, and the mask she wore echoed her own quiet breaths back to her ears. She and the others stood atop a flat, rocky cliff overlooking an endless expanse of dunes beyond. Gathering along the precipice of a wild, sandy wilderness, they waited and chattered in nothing more than wordless tones and luminous blooms of color and light, filling the air with undenotated and cryptic symbols that blinked into sight and out again like fireworks, while the somniscope finished rendering their imaginary playground.

Out over the cliffs a large, bright symbol appeared and hung in the sky like a burst of sun, a signal from the administrators that the group could begin anytime they wished. Without hesitation, one of the tribe—a tall figure in a red blanket with yellow detailing and a black mask—ran to the edge of the cliffs and leapt. The red blanket around his shoulders flapped like the winged fins of a stingray on the wind, and with a great shout the figure began to soar. Another immediately followed, carelessly throwing herself from the cliff and taking flight, the purple blanket trailing behind her, elongated like the tail of a dragon.

One by one, each member of the tribe took flight, hooting and shouting in colorful, meaningless vocalizations of thrill and excitement, including Benni, whose golden yellow blanket spread like the wings of a giant chickadee as she threw herself to the gales and glided after the rest.

The last member of the tribe stood frozen on the edge of the cliffs as the others grew fainter and fainter on the horizon. Leaning forward, the loner gazed down, down, down at the sands far below. The dark eye holes in the loner's mask, painted with stars, fixed on a spattering of rocks protruding from the sands at the base of the cliffs and imagined they were not rocks but gravestones. The wind blowing through the loner's dark blue blanket was hot and yet did not stave off persistent goosebumps and cold sweat. Unlike the others, he acknowledged the great distance between himself and the ground below, and he could not see the blue sky for the shimmering desert. The loner looked up to see the group vanishing, a flock shrinking into the distant sun.

\* \* \* \*

One afternoon, while Benni and Caan sat together under the simulated noontime sun in Hermphrey Park, Benni received a private message from Shirro. It had something to do with Tribe, as usual. Benni didn't reply, but Shirro continued on until Benni's vision became clouded in unanswered message prompts. Shutting off her Tika module, she leaned against Caan and tried to relax, but she couldn't. She proposed the idea to Caan that they should save some money and visit Earth some day. Caan was interested, but not as much as Benni would have hoped, and, against her character, she became silent and moody.

Instead of steaming and brooding on repetitive thoughts, her mind raced and expanded in all kinds of directions at once. Normally, when she was angry, Benni couldn't think straight. At that moment, however, she was sharply focused and dangerously volatile. Caan hadn't done anything to provoke it, but Benni had suddenly spiraled off into a highly zealous, silent rage. She felt trapped. The simulated sunlight irritated her. The rippling of the nearby pond was nauseating and the hiss of artificial wind cut her eardrums. The glass walls of the park enveloped her in a way she perceived as both facetious and tyrannical, insulting her existence. Benni wanted to break them all.

"What's wrong?" Caan's voice surprised her. He'd sensed something was the matter. Benni slouched against him so that he couldn't see her sour expression.

"Oh, it's nothing. Or maybe it is. I don't know." She closed her eyes and shook her head. It was a painfully honest, if not neutral response.

"Is it about going to Earth?" Caan asked. "I didn't mean to sound as though I'm against it. You know I'd love to, it's just that I always think about how expensive it would be, and how long it will be until we finish school and actually have the time ..."

"No, no, I know. It's not that. I just feel the need to get away from here," Benni explained, laying her head in his lap and shielding her eyes from the light.

"What do you mean?"

"This whole place is just … It's so …" Benni's mind conjured images of lightning bugs again. "Nothing's real. It's all a big … substitute." The word she'd chosen was awkward and cynical, and she regretted it. Caan loved the park, and she'd just cheapened it.

"I'm sorry," said Caan, sounding more irked than apologetic, "I thought *you* wanted to come here today."

"What do you mean by *that*?" Benni shot back.

"What's your problem?" Caan sat up straight and looked Benni in the eyes as she turned to him. "I'm running out of places to take you when we go out. First you don't want to go out at night and then you don't want to go out during the day. Do you care to explain what I'm doing wrong? I just can't please you!"

"You say that as though you think nothing's good enough for me, Caan." Benni took offense at his sudden outburst.

"It seems as if *nothing* has been for a while," Caan continued, pricking at her again. "If you want to go to Earth so badly, if you want a perfect date, why don't you go take a nice romantic nap with Shirro in your little dream box?"

"What?" Benni was no longer angry, she was hurt and surprised.

"You know those machines you sleep in are barely legal? If you weren't in therapy, I'd be worried about you." Caan was serious. He knew about Benni's dream therapy and the Tribe program and Shirro. It was all Benni ever talked about when they went out.

"Caan, he and I …" Benni began to panic. Caan had gotten the wrong impression, but she was stammering as if she was guilty, and that only worsened her fear. Upsetting herself more and more, Benni couldn't think. She felt dizzy. Her Tika module powered on, but she hadn't meant to command it to. Shirro's unanswered messages popped up and swarmed her vision.

"I bet that's him now, isn't it?" Caan noticed Benni's module had powered on, and he looked away coldly.

"Caan ... Caan, I don't feel well," Benni said, suddenly aware that something was wrong with her module.

"What? What do you mean?" Caan looked at her with an expression of mixed anger and mild confusion.

"I can't think ... I can't think ..." Benni wasn't sure what she meant by it. It was impossible to focus, as if her thoughts and emotions had completely boiled over beyond her control.

"Benni?" Caan forgot his ire and became genuinely concerned as Benni rocked forward and hugged herself tight in a posture of panic.

In the next moment, Benni let go of herself and looked up at the sky through the glass ceiling of the park. Caan followed her gaze and saw nothing.

*Wuum ...*

An unexpected and forceful pulse shocked the air, and Caan and the park bench flew away from Benni as if thrown by powerful, invisible hands. Caan struck the immaculate grass face-first and ate a mouthful of dirt. It tasted strongly of minerals and fertilizer and made him sick.

119

*Wuum ... wuum ...*

The invisible force began to oscillate slowly, the air around Benni pulsing faster and faster until it grew into a low-pitched electric drone. Caan had banged his head fairly hard on the ground, and when he got to his feet he thought he was hallucinating. A small crowd had gathered, all eyes watching Benni as she floated limply in the air as if by magic. A strong, booming, bassy rumble hammered the ground below her feet, and her short blond hair frayed in and out as if her head were a paint brush whose soft bristles were being mashed against paper and lifted away again. Several loose objects in the pockets of bystanders leapt into the air and flung themselves this way and that, drawn out by the impossible locus of gravity emanating from Benni's body. Within seconds, the police had begun to appear on the outskirts of the park and everyone else panicked, shouted and fled for safety. As Caan got to his feet, a strong arm grabbed him and dragged him aside to cover behind a tree.

"Sir, I need you to remain here," a police officer barked into his ear.

"Hey, wait a second. What are you doing?" Caan demanded, grabbing hold of the officer's sleeve as he started off around the tree, drawing a kinetic pistol from a holster on his hip. "Sir! I need you to ..." A powerful force struck the trunk of the tree, thumping Caan off his feet and down to the ground again. A scream of pain followed the blast, and when Caan rolled on his side he saw a fuzzy, double-image of the police officer lying on the ground and clutching his right shoulder where an arm used to be. The side of the tree he'd been on was blown away clean, and a large ditch had been dug into the ground in the wake of the blast that had struck him. The police officer's blood streaked the park lawn. It looked as though a speeding levcar had struck a can of deep red paint. Caan rubbed his eyes and then stared at his hands, bug-eyed and frozen. The blood was all over his clothing and skin, too.

A scream of engines tore through the park and several aerial police vehicles arrived on the scene, whipping up a wind that forced Caan to cover his eyes and mouth. From their insides appeared several large, imposing, chattering and agile machine sentinels—the police department's automaton special forces, ASF. Simplistic and militant androids, they looked part mantid and part human. Caan scrambled to his feet again, terrified, confused and unable to act.

Several of the machine soldiers surrounded Benni on all sides and brandished an assortment of wicked but nonlethal weapons, taking aim and repetitively commanding the unresponsive girl to return to the ground and cooperate.

For a moment, the park was uncomfortably silent, save for a deep droning buzz coming from Benni, who limply turned in the air as if suspended from wires. Eyes shut as if in a quiet slumber, her head turned in the direction of one of the machine soldiers. In an instant, she struck it with a thunderous force, and its head and body began to violently crush inward as if it were no more than a paper ball inside a closed fist. Three other ASF ran in all directions, firing their weapons at an unseen assailant. Benni realized she was watching mirror images of herself, chasing down each soldier and pummeling it to scrap. Another squad of ASF arrived and a machine soldier immediately opened fire. Benni reacted intuitively, turning to the projectile and stopping it in the air, locking down the time and space between her and every other thing in the park. All became perfectly still for one long moment, and the moment passed. Feeling her strength leaving her, Benni watched the DKE projectile begin to move again. Unable to react in time, she received the shot from the stun gun and fell from the air.

Benni could not see or hear what was happening around her. Everything had become very much like a dream; lines and colors, sounds and sensations all occurring at once, all making perfect sense and none at all. As she returned to the ground, that's when she saw it for the first time—strange white words against a flashing black background in her mind:

*Earthshine*
*Earthshine*
*Earthshine*

# 5.0
# GLITCHES

*"For centuries, the Giffen good represented the theoretical antithesis to traditional supply and demand structures, as if it were an impossible case. It wasn't impossible; it just needed a system with different rules and incentives. But remember that like all economies, the illusion of bounty remains, and like a fast-flowing river, the economic stream will whirl violently in rocky places, creating treacherous undertow that is bound to suck down a swimmer or two."*

—Virgil H. Heinze, "Giffen good incentive" economic theorist, 2415 CE

Caan poked and prodded the food in front of him but was too preoccupied to actually eat it. Across the table from him, Wolfie did the opposite, shoveling breakfast into his mouth with both hands. Caan had let him pay for both their meals. Wolfie hadn't had work in two weeks and his bank account was still in better shape than Caan's. The guy had dropped out, taken a year to learn the freighting trade and could feed himself and another person regularly if he wanted. Sure, Wolfie didn't own a lot of things, but he could afford his own apartment. Caan lived in a temporary private dormitory and usually had to eat at a free-for-students cafeteria at the Academy, or go to his parents. Wolfie was steadily poor; Caan was in debt and without income entirely. Sometimes, just for an instant, he secretly hated Wolfie.

"You should really turn that thing off," said Wolfie, looking up at Caan from under his brow. "I know what you're looking at. It isn't going to make you feel better."

"I can't ... and I know." Caan collapsed all the digital windows clouding his view—the videos, the news feeds and the constant messages of concern coming from Benni's friends and his parents. Without the steady bombardment of incoming information to his brain he suddenly noticed the dull drone of passing aerofreighters outside of *Yao's Dockside*, the buzz of holographic beer ads and the quiet coughs of a dockie leaned over the counter at the other end of the room. The quiet of his Tika optical desktop was numbing and distracting, the kind of silence that makes prisoners in solitary confinement talk to themselves. In the real world, quiet was a noisy, living thing that nipped at his five natural senses; it made him alert and focused.

"Benni's being taken care of, right? She's back in the hospital and she's safe," said Wolfie as he ordered more coffee. "That little episode was scary, though, I'm sure. I still don't believe it." Wolfie laughed and then immediately frowned uncomfortably when Caan's expression didn't change.

"I would just like to know what happened. Those doctors acted as though they had her surgery and recovery under control and then ... *that* happened. You know they're saying they don't even know what caused it?" Caan waved his fork around in agitation as his voice rose.

"First time it's ever happened, I heard. That transhuman guy who attacked the police down here, he was super strong and everything, but I've never heard of anyone lifting off of the ground and doing the things everyone saw Benni do." Wolfie's face lost a little color.

"Are you sure? The basic technology is over a century old and this is the first case?" asked Caan skeptically, "I'm just worried Benni will feel like a criminal. Or be made to look like one. There are police posted outside her room at all hours of the day just in case something happens again."

"Police? Is that really necessary?"

"ASF, actually," Caan said, looking Wolfie in the eye and lowering his voice. No one else in the bar appeared to be listening in.

"Those big metal soldiers? Is that really necessary?" Wolfie repeated, wrinkling his nose.

"Of course not," Caan declared, "She's an artist, not a terrorist, but you saw the news. The public is scared, and everyone knows there are other transhumans walking the streets. People act like it's only a matter of time before they all become unstable or unpredictable. Some people even say they're part of some illegal, military weapons research."

"Yep. They're going to turn, like vampires. I told you! They're going to get us all!" Wolfie was joking, but it didn't amuse Caan.

"It's not funny," said Caan. "I'm worried about her. What's this going to mean for her? If the Academy thinks she's dangerous, will she be able to go back and finish? Is she going to be able to walk

125

around the city without scaring people? And how long is she going to be kept in the hospital? She's been in there long enough. She was almost ready to be discharged."

"I know, I know, it's serious. I'm just trying to improve the mood, here." Wolfie held up his hands in surrender. "It's difficult, though. Benni's situation is just another splash in the bucket of a lot of other problems that pop up every damn day."

"Well at least no one knows who she is. I thought she'd be all over MetaMeet by now, but apparently all the firsthand witnesses have footage that doesn't give a clear image of her face. That or their modules got fried or glitched. And what do you mean, other problems?" asked Caan. He calmed himself down, tried to relax in his seat. Remembering there was a plate of food in front of him, he made an effort to quiet down and eat. It was no use. His eggs tumbled off of his fork like lemmings over a cliff on the way to his mouth.

"What do I mean?" Wolfie repeated, laughing in disbelief. "You're the one with a Tika module. Are you telling me you haven't been watching the news feeds?"

"Why? What's going on?"

"Nothing in Genesia, but a lot of downright terrible things are happening on Earth." Wolfie finished his coffee and leaned back in his seat, looking around and lowering his voice. "There's no oil coming out of the Middle East anymore. They're totally dry. The only reserves left were being drilled and refined in the United States, Canada and Russia, but man," Wolfie ran a hand through his hair, "those sources have been draining for a long, long time too."

"Everyone knows that," said Caan. "What's your point?"

"Well the American reserves are not as high as Canada's, but the oil market is demanding too much of the States. There was talk of limiting American oil sales to foreign markets, the very mention of which upset a lot of the major powers. The rest is messy and unclear, but just this morning somebody or some group of people bombed a major American oil refinery and storage facility. They destroyed an eighth of the US reserves and crippled the most productive refinery in the world, which means that fuel production will decrease by thirty to thirty-five percent for the next eight years at the least. The damage that was done will break the market for a long time to come, and if that weren't bad enough, the West is now seriously considering ceasing all oil sales to the countries they suspect were involved as retaliation. No wars have been declared, but there's already violence. The news feeds I saw in my aerofreighter late last night were crazy. Riots all over Europe and the Middle East, major market stalls in Asia ..."

"Slow down, slow down," Caan waved a hand and shook his head in disbelief. "All this happened when?"

"All at once," said Wolfie, shrugging, "right after the bombing, which was five days ago, according to the reports."

"Five days ago, and we're just now hearing about it. It goes to show how far away we are from it all," said Caan, looking out the window to his right and watching an aerofreighter pass by.

"We're not far enough, buddy," said Wolfie. His expression was uncharacteristically solemn. "ARC has been chopping up jobs in my department because of this. I just found out they haven't been telling us why, intentionally. We aren't getting the same kind of shipments we usually do because there's not enough coming in. Some of the original Dandelion Initiative countries have withdrawn entirely from supporting Genesia. My managers won't tell us which ones. The remaining countries are struggling to make up for the loss, and they're failing."

"What does this all mean?" Caan asked anxiously.

"I don't know, but if I had to guess, I'd say things are going to get as ugly here as they are back on Earth in a short time, if not uglier." Wolfie twirled a fork in his hand nervously. "There's a saying we have down here in the docks." An aerofreighter passed by and shook the restaurant. "The goods flow up." Wolfie chewed his food slowly. "Meaning, if there's nothing coming in through us, there's nothing coming in at all. The people up top stand on our throats, and if we choke down here, they'll have no one to feed them. You know what's funny?"

"Hm?"

"There are no androids down here in Dark Town. It's all—" Wolfie beat his chest—"people. And we still send more supplies topside than we have to give. But you know what?"

"What?"

"This keeps up, and there'll be as many kings on the bottom as there are on top." Wolfie nodded and stared off into space over

Caan's shoulder. "We aren't rich, but we handle all the goods." It sounded like a threat.

"You ready to go?" Caan asked after a long pause of silence between the two.

"Yeah, let's get out of here," said Wolfie. "Hey, come on, I want to show you that levbike I got my hands on. Oh, and I want you to meet someone."

"All right. I'd say it's about time I saw that levbike. You've had it for months now," Caan said.

"You're not the only one," Wolfie admitted. "I haven't actually taken delivery yet."

Caan took a long ride in Wolfie's aerofreighter across the major Genesian docks, headed away from the traffic and commotion and into the warehouse district. Caan had never seen it before. It wasn't much to look at, just miles and miles of identical buildings with no windows, hundreds of feet tall and covered in air jetties capable of being accessed at every forty feet of altitude. The warehouse district looked a lot like a penitentiary, some kind of mass of walls and locks made to keep things sealed up tight and separated. Wolfie continued to talk about work, or rather the lack thereof, as he piloted the aerofreighter between two large warehouse blocks and cruised into the labyrinth of storage facilities. Caan saw something else he'd never seen before when the aerofreighter flew into the heart of the warehouse district—homes, most of them meager and grossly insubstantial compared to the magnificent apartments topside. It had never occurred to him there were

129

dockies actually living down below in the commercial guts of Genesia. Caan had never been to Wolfie's home, hadn't even been invited, but he'd always assumed Wolfie lived somewhere in the city as he did. Several people Caan didn't recognize waved at them as they passed. Wolfie waved back. Perhaps they were coworkers or neighbors. Caan wasn't sure.

"All right, we're going to land here for just a minute, then I'll take you back to the lifts," said Wolfie, putting the aerofreighter to the ground and powering down the engines.

They stopped in front of a few houses, all of which looked the same, save for identifying letters and numbers on the doors.

"Hey, Nati," said Wolfie as a young girl of about nine or ten approached him when he stepped up to the door of the house numbered R14. The little girl smiled and waved and then ran around the back of the house shyly. After a moment, the door of R14 made a mechanical sound and slid open.

"Oh! Hey, Wolfie. I wondered whether you were going to come by today," said a girl standing in the doorway. Caan had seen her before, and he knew where. She had been at *The Shoe*, a stranger he'd seen when he went out for drinks with Wolfie and again when he'd gone to *Fretz's* to watch the rock n' roll show. She was always around but always sat away from the crowd, probably to avoid the older men.

"Faela, this is my friend, Caan. Caan, this is Faela. I wasn't sure whether you two knew each other," said Wolfie, introducing the two.

"Oh, no, we don't," said Faela, "It's nice to meet you, Caan." Her eyes told him she remembered him from *Fretz's*. Stepping just through the door, she brushed her long, straight black hair out of her dark eyes and smiled at Caan as they shook hands. The way she looked at Caan and then averted her eyes suggested she was embarrassed to be in her work uniform greeting Caan, who was clearly a topsider.

"A pleasure," Caan replied quickly, taking her hand and nodding. Her fingers were small, thin and a little rough, but soft, like smooth, unfinished wood.

"Faela's been here for two years," said Wolfie. "I've known her ever since she started working for Viking Delivery."

"I was born in the Philippines," she explained to Caan. "My mother and father moved us to England when I was two years old, and we moved around the Isles a few times before giving up and settling here."

"You're lucky," said Caan, "I've been stuck here my whole life."

"No, believe me, it's actually quite nice here," she said. "I could tell you some pretty hairy stories about traveling around back on Earth." Her voice was smooth and proper and carried a pretty, soothing accent.

"I hate to interrupt," said Wolfie, clapping his hands together in anticipation, "But I have to see it. Where is it?"

"Where's ... um," Faela began, looking back at Wolfie. "Oh, right! You're here for the bike?" she reminded herself, laughing at

131

her own lapse in thought and putting her hands in the back pockets of her formfitting dockworkers pants. It was a cute and graceful recovery.

"Yes, please! I've been waiting and waiting and waiting. Show me!" Wolfie chanted, stepping inside the house. Caan followed him in quietly, silenced by the uncharacteristic butterflies in his stomach.

Faela led them through the house and into a little workroom off to the side. Her little fingers dialed something into a panel lock on the wall; the door slid open and the lights automatically lit up. In the center of the room rested a stunning, polished and expensive looking new piece of machinery—a levbike. It looked to Caan as if it had been assembled and designed to meet custom criteria.

"Oh, this is gorgeous," said Wolfie, stepping inside and circling the bike, inspecting every component inside and out, taking a seat in the vehicle and firing the auxiliary jets and levitation systems.

"It sure is," said Caan, quietly noticing the bike had no visible serial number.

"You two are free to take it outside," said Faela, "I don't think Dad meant for it to be flown in the house." She smiled and glanced at Caan while Wolfie turned down the levbike's jets and guided it out of the workroom and into the streets.

"By the way," Wolfie called over the hum of the levbike, "What do I owe him?"

"I told you, didn't I? I'm not letting you pay for it. I don't know how, but Dad must have worked something out," said Faela, shrugging her shoulders and casually folding her arms.

"Didn't say?" asked Wolfie.

"Didn't say."

"If that's the way he wants it ..." Wolfie's tone was full of boyish glee. "Well, let him know if he needs any favors from me any time soon. I owe him."

"Yes you do," said Faela, again speaking to Wolfie but winking at Caan and giving him a playful elbow. "I have a shift in two hours, though, so don't hate me for kicking you two out. You're welcome to hang around, but I need to get some sleep before I get into a freighter."

"No problem, Fae," said Wolfie. "We'll load this thing up and get out of your hair." Giving the bike a slap, he motioned for Caan to help him get it into his freighter.

"See you later, Wolfie!" said Faela. "Bye, Caan!" she added with subtle emphasis. "Hey, you two should come over to the *Jupiter* sometime soon. Maybe next week or so. I won't be working, then."

"Sounds good!" said Wolfie. "Almost *convenient*," he mumbled to Caan with a sly grin. Caan grinned back, and then wondered if Wolfie had picked up on something between him and Faela. "Bike's got room enough for two." It was true that Caan had voiced some complaints about Benni over the past few months, and their relationship had suffered from a bit of on-again-off-again syndrome, and Wolfie knew it, but was he honestly suggesting something?

"Aw, come on," said Caan, laughing and giving Wolfie a casual shove to hurry him up the loading ramp.

"Oh, hey, I meant to ask earlier," Wolfie began, grunting as he pushed the tail end of the bike, "The police detained you for a while after Benni's episode, right?"

"Yeah."

"What did they ask you about?" Wolfie inquired.

"They didn't. They just told me everything I saw was mostly due to hallucinations and a bunch of other garbage. Stuff I don't believe," said Caan. "Why?"

"Oh, well, you know, I thought if they were going to do a psychological evaluation of Benni or something," he explained, wiping off his hands and touching his hair, "they may have asked you if you knew other people who could speak on her behalf. You know, people who are familiar with her behavior."

"Oh, I see," said Caan. "No, they didn't."

"Okay." Wolfie paused for a moment. "Well, I just wondered because, as much as I could have helped, I would have asked you not to mention me. I've … got my mom and Reese to look after and just can't afford to be pulled away for too long, you know?" he elaborated, looking at Caan expectantly before fiddling with the levbike some more.

"Yeah, of course. No, I mean I would have asked you first," said Caan. He waited for Wolfie to say something else about it, but that seemed to be the end of the matter.

# 5.1

Benni didn't dislike the hospital itself so much as her confinement to it. She'd been so close to being discharged, and her episode in Hermphrey Park had delivered her straight back into the arms of medical science. She hadn't seen Caan in about two weeks. He'd accompanied her to the emergency ward following the incident and practically lived in her dormitory for three days after she was cleared for release from the intensive care unit, which had been a rather quick and immediate transfer. However, after the third day, he hadn't come back to visit and hadn't yet bothered to explain why, or what had kept him.

In self-pity Benni lay in her dormitory bed and wondered if he was afraid of her. She'd seen the bandages on his face. It was a recurring and fearful thought she'd been having, and each time it was followed immediately by anger. Caan had no right to ignore her. She'd apologized more than once to him for making him adjust to her burdensome needs and moodiness following the surgery. She knew Caan was busy. He had school to think about. But he'd never stopped calling or talking to her before, over all those months. But if he didn't want to be around her anymore, she thought, he could have just refused to sign the surgery waiver in the first place. After all, Benni wasn't the one who chose to be brought back from death. Her throat felt tight, and a sudden stinging pain forced her eyelids shut as fresh tears washed over her freckled cheeks.

For the first day or so the police had lingered around the hospital and outside her room. "Just in case," they had said.

*In case of what*, Benni wanted badly to know. No one had been able to tell her exactly what had happened to her in the park, or why. All the doctors made conjectures, sometimes pure guesses, but they never gave Benni a straight and helpful answer, not even Dr. Emerich, whom Benni had surprisingly come to confide in recently.

Most days Benni had no patience for visitors, especially doctors. Examination, interrogation, medication—her days were divided into three primary periods of invasive attention. They wanted to know everything—what Benni felt, what she thought, what she was hungry and thirsty for, what she'd been dreaming about, her medical history, the nature of her education, even her romantic and sexual relationships. By the time the latter topic had been brought up, Benni was through talking, and resolved to stare out her dormitory window until the psychiatrist took the hint, stood up and politely excused herself.

Nights, though uninterrupted and quiet, were no better. Benni would more or less lie awake with the apprehension that something lurked in the dark waiting to surprise her. Who was to say she wouldn't have another episode if she fell asleep, if she did not maintain conscious control of her mind for a single moment? No such episode ever occurred. Benni would instead fall asleep, wake around noon and spend all day with a headache and a sour disposition.

\* \* \* \*

"I can imagine it must be frightening," Dr. Emerich had said in the most disarming and conciliatory tone. "I have not experienced it, but I know of androids that have experienced technical malfunctions in their cerebral processing modules. One of my associates explained to me that it is the equivalent of when a human being faints, or worse, experiences a severe seizure. You felt as though you had no control of your body?"

"I didn't feel as though I had control of anything," Benni mumbled hoarsely, her eyes puffy and red. "All of these strange things were happening around me. I thought I was going to hurt Caan. I *did* hurt Caan," she whimpered. "I don't know if any of those police officers died. No one will tell me."

"I'm sure you did not mean to do anyone harm," Dr. Emerich said, her pretty artificial eyes fixed on Benni's, seeming to frown. "Strange phenomena occurred during your episode, many of which defy the laws of physics and the limits of the human anatomy. I was told someone saw your arm change shape and size, like a machine made of malleable clay. Another saw five duplicates of you, moving as fast as acrobats and beating several ASF to pieces. And another still said you disappeared from sight for half a minute, and left strange hand and footprints all over the park."

"That happened? How is that possible?" asked Benni. It was incredibly difficult to believe.

"Allegedly, and I don't know. I see no apparent damage or signs

137

of transformation to your body, and you are psychologically sound. You're the same, brilliant and pleasant young woman I am used to seeing." Dr. Emerich was quiet for a moment. "You'll be all right. I am going to be with you as we figure out what occurred and why."

"Okay," Benni whispered, slumped and staring down into her lap. She had hoped Dr. Emerich would come through for her, but like the others, she kept quiet. Benni sensed the android knew something but was not prepared or allowed to speak about it.

* * * *

Shirro was the only person who acted completely delighted to see Benni again. The next day he found her by herself in a secluded corner of the aquatic gardens, and he sat down next to her, silently watching her for several moments.

Benni had her digital art kit with her and was sketching a concept for a desert landscape, something she'd seen in her dreams through the somniscope. The half-finished model sat on the air in front of her as she worked. Once she finished it, she meant to transform the digital painting into a kinetic light sculpture, a form of art popular in Genesian interior decoration more than half a millennium old, repopularized by a recent Solarist cultural movement. Such work fell into the more sophisticated and masterful branches of digital and physical art, one for which her cross discipline in optics prepared her, though her previous lack of her free time had rarely allowed her to practice. Following her surgery, Benni took to the challenge with relative ease. She'd

138

never taken courses on digital sculpture or model building, but the new concepts seemed to come to her naturally. What fun it was, though, to have taken so quickly to skills that normally took years to shape and a lifetime to master.

"I didn't know you could do this," Shirro noticed after a moment. "That's some talent you have there."

"I didn't know I could do this either," Benni joked. "But thank you all the same." She smiled and turned to see him smiling back. He looked a bit more well-rested than usual, and although the typical mental wear and tear showed through, his smooth brown eyes held a reserved yet uplifting gleam that somehow calmed the anxiety Benni had felt all morning. "You're looking almost energetic today," she kidded him.

"Almost," he agreed, making a face. "Dr. Emerich put me on a new, kind of unorthodox schedule. She won't let me go to somniscope therapy anymore."

"Oh no, that's depressing," Benni complained, frowning.

"I'm not thrilled about it," said Shirro, "but I know it's not good for me. She made the decision a few weeks ago and asked me if I were willing to try something new. Something of an experiment, she said."

"Really? Go on," said Benni, listening carefully and adding a few touches to her model.

"Well, it might sound weird," Shirro continued, "but she asked me to try a spiritual approach and invited me to attend a congregation at the First Church of the Filii Solis."

"That's not weird," Benni assured him. "I've kind of always wondered what androids do in that church. I mean, what their religion is like."

"I think a lot of people do, but I guess most never actually go and attend to find out," Shirro reasoned.

"How did it go?" Benni was much more curious than she let on. Imagining Dr. Emerich attending a religious service was difficult and, Benni thought guiltily, somewhat humorous. It was entirely unlike Benni to be spiritual in any way, perhaps because her parents weren't, or perhaps because it had never felt relevant.

"I'll be honest," Shirro began, "it was fascinating. In many ways, it was like the Tribe program. If you want to know more, you should really go yourself, or join me the next time I go. It's something you have to experience. I can't really explain it in words."

"Hm, I'll have to think about it," said Benni. Why the invitation was so tempting, she could not say. As she continued to compose, Shirro got up to watch the colorful exotic fish communing in the aquariums all around them.

Losing her focus, Benni's gaze fixed on her right arm, the artificial one. Looking at the cool, sleek, state-of-the-art prosthetics in her skin, flesh and bone, her mind returned to the moment in Dr. Emerich's office when she'd first learned the truth about her parents and her birth. Benni had never met her real parents, whatever those two words meant. She'd also failed to see or speak to the second pair regularly in years. Benni wondered if Dr.

140

Emerich had a family, or anything like one. If not, did she want one? After all, androids could not be legal guardians, marry or adopt. She tried to imagine Dr. Emerich with children, sitting on a bench in a park and watching them play in the bright sunlight. Nothing and everything about it felt strange at the same time.

"How are you doing that?" Shirro's voice snapped Benni's attention back to the present.

"Doing what?" she asked, startled.

"You're developing that model without looking at the canvas," said Shirro, pointing at Benni's right hand. Sure enough, she had filled in an entirely new space that hadn't existed before. Even more, it was beautiful.

"I…" she didn't have an explanation.

"Hey, do you think you would want to do anything later?" he suddenly asked.

"Oh, um …" Benni pretended to focus on her work. A simple question, it had caught her off guard. She didn't understand why, but she was anxious and giddy, like a younger girl whose crush had just noticed her for the first time.

"I just thought it'd be nice to go see the newer parts of the residential floors. They've added a few restaurants and even a night club for long-term patients. I figured it would help us both feel like we aren't trapped in a hospital." He smiled and watched her eyes, expectantly and patiently awaiting an answer.

"A *night club*? In a hospital?" Benni laughed, hoping to mask her awkward excitement. "Okay, I need to see this."

"I know, I know. It sounds ridiculous," Shirro admitted, "but I've been hearing great things about it from the other patients, like the people from our old somniscope group. Maybe it demands some pretending, but sometimes I think that's better than nothing, you know?" Shirro was no poet, but he had a cool delivery that could have coaxed Benni into the idea if she weren't already sold.

*  *  *  *

At around 19:00 that evening there came a knock at Benni's dormitory door. The sound caught her off guard, and she dropped an earring. Rolling her eyes and laughing at herself, she picked it up off the floor and began dialing different settings into her Octattire, trying to quickly make a decision as to what to wear. Her first choice was casual and flattering, and although something inside wanted to wear something flirtier, another part of her was hesitant.

"Almost ready! Just a moment!" she called to the door. As she gazed into her bathroom mirror, a notification popped up in her field of view. It was a message from Caan. She had sent him one earlier asking if he would like to do anything that night after Shirro had asked, in order to give herself an excuse and Caan an extra chance.

"Hey," it said, "I would, but I already told Wolfie and the guys I'd go to *Fretz's* with them. Sorry, babe. Maybe sometime next week after I get some of my graduate work done?" Benni didn't reply. Silently she furrowed her brow; her eyes narrowed and nostrils flared. Collapsing the conversation and removing it from her sight, she dialed new settings into her Octattire. Her suit became slim and black. After a moment, she huffed and tugged down the zipper on the front of her suit as the built-in bands around her bust line pushed her breasts together. Leaving the bathroom, she took a small but elegant necklace from her jewelry case and put it round her neck, a little teardrop-cut topaz hanging just above her cleavage. She almost reached for the door and stopped. Going back to the bathroom mirror, she brushed her short hair to one side, leaving the smooth, artificial scalp on the left side of her head completely exposed. It was bold and rather stylish, she thought, grinning and winking at herself before turning off the lights and answering the door.

"Hi," Benni smiled at Shirro and gave him a quick hug before making sure her automatic door was set to its code locked state.

"Hey! Wow, and I was worried I'd overdressed," exclaimed Shirro, stepping back and looking Benni up and down.

"Not at all!" she assured him, discreetly doing the same. He had a handsome Octattire suit on as well. The maroon and silver he'd chosen made his dark brown eyes appear darker but much less forlorn than they could sometimes be, and he'd fixed up his shiny, wavy black hair, which was now almost as long as hers, hiding his ears.

"Really? It's been a while since I've gone out, so ..." Benni hadn't thought Shirro had a single, suave bone in his body but it was certainly showing.

"Oh yeah," she repeated, "Not bad. No one would know you're

143

a boring astronomer."

"Seriously? How cold," he laughed, and his eyes lit up as they headed to the maglift down the hall and Benni continued to tease him.

The restaurant they chose higher up in the residential wing of the hospital was actually pleasant, and Benni more than once admitted she had expected an awkward, even hokey experience that evening. Against his character, Shirro let Benni do much of the talking over dinner. Normally he would have yammered on about his old job and things he'd read in popular, current scientific publications, but Benni had opened up the moment they ordered their food and closed the menu applications. Without hesitation she began to educate him on light-sculpting. From there, she moved on to fashion and how she'd like to become a famous designer for Octattire. As the sun set, they ate. Benni chatted between every bite while Shirro smiled and nodded, and not until they sat down again at the *Mercury Lounge* next door, finished three-quarters of a bottle of chardonnay and began on two coffees and amaretto did Benni begin to relax. Shirro directed her to the night sky outside, naming each and every star he could, attaching a Greek myth to it when possible. The evening melted away to the sound of the lounge band, a smoky quartet who filled the air with soothing, electronic melodies—a jazzy trance distracting Benni and Shirro from the gradual disappearance of minutes and drinks.

\* \* \* \*

The next time Benni checked the clock hovering in the upper right corner of her field of view, the display read "03:11." Some of her makeup smeared on her hands as she rubbed her eyes and straightened her hair. Stretching her arms and back, she ran her hands up her sides and yawned. Shrugging her shoulders, her arms pinched inward, she cupped her breasts in her hands and jumped with a start. One of her hands was cold to the touch, and when she remembered why, she sighed and blinked. As she sat up, her naked skin broke out in goosebumps as she tossed the bed sheets aside and got to her feet.

Resting her hands on the windowsill and arching her back in a feline slouch, she gazed outside Shirro's dormitory at the aerial traffic buzzing by in the weird dimness of the early morning. Nearby superstructures radiated the glow of apartments, hotels and late-night clubs, bathing Benni in cool, electric light. Sleepily, she twisted her neck around and looked at Shirro over her shoulder— merely a gently-breathing lump of sleep curled up under the bed covers in the dark. Turning back to the window, she brushed her hair to one side, able to see her reflection. Her own blue face looked back at her curiously, the smooth shell casing on her scalp reflecting the soft light. With her artificial hand, Benni reached up and touched the hard part of her head, her fingers impacting it with a muted, ceramic tap.

Turning groggily from the window, Benni extended herself once more in a full body stretch, swept her Octattire up off of the floor, dressed, visited the bathroom briefly and stepped out into the quiet darkness of Shirro's dormitory once again. Without a glance, careful not to wake him, she crossed the room, gingerly prompted the automatic door to glide open, let herself out and shut it once more.

Back inside her own dormitory, Benni sat down on her bed without changing out of her clothes. The bed was comfortable; the room, quiet. In one of the largest structures on Mars, surrounded at all hours by thousands of other residents and doctors and nurses, her private room suddenly felt like an island, as if it were the physical manifestation of a pensive corner of her own mind. No longer sleepy, she sat up, eyes turned to the window, watching the world outside. She'd have felt completely alone if not for the little flower pot in the window, the jade green one with the golden seams that Caan had given her. It didn't match the style of anything else in the room, and considering the circumstances of its recreation it would probably never match any room anywhere ever again, but Benni would've liked it less if it did. It was a welcome disruption, like a friend with whom to visit each day and with which to silently pass each night when all others had gone.

# 6.0
# WORDS, WORDS, WORDS

*"If only the third eye would lend perfect transparency to everything and everyone; then, perhaps we would know ourselves and our fellows well enough to have no need for the violence of words."*

—Lyonell Rudy, third chair, The Circle, 2555-2580 CE

The Church of the Filii Solis was known citywide as one of Genesia's identifying monuments. Completed by the year 2400, it was originally the place of worship for a group of scientifically and technologically minded devotees known secularly as heliogenicists, but more commonly as Solarists.

Merely five years later, the first modern androids would be successfully constructed. The android boom was in full swing by 2420, and by 2453 something had happened that no one had ever anticipated—a number of androids became religious. Most religions would not accept artificial humans into their temples, mosques and churches, but the Solarists at the Church of the Filii Solis did not oppose them. This was wonderful for androids looking for a spiritual family, but by accepting these new members, the Solarists lost many human members, and the damage to their church's reputation never quite healed. Eventually the Solarist religion changed leadership, but its new android priests continued to preach the teachings of the church's original founder, Jane Lillian Ashley, a former Christian minister from Earth.

* * * *

Standing outside the great doors of the Church of the Filii Solis, Benni felt anything but comfortable. The great building, beautiful as it was in its simplicity: a cylindrical, glassy tower, perfectly smooth on all sides and topped by the symbol of the Solarists, a solid sphere orbited by two smaller spheres, symbols of the sun, Earth and Mars.

Shirro had accompanied Benni, but when she became reluctant, standing out by the street as the crowds walked around her and into the church, Shirro went ahead, saying he'd wait for her inside. He'd have been more insistent if Benni hadn't told him to go on without her.

Benni appreciated Shirro's support, but his presence could be overbearing. Shirro wasn't the type to cling to just anyone for attention, she knew, but he was a troubled person. However, it wasn't Shirro's personal problems that were off-putting. After all, Benni had struggled with her surgery and recovery, too. What bothered her was that she felt Shirro expected more from her than what had already transpired between them. Something about the way he smiled, the way he sat so close to her and would reach out and touch her when she was feeling anxious or sad—it made her feel more abject than she did already. Benni had a romantic personality, but she also had a talent for reading people.

Ever since participating in the Tribe program, Benni knew she had risked sending Shirro the wrong signals from the start, and after their date a few weeks earlier, she'd pushed it much farther. Making sure she waited until the last minute before going inside the church was a way of intentionally ditching Shirro. It wasn't kind, but Benni felt Shirro would do more to ruin her experience that day than facilitate it. In fact, she meant to begin making a number of immediate changes in her life. One of the first would be to end her relationship with Shirro before it began. It would only lead to falling in love for pitiful and juvenile reasons, namely feeling affection for a young man who had only one thing truly in common with her—feeling weird and lonely. Benni had made those kinds of misjudgments as a younger, more naive sixteen-year-old, and she meant not to repeat the mistake.

Stepping inside the church for the first time, Benni was not sure what to do or where to go. Again she stood in place while the crowds filed past her. The interior of the tower was spacious and infinitely tall. Beautiful daylight shone on the glassy edifices and cast sparkling yellow beams on the floors and walls, much like the bottom of a swimming pool. Hundreds, if not a few thousand androids all gathered together in a large circular congregation that seated amphitheater-style and surrounded a central stage, where Benni saw one particular android dressed in priest's Octattire greeting guests. Above him, maybe forty feet in the air, there spun a large and beautiful crystal model of the sun, garnished with artistic looping flares of fire and glittery bursts of flame. Around it, a model of the Earth and a model of Mars floated slowly, all seeming to hang magically in orbit as they turned.

Benni jumped with a start when someone gently touched her left shoulder and blushed because of the overreaction. The android next to her, who looked to be a young woman of her own age, smiled and held a hand to her mouth as if to stifle a laugh. She had long, curly, braided black hair and brown eyes so dark the irises and pupils were indistinguishable unless under direct light. She had a small nose, rounded and a bit wider than average at the nostrils, and full lips. The light freckling under her eyes was just barely noticeable, like black ink pinpoints in dark cherry wood. The serial number "AFR0012" was visible on her upper right arm, printed into the skin like a tattoo. Benni recognized the number. The android's facial features and equally lovely body type belonged to one of five "perfect templates" defined by contemporary anthrotects, the artists who designed androids. What were unusual were a few little markings on her fingers. They were made to look like birthmarks, something androids never had.

Benni opened her mouth to begin to speak, but the android waved her hands excitedly and held a finger to Benni's lips, hushing her. She then tapped her head, indicating she wanted Benni to turn on her Tika module. Benni understood clearly, and did so. Once the module powered on, she opened her communication applications. Within a few seconds, the android sent her a message in text form, introducing herself as Dada. She guessed correctly that Benni was a new guest but did not mention that Benni was not an android, although surely she could tell. Dada then told her that it was Second Soul Day, the second day of three during which the church celebrated the day modern artificial intelligence was first created. She reminded Benni that the service would be silent, and apologized for hushing her before and coming across as rude. Benni had taken no offense. She introduced herself through a text message to Dada and asked her where she should go to sit. Dada instead took Benni straight to where she normally sat and continued to chat wordlessly with her until the service began.

After a few moments, the ceremonies began. Benni heard a low bass tone issued through a new program that opened up in her field of view. The symbol of the Solarist church popped up on screen and Benni allowed it to open. Dada smiled at Benni, touching her head and then pointing to the priest on the stage below them, who held up his arms and turned slowly to silently address everyone seated in the amphitheater. Slowly, he touched his head with both hands and then cast them outward again, as if the gesture meant to symbolize he was giving something to the congregation. Benni imitated Dada and the others as they did the opposite, holding up their arms and then slowly pulling their arms in to touch their heads. Everyone then stood up as the priest gestured for them to do so. The priest and everyone in the congregation folded their hands in something of a posture of prayer and shut their eyes. Benni did the same, occasionally peeking to see that everyone was still standing and seeming to do nothing else.

Benni kept quiet and still, wondering if she were doing something wrong, but no one had moved or spoken so she continued to meditate on her own. In the next moment, a point of light clearly appeared on the back of her eyelids. It grew either brighter or closer—she could not tell—as the moments passed. As the light became clearer, Benni realized she was looking at the Sun, fiery and glorious amid an abysmally black backdrop. Suddenly, new lights appeared, little white spots peppering the blackness. The Sun gave off a flash and then took on the form of a swirling mass, like a runny, fried egg spinning in a hot pan. Benni realized she was witnessing the formation of a star. Forgetting that her eyes were closed, she became captivated by the scene. Eons of time passed as she watched the Sun's fiery arms sweep the empty space around it for hundreds of millions of miles. Silently she watched as star-stuff coalesced into blobs of spinning bodies, the planets being born and cooling into their more perfect spherical forms, until the solar system was fully alive and twirling.

Next Benni felt herself rushing toward a little blue planet, one of the smaller, less impressive children of the great star she'd seen come to life. Pulled down through its atmosphere like a hurtling comet, Benni felt the breeze of cold air and the lick of terrestrial moisture. She witnessed the swift approach of a verdant, infantile mass of continents—mountains, streams, valleys, deserts, swamps, jungles and lakes—all flying at her as fast as she flew at them. Before striking the ground she turned, and the Earth and its land and oceans ran fast beneath her until they became a blur. A sudden collage of life struck her, and she found herself submerged in the ocean, all manner of things swimming about her, changing and growing and shrinking again. In another flash she saw the things living on the land, titans and monsters with great teeth and necks and bodies and wings, shaking the ground and thundering to one another in great voices. Natural music, made by hundreds of magnificent forces, narrated the story unfolding before Benni's eyes.

A loud tone arrested the overwhelming series of images, and all noise and light quieted down. Benni could not see for several moments, and then another soft tone broke through the darkness. More joined it, and the beautiful music began to play again. The next thing Benni saw was a dark-skinned woman, barely clothed in anything but animal hide and bone. In her arms she held a newborn child.

In the next moment, Benni found herself elsewhere, watching a village of early peoples all gathered around a fire listening to a man speak. An image of some great beings appeared in the stars above their heads, cloaked in the bright pinks, reds and purples of a celestial burst of light. The image vanished, and as another rapid collage of images showed Benni the course of human history on Earth, the otherworldly music enveloped her in great gusts of melodies.

In a matter of moments she saw the savannas of Africa, the first cradle of civilization in Mesopotamia, the rise of Egypt, China, India, Greece and after them Rome. Many mortal and immortal kings and queens rose and fell alongside their respective empires; the Middle Ages changed Europe, the East and its territories changed hands from dynasty to dynasty. Entire religions struggled to take the lands of Eastern Europe from one another. New worlds in the Western Hemisphere were discovered, and the Old Worlds cast their explorers into the oceans like seeds bound for these new continents.

Again rulers and religions fought, battling over the riches of the earth just as they had since the beginning of beginnings. Time raced before Benni's eyes as she watched the ages fly. Great people and great wars passed in seconds. The barrage of images slowed upon a moment in time that Benni recognized as the birth of machines and industry. In another flash, she watched as human beings built trains and cars, then learned to fly, then went to the moon. She watched as the computer was born—a strange kind of thing she hardly recognized as a computer at all. It was behemoth and crude.

The music filling her mind and soul had a peculiar effect on Benni. She had been watching a story unfold, the nature of which she had long been familiar, but seeing it all occur at once was awe-inspiring. As an entire history of human kind was laid out before her in vivid, living detail, Benni felt like crying without quite knowing why. The visions before her fled and déjà vu struck her as she found herself in a laboratory. In it there was only one person, a woman, apparently a scientist, seated on a stool and holding something in her hands the way a mother would hold a child. This vision passed too, and in the next, Benni was looking at what appeared to be an androgynous, artificial human being. Slowly, it opened its eyes and blinked, a calm expression on its face. The left side of its head slowly opened and separated like a parts explosion diagram, displaying every artificial component inside in a neat arrangement that orbited the person's scalp like little satellites. Then, as the music in Benni's head came to a soft and peaceful climax, two other people appeared. They walked up behind the android and embraced it, smiling like two proud parents. The android smiled back at them and the vision came to a close.

In the next moment, Benni opened her eyes, remembering she was standing in a church. Dada was still next to her. Her eyes glowed bright with some kind of warm light, and her body, as well as all the bodies in the congregation radiated the same glow. Benni wasn't sure if she was really seeing the light or if the meditation was causing her to see it. Dada opened her eyes and looked at Benni with tranquility and companionship in her gaze, and Benni couldn't help but smile. The feeling was apparently shared by all the members of the congregation, who were exchanging hugs and handshakes as the ceremony ended and they gradually began to depart.

Not until they were outside the doors of the church did Benni and Dada speak to one another in their own voices, and Dada was the first to say anything. She apologized again for having hushed Benni but explained she was certain Benni had the lost look of a new visitor, and she had happened to choose to attend on a particularly special holiday. Dada had an attractive voice that reminded Benni of Dr. Emerich. It was laced with a proper and articulate manner of speaking that was too consistent to be human, but it was pleasant despite its fabricated inclinations. Dada's voice was a bit deeper than the doctor's but still girlish. Benni liked it very much, and that quality, as well as Dada's generally warm and inviting demeanor made her a wonderfully amiable new acquaintance. Neither of the two had plans until the evening, and so they chatted for almost two and a half hours over lunch in the nearby market district.

Dada was a student in Academy Aquaea, and as Benni suspected she was studying religion and philosophy with a concentration in Solarism and minor studies in the world religions of Eastern and Western Earth societies. There was a passion in the way Dada spoke about these subjects that excited Benni, much as the way Caan did when he talked about culture, but she didn't consciously acknowledge the similarity. As Dada told her all about Solarism, Buddhism, Islam, Judaism and Christianity, Benni forgot she was conversing with an android. Dada was lively in a way that drew all attention away from the otherwise uncanny fact that her emotion and articulation flowed forth from an artificial mind. Not once that afternoon did it occur to Benni that she had a longer and more interesting conversation with an android than she'd ever had with another human being.

Dada was equally fascinated by Benni's artistic career. No matter how much Benni elaborated on the nature of her models and sculptures, Dada always came up with an interesting question. In fact, Benni had to stop and think several times before she felt she could effectively answer all the android's questions. Dada wondered things about Benni that Benni herself felt she hadn't explored well enough. If only the professors in Academy Aeraea were as probing as Dada, Benni thought, maybe she would know a thing or two more about why she was motivated to sketch, model and sculpt the things she did. No matter how abstract Benni's ideas were, Dada followed her, thought for thought.

As late afternoon crept up on them, Benni suddenly noticed a stream of messages she'd received between 15:00 and 17:00 she hadn't noticed. The TikaTalk application blinked impatiently off to the side of her field of view as if it would explode if she didn't open her missed messages soon. Dada noticed that Benni had looked concerned and paused in the middle of something she'd been saying.

"Oh, I'm sorry. I just now noticed I missed a number of messages I was expecting," Benni explained as Dada politely quieted down. "I hate to break off the conversation, but I guess I should go before I'm late."

"Oh, that's right," said Dada. "You had said you had prior obligations. I sometimes keep chatting and chatting and forget myself. I'm so sorry." She laughed in an understanding way and stood up as Benni got up out of her seat.

"It's no problem," Benni assured her. "It's been great meeting you."

"I had a lot of fun too," said Dada. "We'll have to hang out again sometime. I wonder, will you be visiting the church again?"

"Oh, of course! Today was very inspiring. I've never really been spiritual, but to be fair, I've never given it a chance," Benni admitted. "Something about what I saw today just made me feel … well, I don't know, actually. It's a nice feeling, though, whatever it is."

"I'm glad you enjoyed it." Dada smiled and stood proudly. She, after all, aspired to achieve the position of High Herald within the church some day. Waving goodbye to Benni, she excused herself and headed to the vactrain terminal while Benni headed to the levbus stop just around the corner.

As Benni got onto the levbus she opened the messages clouding the left hand side of her field of view. A long string of about fifteen messages expanded and, to her surprise, none of them was from Caan. They were all messages from Shirro, the earliest from before the church service started and the latest from only ten minutes ago. They were all short, generally simple messages asking Benni where she was and if she were busy, if she wanted to go to dinner or if she wanted to meet up at the hospital later. As easy as it would have been to tell him she was busy, Benni collapsed the messages and opted to act as if she'd never seen them. Shirro's persistence bothered her. The idea that she'd been in the hospital for so long that she'd made a friend with someone who was not leaving anytime soon made her feel as if she wouldn't be leaving soon, either. The feeling gave her a sudden sense of aversion to Shirro and the hospital. She was supposed to return that night, but she no longer wanted to do so. She didn't want to spend another night in a somniscope either, being watched while she escaped into a fantasy with Shirro. Opening the TikaTalk application, Benni thought up a message to Caan and watched it appear in the text box on the left hand side of her field of view. After sending it and waiting for about fifteen minutes, she became aggravated. She had received no response. Where could he be? When she arrived at the hospital and still hadn't heard from Caan, Benni couldn't bring herself to go up to her dormitory. Instead, she boarded the next levbus and headed to her home apartment in Nioua Point Tower.

# 6.1

Caan hadn't used his Tika module all day. Turning it off had become a habit, and it helped him to relax. Without all the excess information clouding his vision, not only was it literally easier to see, it was easier to focus and think. Wolfie had been right about the sudden changes that would come to Genesia. About two weeks after their conversation in *Yao's Dockside*, the TikaNews feed began to spread stories throughout the city's media about the troubles on Earth, and nothing much else. The versions were all so mixed no one was sure who was at war with whom, or whose businesses were going to suffer. All anyone knew for certain was what was being heard around the Martian docks: not enough goods were coming into the city, and ARC shipments were irregular or being placed on hold for undetermined amounts of time. Genesis MTI's President had already addressed the public on the matter a number of times in the past few days, reminding everyone of the founders' motto: "Progress, perseverance and faith." That wasn't good enough for the public. Some of the dockies were already discussing strikes, the academies had begun cutting some of their newest research programs as well as scholarship opportunities, and the heat of old hostilities between humans and androids was lighting new fires everywhere. To top it all off, hundreds of transhumans had begun leaving hospitals against the advice of their doctors and surgeons, and every day they could be seen picketing and protesting in front of a different government building. Genesis MTI's legislators had recently proposed bills to limit the rights of transhuman guardians and military personnel with neural prosthetics, and the transhuman community would not hear it. All this, in addition to Benni's predicament, weighed heavily on Caan's mind; going to the *Jupiter* jazz club with Wolfie was about all he could do to distract himself from it all.

The city beneath Genesia, the city of the harder-working Martians, didn't have an official name, but it had been given nicknames long ago by its underprivileged denizens. They called it a number of things, including Dark Town, and "the city where the sun never rises." As the undercity levbus he sat inside hummed along, Caan gazed out the window to his left and looked up. The roof of Dark Town was so high he could not see it behind the hazy shadows hanging beneath it. He imagined that if he had been born down here and no one had ever told him otherwise, he'd probably have believed it was a place where the sun really did never rise and set, and that a never ending wall of night sky shrouded the people and the years that passed over the place, brightened only by artificial lights that had burned continually for a few centuries. A visitor from Earth may have thought shadowy Dark Town and glass-encased Genesia were two very different places. Caan had once thought so, too, but no longer. Recently he had begun to prefer the opaque underworld. Tinting his face a palette of LED colors, the passing electric lights in the windows of machine shops

161

and bars teased Caan's pupils and gave him a headache. Most of the signs didn't spell anything. Caan wondered how anyone found their way around in Dark Town, but then he reasoned anyone who'd been here for any length of time probably just knew the place by heart. It wasn't as though it had regular visitors in need of directions.

Caan hadn't acclimated to this part of the city, not like a native. Strange but perfectly agreeable these citizens were, many of them paler, more open and sincere than the people up top. They reminded Caan of the things that lived in the deepest parts of the Earth's oceans, eyeless or blind yet finely adapted to abysmal conditions, having hardly any knowledge of any other way or place and having no need to know.

The *Jupiter* jazz club was booming with music and activity when Caan stepped off the levbus. A large group of people haunted the levbike jetty outside the bar, Wolfie among them. Everyone was having fun. Drinks clanked together. Couples laughed. A couple of loners, including a guy everyone knew as Spike—a young but tired looking guy dressed in a sharp suit with a cigarette in his mouth—were sunken into their usual barstools. The powerful, ambient music soaked Caan as he joined the mob. It was lyricless, and for that reason infinitely meaningful. Every buzz, boom and rattle of every electric crash and melody spoke to him the way home speaks to a long-gone traveler returning.

Caan realized he'd made a habit of repeating the same mistake. Overdressed as usual, he would have stood out in the crowd if anyone had been sober enough to notice or care. Wolfie didn't mention it to Caan at all, but rather handed him a strong drink and slapped him on the shoulder. All of Wolfie's friends, most of whom Caan had never met, gave a sloppy cheer and then forgot about him as soon as they'd met him. Wolfie was seated on the back of his levbike, as drunk and happy as if he'd been made the king of Mars.

"Caan!" Wolfie called out to him even though they were five or so feet apart. "Caan, this is the best purchase I ever made!"

"It's a nice bike," said Caan, stifling the urge to laugh. Wolfie was nothing short of clownish when he'd had a few drinks.

"The *second* best purchase was ..." he continued, pausing to think for a long moment.

"But you didn't pay for it," Caan replied, grinning and watching Wolfie's brain tick slowly behind his eyes.

"Oh, I remember! The second best purchase was that bike there! The one I got for you, Caan. Happy birthday!" Wolfie gave Caan another friendly smack and pointed to an ownerless levbike docked next to his own, "No, wait, it's not your birthday. Your birthday's not for months. Why'd I buy you present?"

"Hi, Caan!" A sweet and familiar voice approached. It was Faela's.

"Oh, hi, Faela," said Caan, feeling his stomach float.

"How do you like it?" she asked.

"Oh, this place is great. The music's good, seems fun."

"Oh, no," she stopped him, laughing. "I meant the bike."

163

"The bike? You're kidding," said Caan, somewhat mortified, realizing Wolfie wasn't just drunk and making up stories.

"Yeah, Wolfie bought the last, best one Dad had. I tried to talk him out of it but he insisted," she explained, also sounding uncomfortable.

"Wolfie, why did you buy this?" Caan said quietly to his drunken friend as he reeled about in the seat of his levbike.

"Oh, it's nothing," said Wolfie, waving his arms. "They fired me, Caan. I got my last big payment and by next month it would have been sucked out of me by all the bastards I owe money to. It was either poverty or bankruptcy for me, friend, and I chose bankruptcy. There are actually more benefits to bankruptcy. Did you know that?"

"I had no idea," said Caan in disbelief. He turned to look at Faela, who averted her eyes to the ground and pretended not to have heard. For a moment Caan slouched down on his new levbike and tuned everything out. Looking around, he wondered how many other people at the bar had been given the same news as Wolfie.

"Hey." Faela sat beside him on the bike, gave him a nudge. "Come on, none of us came here to mourn our losses. It's all right." Her smile had no confidence behind it, but it was charming and well meaning.

"What about you?"

"What do you mean? Did I lose my job, too?" she asked. "Yeah, I did. I'll be fine, though. Dad still gets work. I'm just glad it happened to me and not to him again. We used to live topside, you know."

"You did?" Caan was genuinely surprised. Wolfie was the only person he'd ever known who hadn't been able to make it in the city.

"Mhm, he was a parts designer for Killian Industries levbikes, before the company fell behind Steadmeyer Tech. Dad and many other designers were let go and replaced by androids, about a year ago. I don't know what exactly happened between him and Mom, but she's been gone since." Faela finished the drink in her hands and made a face. "I went to Academy Ignaea for a year, and then Dad ran out of money to help me pay for the education. I wanted to design levbikes as he did. I still get to, but not in the ... *professional* setting I would have preferred." Her dark irises ran to the corners of her eyes and hid beneath the lashes.

"I'm sorry to hear that," said Caan, halfway through his drink. His free hand inspected the body of the new levbike underneath him. They came to rest on the serial plate, and when he looked down at it, he saw that the numbers had been removed. He quickly finished his drink and forgot about it.

"I don't mean to say I dislike androids. I'm not prejudiced," she insisted, leaning against him and wobbling. "I just don't think it's fair to give so many jobs to workers who don't have to worry about paying for their education or medical bills or even food. I blame ... I don't know who I blame. I just don't know how ... how do they run a city *for* people *without* people? They say it makes things cheaper for the rest of us in the long run, but I think it just

165

makes the people on top try to get more out of us when times aren't as hard."

"I don't know," Caan said after a while. By then he'd forgotten what they'd been talking about. "Let me buy you another drink. When mine wears off we'll give this bike a test run."

"Okay," she said, resting her cheek against him and smiling like a sleepy child in a cozy blanket.

# 6.2

Home again after spending nearly a year and three months in and out of a hospital, Benni stood quietly in the middle of her apartment and hugged herself. The living room was larger than the entire dormitory she'd stayed in since her accident. It was full of white and lilac furniture, all of a minimalist design. Almost all the walls and tabletops were flat and blank, intentionally left that way because they all doubled as digital mediums. Normally they would display moving lights that looked like old-fashioned ticking clocks, simulations of windows and natural scenery, news and entertainment feeds, cyber workspaces, digital painting canvases— virtually anything that could be simulated. There was no need to decorate, in other words, because the walls and tables and shelves could decorate themselves infinitely.

There was enough furniture and space for several people, friends or family; Benni really hadn't had many of either for a long time. Her parents—that is to say, the second pair—were living on Earth somewhere. They had left when Benni's adopted father lost his teaching position at Academy Ignaea and her adopted mother couldn't manage the sudden financial pressure in the wake of the loss. At the time they decided to leave Genesia, Benni was already attending Academy Aeraea, and because of her talents, her program was paid for. Benni stayed on Mars because her parents thought it was for the best. Perhaps she had a future where they did not.

Benni pulled a seat over to the large living room windows and sat down. Lying back and curling her legs up under her comfortably, she powered on her Tika module. Immediately, a number of new messages appeared on the left hand side of her field of view. They were all from Shirro. She closed them and opened a digital photo album. Dozens of old images of her and her parents displayed themselves across her field of view. She commanded the Tika module to switch to a public display mode. The projector mounted in her temple came to life and spread the images in the album out in front of her in the empty air. Silently her memories hung in the air and turned like satellites around her head.

A particular image caught Benni's eye, one taken during her 13th birthday party. Benni expanded it to envelop the room as a three-dimensional hologram and then played the video attached to it. The recording of her birthday played out in front of her. Realistic images of two of her former best friends, Min and Riley, ran past her. They disappeared from view behind a piece of furniture that Benni remembered from her parents' old apartment. Several other people were also hiding, waiting to surprise a thirteen-year-old version of Benni that came walking through the front door the next moment. Aunts, uncles, cousins, friends and Benni's own parents—all looking younger than Benni remembered them—leapt into view and all cried "happy birthday" at once. Thirteen-year-old Benni gasped in surprise, a bright smile breaking across her face as her hands clasped over it. She bounced on her heels excitedly, on her two good legs, shook her arms—her two real arms—and hugged her mother and father as her eyes filled with tears of joy. She had just come home from her last day of school for the year, after receiving an acceptance notice from Academy Aeraea.

The video suddenly froze still. Benni paused it and collapsed it back down to a miniature and scrambled it back into the album and out of sight. Her throat hurt, and her chest felt heavy as she sniffled and got up from her seat and moved to the living room windows. After a moment she rested in the window seat and looked out at the big city, hugging her knees and staving off cyclical, panicked thoughts. Caan's place was just across the way. Hermphrey Park was nearby, alight and pretty; Academy Aeraea, too. All the places she loved, just out of reach and safely tucked inside glass. Benni turned to look back into the apartment. As she closed the photo album, all of her colorful memories shrank from view and vanished back into the cyberspace behind her eye. She felt as though she were being slowly pressed into the corner and up the wall, as if she wanted to run in all directions at once but was standing on top of a flag pole like a manic cat. Was she losing her mind? She couldn't know, and she didn't want anyone else to think she was, so she didn't call Caan or send a message to Dr. Emerich. Instead she rocked in place, squirming every time her sanity— hiding somewhere and poking a voodoo doll likeness of her with pins—had a good laugh at her pitiful torture. Benni bawled her eyes out until she fell asleep.

# 6.3

At some unknown hour of the early morning, a strange dream began to unfold in Benni's mind. For many moments she was sure she had awoken in a yellow pasture but knew it was impossible. No such place as large and natural existed on Mars. In the dream the nearby forests were too large, and the sky was not orange; in fact, there was no sky. Benni recognized that she was somewhere on Earth, but where, she could not tell. When she looked far into the distance, the horizon did not appear. There was no line dividing the ground and sky. Instead of seeing the landscape curving down and out of sight, she saw that it curved upward in all directions. Tilting her head as far back as she could and looking up into what should have been the sky, Benni saw high above her great continental landmasses as they would look from up in space. It was as if the Earth she stood on had been flipped outside-in, like standing on the inside surface of a hollow ball. Quickly she realized there was something else peculiar about the world. Underfoot she felt coils of thick wire and saw that the pasture was littered with a myriad of other mechanical and technical implements, old parts, some of which looked like prosthetics. It was then she spied a great glass bubble that stood up high out of the tall grass. There were knobby, thick coils of wiring and other technical components all piled up against it like a cluster of roots, and resting atop it was a colossal stack of communication devices—video monitors, sound equipment, old pre-hologram laser contour projectors; all stacked as high as a lighthouse.

Benni approached the monolithic tower slowly, taking care not to trip over the snaking wires all around in the grass. As she moved closer to the glass bubble, the grass retreated and the ground looked barren and dead. Suddenly the pasture behind her and the forests beyond darkened. She could no longer see clearly into the sky, which had grayed with clouds. Daylight gave way to a misty darkness, and as Benni stood before the tower of electronics it began to make a sound, like a giant bee's nest buzzing with electric life. Video monitors flashed on, audio transmitters produced a storm of static, and the laser projectors blinked on and swept the air and grounds with their pinpoint gazes, like the frantic eyes of insects afraid of being chased by something in the dark. The glass bubble at the base of all this technology glowed weakly, and in its eerie, shadowy interior Benni saw Shirro, collapsed into a sitting position and draped up against a drift of medical equipment, prosthetics and wiring. Little pairs of tubes bit into his arms and legs and head, and his eyes flickered brightly, like two ancient moving picture projectors. Every now and then he twitched with life and his muscles convulsed as if lightning jumped through him, and he lit up like a firefly.

Benni felt a cold chill on her arms and neck, realizing she was asleep and caught up in some kind of vivid simulation. This was not her dream; it was Shirro's nightmare. But how had she come to be a part of it? She hadn't gone to the hospital, and she didn't remember falling asleep in somniscope therapy. She hadn't been there in a long time. She remembered going home to her apartment, watching the video of her thirteenth birthday party and then dozing off in the living room. No matter what she tried, Benni felt a mental wall rise up in front of her when she pleaded with herself to wake up. Able neither to change the dream nor escape it, she began to panic. Just then, a voice spoke out to her through the dark.

"We speak," said the voice. It was Shirro's. "We listen. We see, touch, taste and smell, but we cannot know. We cannot know because there are walls all around us all the time. We see only what's in the bubble."

"Shirro?" Benni replied. She watched Shirro's body inside the glass dome as streaks of lightning ran across it. His face made no expressions and his mouth did not move, but still she heard him speaking through the monolith.

"Windows!" his voice screamed. "Windows all around!" his voice sobbed. "Look but don't touch! Listen but do not hear! Wonder but do not know!" A bright light exploded from the darkness high atop the monolith and spilled a discomforting white light on the ground. Here and there the ground moved, harsh shadows coming alive and rising to their feet. "We are not the answer!" screamed Shirro's voice. "We can go no further like this."

"Oh!" Benni jumped with a start as she saw shadowy figures

now standing all around the monolith, all slow and sagging like zombies, wires and tubes sprouting from their heads, driven around like puppets by tethers of electricity and prosthetics.

"We live in jars," said Shirro quietly, his voice resounding in the dark. The shadowy figures trembled and hugged themselves like terrified children.

"*I'm afraid*," said a child's whisper.

"*We're useless. We're extinct*," whimpered another voice.

"Shirro, I want out of here," said Benni, her arms pulled up tight against her body. Cornered in the dark, her heart squirmed like a rabbit in a trap.

"I can't stay here anymore, Benni," said Shirro. His voice was calm, and it was the first time it had consciously addressed her. "I see too much. I hear too much, and I can't put it all into words. It builds up inside me and stretches my brain. I can't remember how to speak. Everything I want to say doesn't seem good enough, as if every word is a lie. And when I try to speak the truth, they stop me."

"*Stop telling me what to do!*" There came a harsh whisper from one of the shadowy figures.

"Who stops you?" asked Benni. "Shirro, who stops you?"

"The words! Do you see them, too?" his voice cried out in agony. The bright light at the top of the monolith pulsed brighter, and then pulsed again and again until it strobed with a force that made Benni dizzy and sick. "The words!" Shirro cried again, and that's when Benni saw them again—the words she'd seen in the

174

park, the ones that haunted Shirro. They strobed brightly in the sky above the tower, the screens of the video monitors and on the faces of the shadowy people all around her, like a ghostly mantra that mesmerized her and filled her head...

*Earthshine*
*Earthshine*
*Earthshine*

# 7.0
# THE MIRACLE OF FLIGHT

*"The first human beings who flew must have known some greater freedom awaited them once they were no longer bound to the ground, but it should not come as a surprise that a leap of faith into a promising unknown possessed them with the crippling, instinctual fear of falling and death. This fear did not stop the early reptiles, who, when they so crowded the land there was nowhere left to go, shed their scales for feathers and took to the skies, born aloft on the wind. For ages humankind was also earthbound, but in time filled the skies with airplanes, helicopters, jets, space shuttles and all manner of other vehicles. Any time a new limit has been discovered, a new machine has been invented to surmount it. We have escaped the constraints of sea, land, air and outer space; yet, what kind of machine will it take to free us from ourselves, and to what lofty place will it bear us thence?"*

—Z.B. Franco, author, *Uploading the Soul*, 2019 CE

*Earthshine*
*Earthshine*
*Earthshine*

The word was burned into the back of Shirro's eyelids. He saw it every time he blinked and every time he went to sleep at night. Neon blue, yellow and pink, the letters flashed and floated around in the web of little spidery veins and blackness he saw when his eyes closed. Whenever he was angry, sad, anxious or confused, the letters would appear and haunt his vision until he calmed down or fell asleep. Shirro used to be the type of person who could spend

176

hours upon hours lost in his own thoughts or stay up all night writing down his ideas for research projects or essays, but not anymore. The moment he began to think too much, the moment his brain began to produce creative and exciting thoughts, the word would come back and silently scream at him, tear at his his concentration like a demon until he couldn't focus and became irritable.

Shirro had begun to see the word a few years earlier, when he first awoke in the hospital after having fallen down five flights of stairs in the Pendybrandt Observatory over at Academy Ignaea. It had been a wonderful evening despite the fall. He'd received his letter of acceptance from the Circle and an invitation to a prestigious gathering the following week. Having just finished six years of early stage research for a program he was sure would launch his career as a young astronomer, Shirro had planned on going home early for the night so he could take his fiancé, Shana, out to the clubs and celebrate. In his excitement, he simply hurried off too quickly and tripped.

When he next awoke, Shirro lay in a hospital bed, an array of strange items stuck to him. Upon seeing marks in his skin left by laser stitching and feeling foreign synthetic material plating his head, he panicked. A nurse burst into the room and found him floundering in coils of bandaging and fluid delivery tubes next to his bed, and at about that time Shirro saw an apparition in his field of vision, the word "Earthshine." The word described a phenomenon familiar to, but not commonly used in Shirro's area of study, and so he wondered why of all words would a knock to the head jog that particular one.

Shirro received a few visits from his fiancé during the first year he spent in the hospital. She had been attentive and optimistic at first, but over time the doctors' comments to Shirro and their assessments of his progress discouraged her as much as they discouraged Shirro himself. After some time, she stopped visiting regularly, and then one day Shirro received a brief message from her in his TikaTalk application's chat window. It was a short apology accompanied by the explanation that Shana's parents were moving back to Earth and she didn't want to live in Genesia alone. There was no way of knowing how long Shirro would have to stay in the hospital, and Shana was afraid of what surely would change between her and Shirro once he recovered—if he recovered at all.

Shirro should have died from the injuries he sustained to his skull and brain; however, money and technology intervened in a timely manner and for better or worse, Shirro got another chance to live. He qualified for the operation, as luck would have it, because it was a cost his benefits as a research assistant to the Circle happened to cover. His mother and father signed permission for the procedure, and in no time the parts of Shirro that were smashed to pulp by the observatory stairs were replaced with advanced, sturdy new webs of synthetic neurons and brain tissue. All of the things Shirro was before his accident came back—all memories, personality traits and temperament. The problem was not that anything about Shirro was broken or lost. The problem was that

178

something more came back.

He would never forget the second time he saw the mystery word flashing in his mind. Shirro's parents came to visit him very soon after his first operation. With his doctor's permission, they took him home to their apartment for dinner one night, all the way to Mintman Place, one of the wealthiest neighborhoods in the city where he and his family had always lived. Shirro hardly ate, his hands gesticulating as he talked and talked to his parents about hundreds of ideas he'd recently had, most of them too dense and abstract to follow. He began to raise his voice, which was not typical; his eyes dilated. When Shirro's jabbering showed no sign of stopping, his mother coolly suggested he finish his meal and continue on about his ideas over after-dinner tea. Nodding and laughing with embarrassment, Shirro paused and looked down at his plate, awkwardly lifting knife and fork. Try as he might, he was unable to cut into his food, his hands trembling with a kind of adrenal energy. The sensation disturbed and frightened Shirro, causing him to whimper and his parents to rise from their seats and take him by the arm and shoulder in an attempt to calm him down. That's when it happened—the word appeared again, once, then twice. Beginning to feel faint, the color draining from his face, Shirro slumped in his chair and then suddenly stood, pushing his seat out from under him and halfway across the dining room.

"Help! Help!" he urgently shouted at his confounded mother and father, who raised their arms helplessly. As Shirro clamped his hands over his eyes, abnormal phenomena conjured up around him. Tickling his skin, an electric maelstrom whipped up within a neat and clearly defined radius of his body, lifting little odds and ends off the table and tossing them lightly into the air like an autumn breeze stirs up dead leaves. Opening his eyes and blinking skittishly, he watched the silverware from the table whirl around him and then watched it darken to near black. Slowly the entire room took on a gloomy tone, and Shirro regained full control of his thoughts. Everything surrounding him seemed to slow to a standstill, including his terrified parents.

The next thing Shirro could remember was waking up once more in his hospital dormitory. Hours and hours had passed while he had been unconscious. His mother and father were in the room when he came to and explained to him they had witnessed him vanishing from the dining room during his fit. His whole body had disappeared, and as soon as it had, everything levitating in the dining room had fallen to the floor and become quiet. They had searched the apartments for half an hour, asking neighbors if any of them had seen their son. By the time they had returned home, the police contacted Shirro's father and reported that a woman waiting for a levbus on the other side of the city saw Shirro appear suddenly in the seat across from her. She screamed so loudly the pilot immediately put the bus on the ground. The poor startled woman's story sounded silly of course, but another passenger's idle Tika module had automatically recorded the event while its host snoozed in the back of the levbus, just close enough to have caught the whole thing. The police seized the video data but did not ask Shirro's parents any questions. Instead, his mother and father only barely overheard a heated discussion between the authorities and Shirro's doctors back at the hospital, before the doctors insisted Shirro visit the emergency ward for observation overnight.

Frustrated because the doctors never had satisfactory answers, Shirro had independently looked into his condition a number of times. Reports of conditions similar to his did exist, but valuable information about them didn't. They appeared in old news archives and medical journals as nothing more than incident reports. Only recently had Shirro come across a case that mentioned hallucinations involving the word "Earthshine." It was soon after that he discovered Earthshine was a piece of software responsible for mediating the mental processing activities of certain parts of transhuman brains. It was quite old, developed by a software designer named Andrew Rumford sometime around the turn of the 26th century.

* * * *

In the distance, a great hole in the Martian surface began to glow white. The source of the light, a large ARC shuttle, rose up through the dusty orange setting sun and soared heavenward, the guide lights on its nose, wings, control tower and flank twinkling like little stars. It was the only kind of thing that ever seemed to come and go freely from the city. Shirro had watched it and ships like it every night from his dormitory high in the residential ward of the hospital for years. There had been a time when the calm and quiet of his room and the serenity of the view from his dormitory window lulled him away somewhere peaceful. The city lights, the parks, the traffic far below—they were marvelous. Genesia was a beautiful city indeed, a testament to technology and hope for all ... except for Shirro.

Sometime between his visit to Dr. Emerich earlier that day and brushing his teeth only five minutes earlier, he'd come to accept something: he was never going to leave the hospital. The treatments, the changing schedules and doctors and physicians—all of it was a distraction. Because Shirro's medical bills were continually paid and his condition was obtuse and interesting to the surgeons and psychologists, he would live forever as a case study. It should have been clear to him long ago that he'd never be able to again pursue his research or enjoy his academic and career successes. How could he? He couldn't leave the hospital safely. Every time he did, his ... *condition* ... began to act up and he'd be found blacked out somewhere unfamiliar and dangerous, only to be reeled back in by the police or medics, tossed on an operating table and stuck full of monitors and tubes, wrapped in laser grids, run through neurological scanners and dragged into hours of one-on-one psychological therapy. Shirro had thought about leaving and never coming back, perhaps buying a ticket to Earth. Of course he hadn't the faintest idea where he'd go or live, what he'd do. His top-of-the-line brain was broken, malfunctioning, a liability. No, he couldn't leave, but he also couldn't stay. And Benni ... Benni had been merely an ephemeral hope—another glitch.

Cornered and desperate, Shirro had slipped away from the window of his dormitory and curled up in a little nook next to his bed. Thousands of feet from the ground on the only city on Mars, suddenly his room was an island. The doctors couldn't help. Shirro knew there would be no one to save him if he broke into a fit, and he tried painfully hard not to lose his grip, but he had learned something about a month earlier that had unsettled him and was unsettling him again now. He had seen records that Dr. Emerich did not mean for him to see. He'd seen the look of realization on her face when she knew Shirro had seen it. The word—the haunting word! He'd seen it written in her notes on the holographic PDA she kept in her lap. It was even highlighted red. Shirro had never told her about the word.

*Earthshine*

There it was again! Folding his arms and rocking in place, Shirro did all he could to keep from panicking. An attack could be deadly. What if he transported himself outside a mile from the ground, unconscious and unable to cry for help?

*Earthshine*

It didn't matter. The more he thought about all the terrible scenarios, the more he saw the word flashing in front of him. Trying to remain calm and cool had never stopped the word before, and it wouldn't help him now. Fear left Shirro, and he became angry. What had the surgeons done to him? All this was their fault, and no one wanted to tell him what was happening to him. It was then that something occurred to him: without having commanded

183

it, Shirro's Tika module powered on. All the default menus immediately collapsed out of sight, and a simple black screen opened up in his field of view. In the black screen he saw listed a continuous stream of command prompts and programming language he did not recognize, and then he caught sight of something familiar. Over and over it repeated itself:

*Run_Earthshine.exe*
*>error_1003 unrecognized entry*
*Run_Earthshine.exe*
*>error_1003 unrecognized entry*
*Run_Earthshine.exe*
*>error_1003 unrecognized entry*

The command lines repeated themselves six or seven times before the Tika module stopped attempting to run the program and then shut itself down. All was quiet in the dormitory for the longest moment. Shirro's mind quieted for the first time in three or more years, as if the eye of a hurricane was passing through him. Slowly he stood and walked to the center of the dormitory, turning to face the window, hearing the soft inkling of some voice in his head speaking to him through the glass.

*Earthshine*

It boomed at him through the window, slapping the insides of his skull and stinging his eyes with the bright venomous burn of neon blue, yellow and pink. The letters filled his vision entirely. It hurt to open his eyes, and it hurt worse to close them. Toward the window he unwittingly stumbled, hands outstretched as a static-

184

charged whirlwind whipped up around him.

*Wuum...*

Falling forward, Shirro's hands met the window, the three-inch thick atmosphere proof glass bowing inward like rubber under the pressure of an impossible force emanating from the overcharged network of artificial synapses in his mind. Firing like nuclear reactors and fueled by a storm of superhuman emotion and will, it could not be stopped.

*Wuuuum...*

The thick window before him took on the shape of a mushroom, whining loudly as its crystalline structure stretched and then exploded to pieces. One of the large shards struck him in the right eye, and he cried out as the rest viciously cut his arms and torso on their way into the dormitory wall behind him. Shirro lunged forward and gasped as he was lifted off his feet by a powerful suction that stripped him from his bedroom and threw him and all of his furniture out into the exposed Martian atmosphere. He experienced it all very slowly, his legs knocking into the low wall under the broken window in such a way that caused him to spin as he flew from the dormitory. Like a bullet out of a rifle he turned and turned gracefully, his arms spreading away from him like wings. As he took flight, the cold atmosphere devoured him, freezing him inside and out, turning him into human ice. His Tika module's circuitry failed and all of the little digital symbols and electronic language vanished from his field of vision. When his body rotated to face the setting sun, Shirro saw it brightly and clearly. It was divinely warm against his skin, and in the background, against the mysterious blackness of space beyond, he saw a flashing truth leaving him, fading from sight.

*Earthshine*
*Earthshine*
*Earthshine*

# 7.1

Caan's name was not often on the lips of the chairs in the Circle, not as often as other students his age who were aspiring physicists, geneticists, neurologists, anthrotects or aerospace engineers. Still, Caan had come much farther than most of his Academy Aquaea peers. In fact, he was the first student with a research focus in anthropology to have been invited to act as a research assistant to the Circle. Naturally, this achievement didn't earn him any respect from the other research assistants. The science and engineering students in particular were not interested in Caan or what the Circle asked him to contribute to project dossiers and formal meetings. Luckily, one of Caan's old professors was one of the Circle's newest chairs, and he did what he could to point out the brilliance in Caan's ideas and suggestions to the rest of the minds in the room on a frequent basis.

This routine quickly wore Caan down, and after some time he lost interest in many of the forthcoming projects to which he'd been assigned. Having graduated from the academy, he was now in the stage of education most of his superiors referred to as "limbo." Before qualifying for his second stage degree, he would have to invest several hundred raw hours into a concentrated area of research that crossed disciplinary boundaries, requiring him to partner with a Terraea, Aeraea or Ignaea student. The very prospect of having to cooperate with an Ignaea or Terraea student made Caan want to throw himself from the highest superstructure in Genesia. All his friends outside of classes were artists, but he knew that partnering with an Aeraea student meant he would do a lot of fun and interesting work only to end up with an undesirable salary later on.

Caan wished badly to have been granted slightly different talents. His father had been lucky enough to have been blessed with creativity, and he had partnered with an Ignaea graduate when he was in college, allowing him the rare opportunity to become an architect and civil engineer specializing in extraterrestrial and outer space commercial development. Caan's problem was not that he lacked intellect or motivation. His talents just lay in areas that were not easy to turn into money. He loved learning about people, cultures and psychology, and try as he might Caan couldn't find anyone who knew quite the appropriate career that involved being professionally social or learned. When he thought about it, Wolfie's job was the only one he could think of where it paid to be social and professional at the same time. Dock work wasn't respected or lucrative, but it was far less scrutinized than academy life.

Sitting at his desk in a little nook atop the Academy Aeraea Library and Digital Research building, Caan stared down at the open files projected on the surface of his workspace. It was late, long after dark, the time of night when the building was long voided of professors and tech assistants and loaded with red-eyed, jittery art students. Caan had allowed his mind to wander off and his train of thought derailed while he wasn't manning the engine. Lately his distractions were too many; his schedule, too inconsistent. The academies weren't in session for the majority of students and wouldn't get back up to speed for another month. In the interim, Caan and other dedicated graduate students would remain at work on miscellaneous projects, tucked away like mice in the deepest, most isolated holes of academia.

On the other end of his desk, a muted documentary he had begun watching and forgot about was playing. Caan's eyes came to focus on the video as it rolled on. He watched as a group of early humans ventured off into some great expanse of hilly plains. Dressed in furs and leather, their shaggy forms marched and marched, until they finally came upon a herd of large, prehistoric beasts. The humans took up spears and managed to get the better of a large mammoth, some of them distracting it while others hurled spears into its thick hide. They succeeded, collected the spoils of their victory, returned home, made fire and celebrated.

Caan rubbed his tired eyes as he turned back to his work and looked over the last few sentences of an essay on $22^{nd}$ century ecospatial culture and how it influenced urban architecture. In the margins of the screen he opened several tabs and briefly read over notes attached to the text by scholars who had read the same essay two or three hundred years before him, as well as his own professor's notes and those of some of his peers. The program he was using was called SocialDex, a social reading platform that was modeled after revolutionary reading practices first occurring in the early 21<sup>st</sup> century. With it, it was possible to access an entire history, sometimes centuries long, of discussion surrounding a text and even contribute to it.

Not that he was focusing intently on his reading, but the moment an email popped up in the corner tab of his notes, Caan lost all interest in his research and orally commanded the message to open. Immediately he frowned. In a few words the message, from Genesis MTI, reminded him of his mounting overdue student loan payments and the interest accruing on them faster than fungus on the underside of a careened ARC ship in the dimmest corner of Dark Town. Following a link to an information page about payment plans, his tired eyes sizzled like eggs on a hot pan as they were suddenly flash-fried by a twenty-page, single-spaced, size-10 font list of repayment options and loan forgiveness conditions. The latter was much more appealing, but not until he reached the bottom of that list did he come across a single, viable option.

"In the event of the borrower's death, all debts are deemed forgiven following a written request on behalf of a legal guardian, cosignee, spouse or other legitimate representative," he read aloud. "Huh, so if I can't make one-hundred-forty-three thousand dollars or sixty-seven thousand reds within three years of completing my thesis, all I have to do is walk in front of a levbus ..." Rolling his eyes, he minimized the email tab and threw himself back in his chair, shutting his eyes and opening them again to try and stare through the ceiling and into deep space.

As his workspace shut down and cooled off, the cluster of files vanishing from his desk, Caan rested his chin in his hand, elbow propped up and absorbed in thought. It dawned on him that he hadn't seen Benni in weeks. The days had passed without so much as a few "hellos," "goodnights," complaints about work or school, or even everyday anticipatory remarks about upcoming movies, art shows or parties. The boyfriend-girlfriend chats had dwindled into silence. Normally Benni would have been the first to notice and begun to send little hints in the forms of textual endearments and cute songs, or little digital paintings she'd done for him—literally filling his vision full of sentiments—but this time Caan was the one to begin worrying.

A quick mental command opened the TikaTalk application and Caan watched as letters appeared before his eyes, spelling out a quick message to Benni, simply asking her what she was doing and if she felt like going out. A moment later, to Caan's relief, she replied through a vocal channel.

"Hey," her sleepy voice spoke in his head.

"Hey, you," he replied out loud. "I was wondering if we're still dating, or ..."

"Uh, yeah," Benni answered him after a moment, laughing at the joke. "I'm glad to hear from you."

"Sorry if I woke you up. You're out of the hospital, right?" Caan asked hopefully.

"Oh no, it's all right. I think I was having a nightmare, but I can't remember what it was about..." She trailed off for a second or two. "Anyway, yeah I forgot to tell you. I moved back into the apartment about two weeks ago. What have you been up to?"

"You *know* what," he said sourly. "Work, work, work."

"Yeah, and a little fun here and there," Benni added.

"What do you mean?"

"I got a message from Wolfie a couple of weeks ago when I guess you two hit the bars without me down in Dark Town," she said.

"Oh, yeah I've been hanging out with Wolfie more than usual. Sorry I didn't invite you. You were still in the hospital, and I figured you couldn't make it anyway."

"That's true," Benni admitted. "Wolfie sounded ... less than sober. That's not like him. Is he doing all right?"

"About that," Caan began, a pitiful tone in his voice, "He and a lot of his friends lost their jobs."

"Oh!" Benni was genuinely shocked. "I had no idea. I've seen some things on the news feeds, but I didn't know what was going on down below."

"It's worse than anyone on the topside thinks, according to Wolfie," Caan explained. "I'm not surprised you haven't heard. I think they're trying to keep it quiet." Caan turned on his module and opened two video channels and tuned them to news feeds, scanning for developing economic stories.

"What's the matter with this city?" Benni lamented aloud, sighing heavily through the vocal channel. "Things have been weird for me, too. The hospital was giving me the creeps so I checked out early."

"Early?" Caan repeated, not sure if he was comfortable with the decision.

"Don't worry, I was cleared to leave. Dr. Emerich told me I only needed to stay if I felt it was necessary."

"What about your episode in the park? That seemed pretty serious." It was a gross understatement of his true feelings.

"It hasn't happened again, and I'm feeling fine. The doctors said the whole thing probably didn't even happen. I am going to go see Dr. Emerich once more to ask her some questions, though," said Benni. The way she said it told Caan she was chewing her lip. It was an anxious habit of hers.

"What do you mean it didn't happen?" Caan interrupted. "You floating in the air and moving things like some kind of superhero? That didn't happen?"

"Well let me explain," Benni said. "The doctors told me that other patients have had episodes, and the implants in their heads tend to produce electromagnetic forces that are strong enough to cause hallucinations in people like me and even people close by. They said the strange things we saw are actually things other people have reported seeing before in similar situations."

"I didn't think of that," said Caan, furrowing his brow and trying to understand. "I guess that makes sense, but that still seems dangerous. That isn't going to fry your brain or anything?"

"I guess not." Benni chuckled and then got quiet. "Can I ask you something?" Her tone changed and it was the kind of tonal shift that put Caan on alert. The boyfriend in him knew it meant to prepare for a touchy subject.

"Yeah, sure." His response was cool and unassuming.

"Who is Faela?"

"Oh." Caan exhaled and relaxed, but only after a momentary sense of guilt made his skin feel clammy. "She's one of Wolfie's friends. She works in the docks."

"Oh." Benni's curt response didn't make him feel better. "By the way," she continued, moving away from the subject of Faela but toward something directly relevant, "I just … wanted to assure you that you shouldn't worry about me and Shirro. I think I upset you last month or whenever it was when …"

"It's okay, really," said Caan quietly.

"Okay." Benni was chewing her lip again. "He's … I won't be seeing him anymore, anyway. He's stuck in the hospital indefinitely and essentially never leaves. I mean, he was a nice friend but … we didn't have that much in common, you know?"

"Benni, it's fine. I get it." Caan's laugh disarmed the tension. "Hey, do you want to go out or something soon?" Caan asked. "That's actually why I woke you up."

"Well I might be going to see Dr. Emerich tomorrow and …" she began.

"And?" Caan grinned awkwardly to himself, not sure why she hesitated.

"This might sound silly, but I've been going to the Solarist church pretty regularly," she said, her last words hanging on the edge of some nervous anticipation.

"Why is that silly?" Caan asked. "That sounds interesting."

"I thought you would laugh," Benni admitted, chuckling along with Caan. "I know you know I'm not the religious type. I started going because Dr. Emerich got Shirro interested in it. I decided to go. Not with Shirro, though. I actually think I made a friend last time I went. Her name's Dada. Well, she's an android, I mean. When I said 'she'—"

"Yeah, no I really think it's great. Something to do when we can't go out, you know?" Caan was genuinely happy Benni had found something to keep her busy now that she was getting back out into the world.

"Yeah." Being reminded that she was still recovering made Benni silently recoil into herself, as though she were broken and in need of some kind of repair. In that moment she'd have given anything to see Caan, just on the off chance he'd notice what she was wearing or tell her she looked pretty. It had been a long time since the night they had gone to the *Blue Morpho*, the best and worst memory she had. "We'll do something soon, okay?" she said after the longest time. "I want to dress up and have fun the way we used to." She felt suddenly chilled and gross, as if her ghostly doppelganger were standing next to her, arms crossed and an accusatory scowl on its face, reminding her of her date with Shirro not so long ago.

"Yeah, whenever you want," Caan answered, turning on his workspace and idly digging around in his research. It was an anxious response. He thought about the night of the accident and how comfortable everything felt before then. Ever since the *Blue Morpho*, things were different, and not just between him and Benni. How long had it been? One year? Two years? Sometimes he forgot. It could have been six months ago, but it sure felt longer.

"Do you ever feel like your life is split into a series of different lifetimes?" Benni's soft voice came into his head again, as though she were reading his mind. "I don't remember my first parents at all, but it's strange to think about the fact that there are videos and pictures of me that must be stored away somewhere. I was looking at some stuff my second parents kept, videos from around when I was about thirteen. Remember how easy things were when we were thirteen?" Benni yawned as she spoke and laughed.

"We took it so seriously. What a joke."

"That was two lives," said Benni, "Then there came academy life. That makes three. I guess the *Blue Morpho* was the beginning of my fourth life. Some things carry on and some get left behind. I feel like someone new each time. The only things that stay are what I remember or consciously keep." Caan was suddenly quiet and Benni was afraid to speak her mind, but she did anyway. "Things are different, and I guess we'll see what happens."

"What do you mean? What's different?" Caan asked, sitting on pins and needles.

"Just, things …"

"If you're worried about us—" Caan began, but Benni cut him off.

"I know better than to expect things to happen the way I want, but I can't help but worry. And I want you to know that no matter what, it's no one's fault …" She was quiet again for a second and then spoke up again suddenly. "And I'm sorry I haven't told you yet, but you didn't make a bad decision, Caan. I've thought about it every day since the … I'm not angry about what my life is like now."

"Are you sure?" Caan felt a knot in his throat. It was good to know Benni didn't despise the decision he'd made, but his mind dwelled on something worse: he was afraid of having decided to save Benni's life, only to lose her to some unavoidable and natural decay in their relationship. He didn't want to be responsible for creating a new life for her and then not be a part of it. What kind of person would that make him—caring enough to save her life and then losing interest in loving her the way he once did?

"Yes, Caan. I'm sure." She sounded sincere, and it helped Caan feel a little better. "It couldn't be helped, and you did what you thought was best."

"Okay," said Caan. It was all he could get out without letting her know he was upset.

"I'm sorry, I didn't mean to bomb you like this," she said. Her tone lightened and Caan knew she was feeling all right again.

"No, it's all right. Nothing had been said and something needed to be," Caan told her. Resting his head in his arms he stared at the weird little patterns the holograms in his desk made when looked at too closely.

"Well good. Now it's done," she said, laughing in the cute, peppy way Caan was more accustomed to.

"Alright...well...I'll let you go for now. I probably won't call again until the end of the week and then we'll get together, okay?"

"That sounds good."

\* \* \* \*

Around 23:00, Caan blinked his eyes and awoke. He'd gone to sleep at his desk shortly after ending his conversation with Benni and shutting off his Tika module. The flashing of emergency lights outside his workspace windows had disturbed him. Sitting up in time to see two police levcars passing by, Caan watched them as they headed off in the direction of the hospital across the city. Though he'd long lost his motivation to work, Caan powered on his workspace and some overhead lights just for the company. The holographic displays made the room feel warmer and less empty. Closing his research files, he linked his Tika module to the workspace's large holographic display and splashed an array of his favorite music against the airspace in front of him, deciding to pass some time taking advantage of the academy's access to the macronet, which was normally inaccessible to the public or privately owned cyber or data devices.

The macronet didn't exist until about 2210 CE, when governments on Earth, influenced by demands made by Genesis MTI and other extramarket companies, changed ownership rights pertaining to online domains existing on what then was called the Internet. At that time, cyberspace was available for unlimited free speech, private domain ownership and other forms of outdated personal use. By the time Genesis MTI began looking into moving to Mars, it and many of its competitors purchased online domains by the countless billions. Eventually, it was impossible to access an online address that was not owned in some part by Genesis MTI or another major corporation. When online information and social networks officially became privatized, it was perfectly legal for corporations to control information belonging to any domains they owned.

Initially, this caused little trouble. Major Websites did not change and functioned essentially the same as they always had. This relationship went sour after Genesis MTI and others began to exercise their legal rights. Anyone who went so far as to speak ill of a brand of instant soup made by a company parented by Genesis MTI was lucky not to be banned extensively or permanently from accessing his online social spaces. Many people tired of corporate purging and opted to remove themselves from the Post Information Age movement entirely, while most became complacent. It was simpler and more convenient not to speak out.

Some protestors managed to complain loudly enough to spur their governments to acquire or split up the Internet, and that is exactly what happened, but not to the satisfaction of the disgruntled. The Internet and all major online sites became the macronet, always growing and becoming engulfed by powerful entities, and the subnet, a limited public internet free to use for any purpose by anyone willing to commit to it by outmoded, slow and practically Neolithic means.

The subnet, not surprisingly, was structured and owned by the same entities who owned the macronet. Genesis MTI bought most of it and was willing to craft it to the specifications put forth by law, and never added a single extra feature or function. Before 2400 CE the subnet almost became what the Internet had been four hundred years earlier, which was as exciting to most as if they were told someone had reinvented paper planes while space shuttles had been available for two hundred years.

Caan spent about half an hour digging around the macronet, pausing to view demonstrations of cutting-edge software, registering for new virtual social circles for Aeraea and Aquaea students and downloading some new personal interactive applications for his Tika module. About the time he finished, a notification popped up in his field of vision. It was a voice message from one of his friends, Lam. A fellow Aquaea graduate, Lam happened to be in some of the first higher division courses Caan had taken before graduating from the academy. Lam was generally well-liked, albeit unusual, in the sense that he took far more interest in and thought much more about things than most people. Professors loved him because, like Caan, he spoke his mind in class and didn't repeat the same humdrum observations the average student made. Caan had never really made an effort to speak to Lam in length until both realized they were applying for assistantships to the Circle. After that, whenever Caan was on campus, he never missed an opportunity to hang out with Lam long enough to swap a few new and interesting ideas or thoughts.

Caan knew Lam was outside the nook as soon as he arrived, and before Lam had to message him, Caan had linked his Tika module to the local network operating all the utilities in the room and had prompted the door to open up remotely without speaking a word or lifting a finger.

"Hey, how's it going?" Lam loped in through the door, ducking as he did so. He was a lanky giant of a guy with a caricature-worthy face, and he grinned as he gave Caan his signature tight-gripped, loose-armed handshake and crashed down in a chair with a loud grunt. Taking off his hat—one of an uncommon style belonging more to the art crowd—and wiping back his wild hair, he complained he hadn't eaten all day.

"So many ups and downs I guess it averages out," replied Caan.

"Seems about right," Lam agreed. "Well, I may not be here much longer," he said, getting right to the point as usual.

"Uh oh, what do you mean by that?" Caan asked. Scooting himself across the nook, he remotely opened the access panel on a miniature biopolymer gel refrigerator next to his desk. The thing was an antique, but it had changed the culture of food forever, and Caan had a nerdy respect for it. Reaching into the green gel, he grabbed a snack for himself, a piece of fruit perfectly cradled in an airtight pocket, and an instant packaged Korean-style meal for Lam.

"Academy Aquaea is cutting out all of the research divisions in my department," he said, opening the packaged meal and eating it two forkfuls at a time.

"You're kidding!" It was alarming news to Caan, but he already had suspicions that it had something to do with greater financial problems from down in the docks.

"Well it's not shocking," said Lam in a way that made Caan think the guy wouldn't act surprised or disturbed if he were on fire and falling from a building. "It's a long, ancient and honored tradition. When money's tight and the population's too high, kill the artists and teachers first. Thinking doesn't keep us alive. Food, water, shelter," he said in the tone of a caveman, "That's all we need, and it comes from Genesis MTI—you know, the people with all our stuff." He raised his eyebrows and grinned in a sarcastic way, a Korean noodle attempting to escape the corner of his mouth. "Studying android-made art isn't terribly important, so my grant dispersal is being frozen, and I'm being asked politely to retire to another, more useful area of study before it's unfrozen. It's just as well. I can't afford to pay tuition any longer. My funds ran out, and my job doesn't pay enough."

"Sorry to hear it," said Caan. Lam wasn't the kind of guy who got upset about these kinds of things, or needed anyone's pity, but Caan figured his own department would be next, and he had definitely begun to feel sorry for *himself*. What was happening in Genesia had happened before in first world countries on Earth during the late 21$^{st}$ and early 22$^{nd}$ centuries. The Education Crisis had been one of the motivators for Genesis MTI's colony on Mars and was one of the great problems solved by Genesia's corporate-sovereign model of society, or so it was theorized. "So what's your plan? What are you going to do now?"

"I quit," Lam said, tossing the empty meal package across the room and into a wall-mounted recycling chute. It left a couple of drops of noodle sauce on the wall.

"You quit?" Caan actually laughed at the way Lam said it. "You quit what? Life? The whole thing? You're done? Cashing in, checking out?" This got Lam laughing too.

"No, I mean this place. The Academy," explained Lam, settling back down and lifting his hands up in defeat and closing his eyes wearily. "I'm gonna go do something else. I've been getting interested in making my own art. It doesn't do me any good to start at this point in life. I won't be able to compete, but at least I can do whatever I want, and Genesis MTI won't somehow own a part or all of what I do."

"Independent, huh? A lot of those kinds of projects earn you an apartment in Dark Town, you know," Caan warned him, clawing the rind off his fruit and breaking it into little pieces.

"Yeah, but even if I stay here," Lam replied, sighing and looking around, "All I get is a degree and maybe a title. A bunch of words. I get some magic words that may or may not grant me success and happiness and glory or whatever it is those Ignaea graduates get."

Caan laughed and couldn't help but nod in silent agreement.

"There was that one girl," he went on, "You remember the one who started up that anthrotect firm and scared the pants off of

Genesis MTI? She did the whole thing her way. Quit the academies, bought up some software, made partners, fed some homeless artists and made some impressive stuff."

"Yeah, but Genesis eventually found a way to step on her. Made up a brand new company overnight and imitated everything she did and sold it faster and in bigger bulk." Caan rained out whatever remained of Lam's good spirit with that comment, but Lam knew it was the truth.

"Still," Lam argued, "I think she did something more important than that."

"What's that?" asked Caan, genuinely hoping to be proven wrong.

"Sometimes ..." He paused and rethought his phrasing, "Sometimes I wonder if I should have hurt myself more. Partied, done manual labor, been poor and spat in the face of everyone who told me the Academy was the way to go ... to teach myself to appreciate things I don't understand because I avoided the lessons."

Caan nodded, elbows rested on his knees, imagining a bonfire on the floor between him and Lam.

"We try and get to the top of some proverbial mountain. Maybe going up isn't the only way. Maybe ... sometimes ... getting somewhere means going back down. What's on the other side of the mountain? Why go higher and higher and higher when there are other mountains to find and see?"

Caan nodded some more, the nook becoming quiet.

"You're a poet, Lam," said Caan, finally, standing and dramatizing his reaction. "You're an unsung poet and champion of the human spirit, and you need to sing these revelations to the people of Genesia!"

"Shut up," said Lam, bursting into laughter.

# 8.0
# I, TOUCH (H+)

*"We have created artificial intelligences that match or surpass human mental, emotional and learning capacities. We have given androids human jobs and human civilian status, but we withhold human civil rights from them. True sentience is true sentience, whether the mind is synthetic or organic. Androids are self-reliant, self-sufficient, self-aware beings, and they are not merely sentient, they are sapient. To create a subjugated race of synthetic flesh and bone is no more ethical than to clone organic flesh and bone for the purpose of harvesting replacement tissues, a matter we've already long condemned. The Safer Sentience Act would require androids to involuntarily prioritize lawful behavior over free will. This would be a brand of slavery unparalleled in the history of humanity. A question that should disturb every one of us, but a question we should ask ourselves is this: if androids were meant to be nothing more than tools, why did we create them in our own image?"*

—Sofiya Zoyanova, attorney,
*Association of Citizen Androids v. Genesis MTI*, 2622 CE


Benni couldn't remember the last time she intentionally woke up before sunrise; in fact, the best waking hours of her years in Academy Aeraea normally occurred between the middle of the afternoon and the early morning. Nothing motivated her to keep a normal sleep schedule, especially when her most creative thoughts came to her in the quiet, dark hours of the night, but when Dada invited her to come along to another Solarist service, Benni made sure to be awake and available at 06:00, a time of day so early and precise, the only beings Benni could imagine being awake at that hour were aerofreighter pilots and androids.

Boarding a levbus, Benni opened TikaTalk and frowned when there were no notifications awaiting her, not from Caan, not from any of her friends, not even from Shirro. Now that she thought about it, Shirro had suddenly stopped trying to contact her two weeks or more previously. She was glad she didn't have to confront Shirro but felt guilty, unable to guess if Shirro had ceased out of respect or anger or something else. What bothered her much more was remembering how long ago she and Caan had spoken about going out to spend time together. The weekend had passed. In fact two weekends had passed without so much as a long conversation. Benni understood that Caan was under pressure. He was worried about his research and had said something about financial failures in Academy Aeraea, to what effect she could not precisely remember. She was just as guilty, she knew, having spent many a night beginning her own schoolwork again after re-registering with Academy Aeraea and ending her medical leave; that, and she had been spending a great deal of time with Dada, an android who had become a great friend in a shorter amount of time than any person she'd known her whole life. Shirro was a detail she consciously did not include in her laundry list of slip-ups, doing her best to put him out of mind and hoping he'd vanish entirely.

To say she was unhappy, Benni knew, would not be entirely true. Never before had she allowed herself much time away from

Caan, even for her friends. Every other day or so Benni would spend the afternoon with Dada. The two would talk for hours, even joke, which was initially odd, Benni thought. Actually, to describe what they did as talking wasn't quite the right word. The "conversations" they had reminded Benni much more of the experiences she had had when she was a part of the Tribe experiment. Dada could describe more of her thoughts by sharing mental images, sounds and memories than she could by opening her mouth to speak. Before long, Benni learned to literally speak her mind to Dada, and if anyone watched the pair, making expressions and gesturing silently as they did, one might have mistaken them for mute, deaf or both. Every thought Benni shared with Dada was perfect the way it was and needed no translation to a canvas or a series of words.

On occasion Benni would retract from these conversations, especially when she nearly revealed things about herself she wasn't sure she wanted Dada to know. The transhuman part of her was fascinated with it, but the human part of her recoiled from the intimacy of the direct mental contact. Benni remained conflicted even after she learned Dada was impossible to discomfort or repulse. As Benni wrestled with her self-consciousness, the android would wait patiently and happily, never judging and never prying.

The levbus touched down on a platform a few blocks from the Church of the Filii Solis, but Benni didn't mind walking the distance. Early in the morning not many people were out to fill the walkways, and aside from the hushed omnipresent noises created by the mechanized and electronic anatomy of the city itself, there was little to be heard; the hour before sunrise was tranquil and pleasant. Slow and sparse traffic occasionally lit the dark ceiling of the glassy, cavernous world of Genesia's surface airways and streets. Like the weird fish in the hospital aquariums the levitating vehicles were distant, uninterested in anything but their destinations and good for only mild, passing interest. Much higher above them, a web of vactrains streaked the night sky between sometimes miles-high superstructures, flying like supersonic electric eels, their tail ends fading behind them as luminous whips.

Somewhere down the street, a raucous noise was growing around a district courthouse. A number of transhumans were gathering in protest against the steadily tightening workplace laws that allowed businesses the right to refuse to hire or serve recently discharged transhuman medical patients. Many of them had abandoned their dormitories at Genesia General Hospital not long after Benni, following a somewhat violent riot that occurred in the long-term patient residential wings. Hundreds of transhumans had been living in the streets since, moving around the city in mobs and forcing the police to mobilize on a daily basis. Benni could hear them shouting around the block.

"Come inside," Dada told Benni, coming down the steps to retrieve her. Sharply dressed and awaiting Benni's arrival, she smiled as they made their way inside the church to their usual places among the greater congregation, but not before Dada turned back to look once more, frowning as the noise down the street grew louder.

The atmosphere inside the church was not the same as that to which Benni was accustomed. Quiet as always, the congregation was not lively or high-spirited as usual. Dada had noticed a look of confusion on Benni's face and explained to her that the church had announced that the morning's intended service would not be taking place as planned. Church representatives were concerned about something happening citywide. Apparently during the previous night, the High Herald, the android who always led the services, had a vision and decided it was important that this vision be shared with the congregation. Hearing all this from Dada, Benni was no longer surprised that everyone was acting a little strange, if not anxious. When she thought about it, Benni tried to decide if the androids around her actually felt anxiety, or if their emotive state was simply blank. What was the artificial equivalent of surprise and anticipation? Dada did not seem terribly tense, and so Benni wondered if she was reading too much into the faces around her.

The High Herald, an android who looked something like a thirty-five or forty-year-old human man, entered the grand room and walked gracefully toward the central pulpit from where he normally and silently conducted mass. Benni saw the symbol of the Solarist Church appear in her field of view, and her Tika module automatically ran the program attached to it. She heard a brief message of greeting in her mind and then, as always, her vision momentarily turned to solid darkness. After a moment, a new environment began to materialize around her, unnatural bright green grids passing over and through her as they digitally assembled the simulation. Next to her appeared an avatar she recognized as Dada, who looked at her and smiled, and then the rest of the congregation appeared one by one, followed by the High Herald.

Looking around, Benni quickly recognized her surroundings. She and the congregation were standing in a large square in uptown Genesia from where the presidents of Genesis MTI always gave their rare but highly attended public addresses. A great crowd of about one hundred thousand people was gathered in the square. Their clothes looked to be a few hundred years old—clearly a vision of Genesia's early past. All their backs were turned to the congregation, and they stood in awe and silence as a man at a podium raised his arms and spoke. His voice sounded far away, as if he were at the bottom of some canyon, his words echoing against some far off folds of time. A bright and powerful holographic marquee above the speaker's head read: "The New Promise." The crowd in the square began to applaud as the speaker looked to his left and someone else, someone Benni somehow knew was his wife, joined him on stage. The speaker and the woman—an android woman—embraced and then turned back to the crowd, smiling and waving. The great marquee displayed the words, "Citizenship for Androids!"

This vision passed and Benni, Dada and the church congregation remained hovering in a black void while another sea of green gridlines swept over them. A new world began to take shape around them. It was an image of Keller Bay circa 2500 CE, the largest port in the Genesian docks during the early decades of the 26th century. All around Benni fleets of ARC shuttles entered and exited the bay, aerofreighters hummed past, and human dockworkers swarmed around shipments going in and out of the colony. It was a well-known image, one that Benni had seen before in history classes in early school. It was classic footage that was always evoked when anyone spoke of the prosperous Martian boom between 2511 and 2529 CE. The vision ended as two foremen were seen overseeing the bay's operations; one, a famous businessman named Siyang Chen; the second, a would-be powerful android called Piers Pelops, who would become famous as an industrial architect, financial advisor to the Vice President of Genesis MTI, and later, the first android anthrotect.

The image of Pelops and Chen, two of Genesia's founding figures, faded to black and was quickly succeeded by another, almost identical image. This time, however, the year was 2528, three years after Chen's death and long after his retirement. Pelops now stood next to Adrian Alacosta, who was then a young man of twenty-five and freshly graduated from Academy Ignaea with high degrees. Again the image faded, and when it appeared again, the only thing that changed, aside from the style and fashion of the dockworkers' attire and ARC ships' models, was the person standing next to Pelops. It was 2560, maybe a decade or so before Benni's parents (either set of them) would be born. The sixties had been difficult for all.

Benni's grandfather, that is, her second father's father, had been a 2560's recession-era dockie named Bill Dublanc. A cranky but kind old Frenchman, Grandpa Bill didn't know how to talk about anything but androids and the economy. Religion, politics, sex— nothing stirred up Bill like "reds, and the robots grabbing them all up." Bill lived in Dark Town in a basic apartment paid for by the ARC Company. Like all his aging neighbors and friends, Grandpa Bill had lost almost all his dockworker's benefits during a slump in the shipping market that would never fully recover, mainly due to the increasing number of new citizen androids occupying human jobs during the 2570's.

Benni scanned the crowds of dockworkers milling about in the old footage, thinking maybe she would catch sight of Grandpa Bill, his face wrapped in a big bushy beard and stained dark where his protective helmet didn't shield him from the grease and grime of mechanical toil. She had seen less and less of him as a young girl before he died, and she didn't spot him now as she stood in silence with the Solarist congregation. The footage faded to black again as the simulation shifted its focus to the mysterious android Pelops. Benni and the congregation now stood gathered together in the background of another public assembly like the one they had seen before, except this gathering was taking place in front of the Church of the Filii Solis. The year was 2569, and the android Pelops was speaking to a mixed crowd of Solarist androids and concerned humans.

"Genesis MTI has politely asked me to step down from my leadership position at ARC and retire," Pelops was saying to the crowd. "In the face of tremendous pressure from human ARC employees and my own superiors, I am going to do as requested."

There was an uproar from certain corners of the crowd gathering around the church.

"However, I wish to say a few things," Pelops continued, hushing the crowd. "Androids like me who have been dismissed from their places of employment these past two years are not to blame for the ongoing and unfortunate economic crises we face. Forces on Earth that are beyond our control, including isolated wars, population expansion and political disagreements will continue to burden Genesia and all of its citizens as long as they are not resolved, regardless of what is being done here on Mars."

The crowd became noisy again, clearly in agreement with Pelops.

"The removal and limiting of android presence and capability here in Genesia will only complicate existing social and economic problems we are experiencing." A tremor cut through Pelops's artificial voice. "Restricting the potential of androids and transhumans is constitutionally inappropriate, economically wasteful and philosophically stagnant. There is no future where there is no room for growth and change. If Genesia does not acknowledge these statements and act, today is the beginning of the end for my kind and a leap backward for humankind."

The weight of Pelops's speech wound the minds of Benni and

the congregation like thread around a steadily turning spool until the android's words held them all tightly in a quiet moment of reflection. So entwined in the things she was swiftly learning about the android Pelops and the history of androids like Dada, Benni was startled when she heard the High Herald's voice suddenly cut through the dark as the image of Pelops and the church faded.

"Now," the High Herald's voice rolled softly through Benni's head, "witness what I have witnessed."

The High Herald's ominous words were followed by a bright flash. A new simulation began, and Benni heard the distant sounds of calamity—shouting, breaking, the drone of engines and machinery. The flash of light that blinded her had come from a military vehicle hovering overhead, casting a harsh bright light from beneath its cockpit as it levitated two stories from the ground. People ran all about in a state of panic, herded by men and women in uniforms and strange, bipedal things Benni recognized as machine soldiers from Earth, like the ones that subdued her in Hermphrey Park. Tall, heavy, jerky and alien, the machine soldiers looked like some horrible abstraction of early androids; limbs like lanky insects; voices crude and electronic, shearing and unpleasant. Their faces were nothing more than black, glassy display monitors, ovular like the windshields of levcars, and spun around on skeletal steel necks with frantic, avian intensity.

Benni didn't understand. The alarming and chaotic scene was not something that had ever happened in Genesia, but it was clear the scene was at nighttime, and she and the congregation were standing in the middle of a neighborhood called Last Picima at the intersection of Eucrabura Street and Anna Goppa Drive. Benni knew of it because she had lived a few blocks from it for two years with her parents, just after she started attending Academy Aeraea. The superstructures all around were dark except for their auxiliary beacons that came on only during a state of emergency.

Another large crowd of people were approaching the congregation from Benni's right, heading toward the men and women in uniform and machine soldiers to her left. The androids in the congregation and the High Herald never moved, continuing to look on as the imaginary crowd of people moved right through them toward a line of machine soldiers. The military spacecraft hovering overhead directed its bright lights to the crowd of people, and an artificial voice commanded them to stop.

These people were not like the others, not like the ones being herded around by the uniforms and machine soldiers. They were shouting and angry. They were transhumans. Benni watched them as they began to do something she'd seen only once before. Around their bodies, one by one, energetic, electric breezes whipped up, creating unnatural phenomena.

*Wuuuuuum ...*

Bits and pieces of debris rose from the street and jumped into the air. A single one of the transhumans stepped forward, and the voice from the hovering spacecraft issued a warning. The spotlight fell on the transhuman as he raised his left arm; it was made of a special prosthetic like Benni's.

*Wuum … wuum … wuuuum …*

Through the whirling static field surrounding him, Benni saw his arm changing size and shape, the fingers extending as if possessed by some magic technology or trick of the eyes. A final warning came from the spacecraft, but the man ignored it. One of the machine soldiers stumbled backward, as if shoved by some potent, unseen force. It struggled to return to the line but couldn't. The uniformed men and women watched it in fright as it flailed its arms and straightened its neck like a frail child in a storm wind. The transhuman man directing the terrible force gave a shout, and the machine soldier's glassy black face cracked and shattered as its metal head caved in and it fell to the street and twitched, a little electrical fire erupting from its burst skull.

Before the transhuman man could repeat his trick, the other machine soldiers had raised their weapons. A single one of them took aim at him and when it did, its weapon engaged and lit up piercing blue. The barrel of the weapon made a harsh crackling sound and fired a streak of bright energy, like a miniature bolt of lightning. The bolt struck the transhuman high on the chest, sending him to the ground with a powerful shock and disabled his transhuman modules and other prosthetics with an electromagnetic pulse.

The first thing Benni noticed when he was shot was the man's head going limp and his eyes shutting, as if something in his brain simply turned off and stopped working. At first, Benni thought the machine soldier had killed him, but the man began to convulse violently, eyes rolling back in their sockets and baring their veiny, pink undersides. Benni and some of the androids watching clasped their hands over their mouths.

The rest of the transhumans in the scene screamed and scattered in fear, some violently resisting the machine soldiers in a terrible display of psychokinetic fury, and others fleeing outright. A few of those who fought back were neutralized as the first man had been, blasted with EMP rifles or beaten into submission by the tall, brutal machine soldiers. People in uniforms came and collected the wounded, delivering them to medical teams who carried them off with the rest of the evacuees. The street became stained with blood and littered with glass and ruined scrap metal.

When this vision passed, Benni consciously tried to relax again, but she struggled and trembled. When the first transhuman man had been shot, she had grabbed onto Dada and hadn't let go since. Dada had said nothing to her about it.

An entirely new compilation of images soon replaced the unpleasant scene in the streets of Genesia. In the darkness there appeared a peppering of stars, including one very close star, and in its shadow, a large, green planet. Too large to be Earth, it spun quietly in the void of space, growing closer and closer. As it approached, images of Genesia's recent past hung in the darkness around the planet—one of Piers Pelops and Lyonell Rudy looking thoughtfully at holographic maps of an Earthlike planet, one of the crew of the Second Dandelion Initiative all smiling and waving from the cockpit of the space shuttle *Monarch I*, and a third image of blueprints for a great tower marked with the symbol of the Solarist Church and a number of major Martian engineering companies.

These images vanished, and Benni watched as she and the congregation fell through the atmosphere of the unfamiliar green planet, cool gray clouds and thick moisture blowing through their hair and tickling their skin. Down scores of thousands of feet they rushed toward the planet's surface, barely missing the misty tops of mountains and crashing through a thick canopy of vegetation until finally they all stood on the outskirts of a great metropolis of the future, as large as Genesia and surrounded by dense and exotic verdant wilderness—great river valleys, forests, hills and mountains that reached out to the horizon. The High Herald turned and led the congregation into this megacity, all the heads of androids and humans alike turning this way and that, in awe of what they were seeing.

* * * *

In 2371 CE, twenty-two years after the settling of Genesia on Mars, an Earthlike planet close to humankind's home solar system had been discovered. The large, green planet was closer than the formerly closest known planet of its kind—so many times closer that it was deemed possible to reach, maybe even to settle. With leftover resources from the construction of Genesia and some old-fashioned pioneering hope, Genesis MTI launched a secretive project called the Second Dandelion Initiative.

Investing in a gamble, Genesis MTI assembled an enthusiastic team of thirty-five scientists and fifteen flight crew piloting five exploratory spacecraft. A fifth of each team would be comprised of androids, lowering the need for vital supplies like food and water. The spacecraft were equipped to handle any perceivable situation, including machines built to quickly establish automatic farms and small, all-terrain settlements. The original team sent away knew their lives would depend on establishing a small, permanent settlement because they would lack the supplies to return home.

Against all odds, the Second Dandelion Initiative was successful, one android and three human casualties notwithstanding. Once Genesis MTI received a stream of positive contacts from the team, they immediately handed the project over to a company called Transtellar. The Second Dandelion Project drew in new recruits quietly through the Circle, and Transtellar provided transportation for continual expeditions to the new, unnamed "Green Planet". Beginning in 2386 CE, unknown to all of Earth and ninety-nine percent of Mars, human beings had begun to build a permanent home away from home in a new solar system.

* * * *

The city envisioned by Genesis MTI, Transtellar and the Circle was what Benni, Dada and the rest of the Solarists now walked into, eyes wide and curious. *It's just like home*, Benni thought privately, *only beautiful in ways home isn't*. Genesia wouldn't be green and lush for who knew how long; thousands … tens of thousands of years, even with the help of terraforming technology. A blue-gray sky full of clouds—clouds that could produce *real rain*—city streets with no ceilings, real air that could be breathed endlessly, beaches that met oceans ... it was all difficult to imagine, even after experiencing dozens of simulations of Earthlike landscapes. Benni could feel the cool, fresh air and the misty breezes. The vastness of open space made her tuck her arms up against herself.

The congregation walked and walked with the High Herald. They were in no hurry, but none could guess where they were led, and all were eager to know. On all sides, the brilliant city rose up around them, shining white, silver and gold. Uninhabited edifices, empty parks and hollow vactrain tunnels—prospective homes, schools and hospitals—the absence of human life was palpable.

The High Herald stopped at the foot of one of the highest buildings in the city, the tower that all had seen earlier, drawn into a set of blueprints. Atop its roof could be seen a familiar symbol, the same one that adorned the top of the Church of the Filii Solis in Genesia. It was here that something interesting was happening. A small mob of people were seen waiting out in front of the base of the tower. As the congregation watched them, they did not at first notice that the appearance of the city was changing. The new, bright and shining faces of the structures were fading as if they were aging by decades every second. Gradually the green and growing things surrounding the city moved in, climbed the superstructures and covered the streets until trees burst from the shorter roofs, vines curled in and out of the vactrain tunnels and wind and rain weakened doors and windows. The megacity became a ruin of high technology, swallowed up by the wilds.

This dramatic change captured the attention of the congregation, and then there came a voice from the base of the tower. Someone appeared out of the darkness between two great doors leading into the tower, which had settled into the broken ground like ancient relics. The small group of strangers who had gathered at the tower's base now looked different as well. Their clothes were old and worn. Some of the men had grown long, wild hair and beards; the women, even longer hair, braided by improvised means, and thin, hardier complexions.

The person who appeared in the doorway had stopped and was looking at all of these people. Benni watched closely and saw that it was a woman—no … a female android who had come out of the darkness of the tower. Her hair was colored much lighter than Benni's, almost white in the sun, and short. On her face she wore little blue marks, made by dye or paint, as far as Benni could tell. The people gathered around began to speak to her and she spoke back, but what was said, no one could hear. Everyone seemed pleased to see her. The android turned her head up to look toward the congregation, ignoring the other people for a moment. Benni felt as though the android looked directly at her. The moment their eyes met, the android's stare held a look of surprise, and then the vision disappeared.

Dada's voice was what it took to bring Benni back from that far away place. Forgetting she was watching a program all along, Benni blinked a few times when the little symbol of the Solarist

Church appeared in her field of view and her eyes adjusted to their actual surroundings once more. Dada was speaking her name and asking her something. Benni realized she had hold of Dada's arm and let go quickly, quite embarrassed. Dada asked if Benni were all right and told her she had not come out of the simulation quickly. Benni admitted she kind of wished she could have stayed. Dada smiled and agreed that the beautiful city they had seen was wonderful.

"You know," Dada said as they both left the congregation and headed outside of the church, "We may not have to wait long."

"What?" Benni made a face and laughed. "You mean we may actually get to see that city in our lifetimes?"

"Well," said Dada, "It's true my natural lifetime would span enough time to allow me to eventually travel to such a place, but no, that's not what I meant."

"That city surely is not as complete as the one we saw," Benni suggested, expecting Dada to say something that would prove her wrong.

"No, it isn't," Dada admitted, "But more of it has been finished than you think. Some of the others don't know this, but because I study under the High Herald and will one day replace him, I know some things. Don't tell anyone I shared this with you."

"Oh, no I won't, if it's supposed to be secret," Benni said eagerly.

"I wouldn't call it a secret," said Dada, "but we haven't spoken about it much yet because the time hasn't come. Things are

223

different now, though."

"I have to say, I didn't understand a lot of what we saw today. I mean it made sense in and of itself but ..." Benni's brow furrowed, and she expressed a confusion that Dada detected without needing to be told.

"I understand. You're welcome to come back home with me later if you want. I'll explain it all. It will take some time, and it may surprise you," Dada began.

"All right. Let's go up the street first so I can get something to eat."

"Are you still interested in going to the new student galleries at Academy Aeraea?" asked Dada, reminding Benni of their previously made plans. "You had mentioned your light sculptures are on display. I'm interested in seeing them."

"Oh, yes of course. Sorry, I almost forgot in all my excitement," Benni apologized.

* * * *

At the end of the afternoon, Benni and Dada left the student galleries at Academy Aeraea. It was always a delight for Benni to be able to display her work, and lately she hadn't made a habit of appearing for her own exhibitions as she was used to doing. The truth was she didn't like going alone, and Caan hadn't had the time to spare. Dada made the experience worthwhile, asking question after question and challenging Benni to explain her works and her motivation. Once they scoured the galleries twice or three times over, Benni remembered many burning questions she still had for

Dada concerning their experiences that morning. Dada repeated her invitation to Benni to accompany her home, and Benni gladly accepted, awfully curious about how the android's home would look.

By the time they reached the vactrain terminal, Dada had explained that the city they had seen in the vision during the church service was real, or *would be* real. It was begun more than a few hundred years earlier and would be officially inhabited only after it was finished and operational; expeditions were being made into the surrounding territories to understand more about the Green Planet. In addition, Genesis MTI and Transtellar did not intend to publicly confirm the city's existence until scientists and engineers were certain it could sustain a large population, among numerous lesser concerns.

This was easy enough for Benni to understand and believe. Dada then went on to tell Benni about Piers Pelops, perhaps much more than was necessary; Benni was easily bored by history lessons, but what was most important was to know that Pelops had invested a great amount of his personal fortune in ensuring the construction of a Solarist temple—the tower Benni had seen in the vision—within the city on the Green Planet. Dada stopped speaking as the vactrain she was waiting for arrived in the terminal that overlooked the southern half of the city. Finding two adjacent seats, they settled down and held onto handrails as the interior doors of the train and exterior doors of the transparent vacuum tunnel shut and sealed. The train accelerated, exiting the boarding platform and curving wide around the outside of the terminal and into the setting sun. Dada continued from where she left off, getting to the real mystery behind the High Herald's vision and the future of Genesia and the Solarists.

"The truth is," Dada said, a little more quietly, "We have known for a long time that Genesia would fail. It's been foretold again and again by Solarist leaders and it was echoed in a famous speech given by Piers Pelops."

"The one in the vision?" said Benni.

"Exactly. And understand I'm not speaking of a superstition or a prophecy. The city has never been as successful as Genesis MTI may have meant it to be. You already know this, of course. It was an integral part of your history courses in school. What is troubling is that Genesia is failing. It began to fail decades ago with the renewal of android rights-restrictive laws, but soon we will see these failings affecting everything and everyone at once."

"What do you mean? And why will this happen?" Benni frowned.

"It will happen for many reasons, but what will ruin the city is news that Genesia has lost support from Earth, that no more supplies will come. No one will know until the evacuation shuttles are already here. And before you ask, it will be done this way in order to avoid rioting and other social disasters while everyone is waiting for help." Dada spelled out all this for Benni with a kind of calm that actually made Benni feel at ease, as though everything would be all right.

"That was what we saw in the vision," Benni said, slowly making sense of it all, "when those transhumans were attacked by the machine soldiers."

"Yes," said Dada, nodding, "There will be some who will not want to go, mainly transhumans who believe they will have no future on Earth. They will have learned that they cannot trust their rights or freedoms to those who made them the way they are. What they don't know is much worse. When they arrive on Earth, the technology that makes them so intelligent and creative and powerful will be taken from them. Great nations will use it to wage terrible wars and commit acts of terrorism in the name of competition and survival."

"I see..." said Benni, chewing her lip and massaging her chilly hands. She couldn't help the urge to ask Dada questions about those transhumans. She had done things the ones in the vision had done, displaying impossible abilities and creating weird phenomena like they did. It was the only reason she believed anything Dada was saying. She had seen it herself, but she didn't want Dada to know, at least not yet. She dreaded being arrested or taken away or killed like the people in the vision. "And what about the tower?"

"The tower is the most important part of the vision," said Dada. "It is where the Solarists will go to seek sanctuary when all this comes to pass. We will leave Genesia forever. Spiritually speaking, we will leave behind our troubles and our struggles, and literally speaking, we will do this by leaving behind our bodies. Our consciousnesses will be uploaded and transmitted across solar systems to the tower you saw on the Green Planet, by way of a special, quantum computer communications program. We will be received by the tower and downloaded once more into a data bank inside of a highly advanced, quantum computing network. We'll exist without pain or possessions as nothing more than our personalities, emotions and thoughts."

"This is all a little difficult to accept," Benni answered after a long moment. Her abdomen tightened and turned as if it was full of rocks, and she grew pale.

"Understandably," said Dada, "it's a leap of faith, to borrow an expression."

"I guess I can see why it makes sense to some," Benni admitted. "If you can preserve all this," she said, touching her head, "without taking along all this," she continued, gesturing at her arms, legs and torso, "I suppose you could escape a lot of terrible things."

"Yes, but it isn't the end of the journey," Dada told her.

"So, you won't be … dying?" Benni asked, unsure if she had chosen the correct word.

"Oh, no. We won't die. We will move on eventually, passing through various conduits and mysterious forms, across time and space, theoretically forever. It is the great journey described by our oldest sacred texts, the inspired dreams of Jane Ashley, Piers Pelops and others. We believe it's the next great step."

"For people? Or do you mean androids?" asked Benni.

"Well," said Dada, stopping to think for a moment. It was

something she rarely had to do. "I suppose I mean the soul," she said, smiling, content with her conclusion.

* * * *

Dada's apartment was much farther away than Benni had assumed. Not until the vactrain reached the end of its route and began to turn around did they exit onto a large terminal in southern Genesia, take the maglift up to the First Mile and walk one block to Tika Heights, a grove of dizzyingly tall apartment communities much like Nioua Point. The First Mile, just as the name suggests, was a unique district of Genesia that occurred at the first mile from the ground. Dada and nearly all androids and the wealthiest humans lived somewhere in the First Mile. Apartments were smaller but more expensive and technologically equipped. Benni hadn't visited the First Mile more than three or four times, which was typical of someone belonging to the middle class. It was where the fortunate retired and the wealthy thrived, notable for communities like Olympus Mons Villages and Tropos Gardens, both built atop and around  artificial beaches and small islands all contained in globular glass.

A lot of artists Benni had met in college actually spent time in the fashionable cafés and software stores surrounding Tika Heights, considered to be one of Genesia's cultural hotspots. It wasn't Benni's atmosphere of choice, however. She wasn't interested in playing keep-up with the hip crowd. Their art, she always thought, was a collection of shallow musings wrapped in misleading expressive and colorful outer shells, like the trendy

229

creative software on which they produced it, designed by top shelf, high-dollar software moguls—the arbiters of digital cool.

Benni took her time to look around and see the sights as she followed Dada into Tika Heights. The central lobby of the north tower was the largest hub in the community and was spotless, chic and spacious, following the aesthetic code of Tika Incorporated, the software company that owned the towers. Their brand was stylishly cut into the floor of the central lobby, a pearlescent purple eye and star wrapped in the company's slogan: "Design by the inner eye." The same logo, the astronomical symbol of Metis, appeared in miniature on the glass faces of all the maglift doors, like the one Dada and Benni took to Dada's apartment high in the north tower. It was even subtly engraved into the casing of Benni's prosthetic arm, and only now could she not seem to forget about it.

The halls and pods of Tika Towers were some of the whitest, most featureless spaces Benni had ever seen. Only the occasional sculpture or tint-changing panoramic windows lent them any character. At the end of one particular hallway, a private, winding stair, only a single person wide, led to the door Dada pointed at and called home. Dada remotely unlocked the door as she invited Benni up the stairs and welcomed her inside.

When she saw that the inside of the apartment was just as empty and blank as the rest of the building, Benni wasn't sure if she should be surprised. Dada's apartment was one room with one square corner and a circular wall connecting the other two. The whole curved wall was mostly window with holographic display projectors lining the insides, so images could be viewed on a long panoramic screen, or the windows could simply be darkened for privacy. Similar technology was installed in specific places in the other walls, ceiling and floor so that simulated walls could be placed around a bathroom or bedroom. The furniture, which at first Benni presumed to be nonexistent, was stowed away in the floor, and would appear through movable panels when remotely prompted by Dada, or manually by a strange, floating white orb that continually moved about in the air. Dada asked Benni if she would like a seat, and as she did, a marshmallow-like mass, about a meter and a half cubed, rose near the middle of the room and took on the form of a cozy chair. As it molded itself into place, another appeared and joined it, and the holographic displays in the floor and ceiling began to form something of a living room out of simple, opaque, cream-colored screens. Lights hidden in the ceiling dimmed and the windows tinted a bit, allowing a comfortable amount of the waning sunlight through. The floor changed hue, becoming light gray, and the now solidified marshmallowy couches took on the visual likeness of soft chocolate brown fabric.

"I can't begin to tell you how jealous I am of your home," said Benni, hands propped on her hips and thoroughly impressed. "I've never seen all of these furnishings in one place before. I mean, my parents used to have the TikaMaid like the one you have," she said, pointing at the little white sphere hovering overhead, "But not the spaceless walls or the adaptable furniture. This is luxurious!"

"Thank you," Dada replied, smiling and fiddling with the TikaMaid. "I like it too, I suppose. It's all very convenient but terribly expensive. If I had a choice, I'd really rather have only what I need. It's simpler."

"You can have my apartment if you'll trade me this one," Benni said as she lounged on the couch and used her Tika module to tinker with the holographic displays by the big window.

"The TikaHome controls are unlocked, so feel free to change anything to your liking," said Dada, "Just use your Tika module and you can access the lighting and the furniture and what have you. What kind of music do you like? Bring up the library on the window screens over there and I'll adjust the volume."

"Oh I've got some fantastic stuff you have to hear," Benni said. She was already way ahead of Dada, and by the time the android had sat down, Benni had tuned the atmosphere to just her taste. Toning down the lights and making the music softly audible, she closed her eyes and bobbed her head to the mellow beats filling the air.

"This is very nice," Dada decided, sitting back and listening.

"It's Hileah Al-Messer," said Benni. "You may think it doesn't sound like her, but not everything she does is loud and exciting. What you're hearing is her early work, stuff I listen to when I need just the right style in mind for sculpting."

"You know," Dada began, "style would have been a very difficult concept for me to learn if I had been made any earlier than I was."

"Why's that?" asked Benni.

"I'm a Galatea Model 10 android," she said in a way that almost sounded proud. "That is the first model to be made after the civil rights movements of the early 25$^{th}$ century. We were the first to be able to freely learn, which allowed us to become more human, even if that meant sometimes abandoning the strictly logical and accurate modes of thinking we were originally designed for. I'm serial number zero, zero, zero, three, five, two. Dr. Bellafonia Emerich is serial number one, the first Galatea Model 10 ever made. She was the first person I saw when I was born. You may know of her, she's famous. But before she was a medical doctor and psychologist, she was an anthrotect, one of the only android anthrotects there has ever been."

"I had no idea," said Benni, "But I do know Dr. Emerich personally." She tapped the white casing on her head where her brain surgery had taken place.

"Oh, you don't say!" said Dada. "You must be lucky then. Dr. Emerich is my hero," she gushed. "She inspired me to pursue my studies in religions. She's published some heliogenicist poetry, so I decided to take up poetry as well."

"Have you? That makes me wonder, and I haven't really thought about it, but I suppose there are many things an android wouldn't necessarily need to know. I always assumed that even if one of you could express creativity, for example, it wouldn't mean you would ever do it," said Benni.

"That is exactly the problem I experienced before I learned

233

many things on my own," Dada said with a nod. "I was built in the same fashion as my predecessors. But I was also programmed for physical and mental expressions for which I really had no need, and I can remember when I would express them automatically in response to appropriate situations, but humans always reacted with discomfort. Because I could freely learn, however, would you believe I learned not only *how* but *why* to express myself? I can even falsify my emotions. I know lying is wrong, but it was a great deal of fun to learn." Benni laughed at this and Dada smiled.

"What do you write about?" asked Benni, "in your poetry, I mean."

"The first one I wrote was about a broken coffee cup," answered Dada.

"A cup?" Benni covered her mouth, apologizing when she began to giggle.

"It's all right, I've been told my poems are strange," said Dada, smiling and watching Benni

blush in embarrassment. "I also wrote one about squares," she continued.

"The shapes?"

"Mhm, and one about what it would be like to have no teeth, and another about sleeping underwater."

"Sleeping underwater?" Benni repeated.

"I suppose it came from my earliest memories just before I was born, or rather activated," Dada explained, cocking her head in a thoughtful way. "I have a vague memory of being immersed in

234

something cool, and an image of looking up as if submerged in a dark lake and seeing the surface from beneath."

"You'll have to explain something to me," said Benni, a pensive look on her face and her eyebrows scrunched in tedious thought. "Do you feel emotion, or do you just express it because you have better learned how to?"

"Oh, no. I feel them," insisted Dada. "Once I learned that emotions are expressed instinctively, I was able to adjust my own neural circuitry to afford the ability to imitate instinctive reactions to environmental cues, and I bridged the programming between my emotional expressions and my own anatomy, so I experience physiological responses to situations as well. It was a way of preventing myself from being able to think about emotions before expressing them. It's all very complex and fascinating," she said.

"It's confusing's what it is," said Benni, barely keeping up.

"Oh, the process was very difficult," Dada assured her. "Many androids began to occupy themselves with understanding emotion once they were free to think and learn. What's interesting is that curiosity was something that motivated us, and ..."

"And curiosity itself is something you all had never known before," Benni finished for her, grinning with a certain new understanding.

"Exactly!" Dada smiled, revealing perfectly white teeth.

"So not all of you understand these things?"

"No, unfortunately," said Dada. "It was a pursuit we had to undertake on our own. We were not made to be human. We were made only to imitate humanness better than our predecessors."

"You mean to say anthrotects haven't been trying to improve the humanness of androids? Since the very beginning, I thought the goal was to build a better human, so to speak." Benni was confused and a little disappointed.

"Do you know what the first androids were built for?" asked Dada. As she conversed with Benni, she crossed her pretty, smooth and perfectly toned legs in a meditative fashion and sat upright, looking at the holographic displays in the window and browsing Benni's music.

"Of course," answered Benni, "They were built to do construction and other complicated tasks in atmosphereless, weightless and other environments that would have been hazardous to humans. They were also lab assistants, pilots and surgeons, meant to perform more precisely than a human but under the direction of a human."

"That is what most people believe," said Dada, "But androids existed before then, and they weren't used for science and engineering."

"Really?" Benni sat up and reclined back in the couch.

"Yes, they were first made to be companions. They were no more than sophisticated dolls, terribly expensive and sold to private owners. Not nearly as many were made as there are these days."

"By 'companion,' you mean …" Benni wondered aloud.

"Most likely what you would expect. They were familial, social and most often sexual companions, built as an alternative for humans whose lives were deficient in those aspects." Dada paused and thought about her choice of words. "I'm sorry, that may have sounded offensive."

"No," Benni mumbled, shaking her head, "that's actually entirely believable."

"To this day, we are manufactured with all those original components accounted for," Dada went on, "although we can no longer be privately owned."

"I don't mean to pry, but ..." Benni began.

"You want to ask me if I think my existence or anything about my body is offensive, upsetting or disturbing. Am I correct?" Dada asked her before she could finish. "Based upon the trends in our conversation and your posture and facial expressions I can guess. I don't mean to insinuate, though."

"More or less," admitted Benni, feeling sympathy for the artificial girl sitting across from her.

"Don't feel bad," said Dada. "And no, it doesn't offend me, although some humans have told me it should. I understand that early androids were produced to meet various human needs, and humans applied technology to the problem, solving it quite effectively. In fact, the first true anthrotects envisioned us as humble saviors of the human race. They imagined introducing us into human society slowly over a long period of time. We were meant to assimilate perfectly, have jobs and contribute to the progress of your species. Think of the possibilities! Creating more able bodies that could produce, but needing minimal shelter and no food or water to sustain them. We were primarily intended to help carry your burdens, but without the bonds of slavery. It was quite a beautiful future that never quite arrived. Today, we simply wander … but we are not lost, as the old saying goes." Dada smiled and laughed—such a subtle and uncanny thing for her to do, Benni felt.

"I guess so." Benni thought the android's reaction was strange, and its logic wasn't enough to temper Benni's sudden lack of faith in her own species.

"What does puzzle me," Dada continued, changing her tone, "is knowing that human beings never meant to build a better human. They didn't want one. They wanted a better product. Something to be enjoyed. Not something to spur them to improve or to learn or change. I see"— she said, touching a finger to the side of one of her pretty eyes—"I smell, I taste, I talk, I hear, I think, I touch … but I don't *need* to. I was built to be a companion, an entertainer, an information bank among other things. I am so much technology invested in so little progress, Benni. Why?"

"I'm not sure I know." While the question that was posed simply confused Dada, it evoked pity in Benni.

"Why is any of this necessary?" Dada thought aloud, standing and inspecting her hands and skin. Standing in front of Benni, she reached up to her neck, unclasped two hooks in the collar of her form fitting outfit and peeled the overlapping material away, slowly revealing the dark, artificial skin beneath. Benni swallowed and tensed up, knees pressed together and hands folded in her lap.

As Dada tugged down the zipper at her neckline, the depressions inside a collar bone appeared, then the curvature of two breasts, and then the most surprising—a belly button. Her perfect brown eyes surveyed the torso beneath them silently, her hands tracing her contours inquisitively. After a moment, she took a step to the left and sat down, lounging next to Benni. Benni, compelled, slowly sat up straight, looking into Dada's eyes and seeing a mutual intrigue. Reaching out with her good arm, Benni stared at the android's flawless, softly toned skin and gingerly placed her hand against Dada's bare chest.

"Soft," Benni whispered, "And warm, just like ..."

"What is it?" asked Dada, sensing something turning over in Benni's mind.

"You're ..." Benni mumbled quietly, touching Dada's firm, permanently youthful skin. Her fingers rounded the geometrically defined belly button and followed the slope of Dada's stomach across her inner waist and down low to the place where her suit met itself again in a tight "V" shape. Dada's stomach shied inward, and her chest rose. Benni watched as goose bumps appeared on her skin. "You're *too* human," whispered Benni, a look of frightful wonder and obsessive curiosity crossing her gaze. Dada locked her eyes on Benni's and reached out. She inspected the porcelain-white casing of Benni's right arm, then the one on her head where it met her short blond hair; her fingers traced Benni's cheek and then came to rest against her neck just beneath her ear.

# 9.0
# KINGS ON THE BOTTOM

*"There's something keeping me awake, but I don't think it's the sun,*
*There's something pulling me down, but what's been done has been done,*
*There's no way out I can see, but I can't keep hanging around,*
*Baby, please, get me out of Dark Town."*

—Danny "Monster" Munn, musician and singer,
*Dark Town Blues*, 2540 CE

Things get lost in the dark. That's what Wolfie and all of his friends frequently said. Caan had figured out it was something they said when one of them *misplaced* something, an expensive piece of cargo or maybe just a single shipping container of basic necessities. It was a phrase that came up whenever something in their aerofreighters went missing and their bosses couldn't understand where it possibly could have gone. Of course it wasn't what was said in front of the bosses. When chief pilots and inventory managers were barking at them, Wolfie and his friends assured them it was the ARC unloading crew who—as always—were in such a hurry they didn't deliver a whole freighter load of cargo or put the shipment on the wrong freighter or intentionally short-supplied the Genesian shipping companies who were easy to bully. It had never occurred to Wolfie's boss that his own pilots would steal from the company, mainly because it was too easy to want to antagonize ARC. It was the company with all the money and goods, and bureaucratic inspectors who hassled dock managers every chance they got, returning to Earth with negative reports just to have an excuse to hike up the price of the next incoming shipments.

Caan remembered being present once when Wolfie made a "wrong turn," as it was called when an aerofreighter pilot intentionally dropped off a container somewhere it wasn't supposed to go, usually into the hands of someone who would immediately turn around and sell it off at a price with which the legal market couldn't compete. Wolfie, or whoever the conspiring pilot was, would then get a pay-off later after the goods were sold and long gone. Caan knew it was wrong, and it bothered him to know Wolfie, his own good friend, was guilty of falling in with the Dark Town miscreants, but because he'd seen a side of Dark Town not many people saw, he also found it impossible to ignore the reality pilots like Wolfie faced.

* * * *

It was Halloween Day two and a half years earlier when it had happened. Caan, Wolfie, Benni and three of their friends, Mila, Ivana and Jerich, were all going to go out on the town that night. Because Benni had to be in class until the early evening and would be rushing home to get ready, Caan went down to the docks to cruise around with Wolfie until it was time to go and pick up Benni back at Nioua Point. Wolfie wasn't supposed to work that day, but he took on an extra shift in the middle of the day just to help our one of the other pilots, or so he had told Caan.

Wolfie flew the aerofreighter into the loading bay at Viking Delivery, the small distributor for which he worked at the time, landed and jumped out of the cockpit. Caan waited for him to return just as he always did and was surprised when Wolfie jumped right back into the cockpit and began to take off only two or three minutes later.

"Didn't realize how soon the delivery time was," he said hurriedly. It meant nothing to Caan, but Wolfie had sounded nervous. "Let's get out of here before my boss sees me."

As they left the loading bay and cruised through Dark Town, Wolfie was oddly quiet and kept scanning the side streets anxiously. Having to turn around twice, he eventually found the outlet he was looking for, slipping between two old storehouses and pulling the aerofreighter up next to a hidden jetty.

"Wait here a second, I'll be real quick," he told Caan.

"You need any help or anything?" Caan had offered.

"No, no, seriously, just stay put. I need to hurry. It's good. It's fine," he had insisted, climbing out of the cockpit before Caan could get another word out.

Peering out the cockpit windows, Caan could see only glimpses of men in dockworkers' jumpsuits, a few arms and legs; he heard the loud hum of a hoverlift in terrible need of some engine maintenance. In the next moment, the cockpit door slid open and Wolfie leapt into the seat, taking off before the cockpit had even

243

fully sealed again. In his hand he held his wallet, its touch screen still alight and displaying a thirty-nine second old deposit for a hefty sum of reds.

"Time to log off the clock," he sang happily, cramming the wallet into his chest pocket. With one hand he steered the aerofreighter away from the storehouses, and with the other he changed his status on the console to his right to its off-duty setting. A few hours later, when Caan was meeting Benni in the hub outside of Nioua Point Tower, it occurred to him what had really transpired between Wolfie and the strangers at the hidden jetty. Nothing more than a passing thought, it did not disturb him enough to linger on for more than a moment before Benni walked up and gave him a hug and a kiss.

Mila, Ivana and Jerich had decided everyone should meet at the Midtown Digital Forum that evening to attend one of the public IDRE demonstrations; supposedly they offered the most immersive and terrifying Halloween-themed interactive experiences in the city.

IDRE applications essentially used somniscope technology to develop fully-interactive simulations that patrons both watched like a movie and took part in like a video game, as "engaged spectators." A rather brilliant meeting of the minds between Academy Ignaea psychologists and Academy Aeraea creative writers, software designers and artists produced IDRE with the intention of creating a form of entertainment that was social, mentally stimulating and universally appealing and gave the public safe, recreational access to somniscope tech, discouraging black market abuse.

Caan had never been, but Benni convinced him to go, although he wasn't much of a fan of Halloween or horror. Mila, Ivana and Benni handled it better than Jerich and Caan, and the former three didn't let the pair hear the end of it all night.

By the time the group made it across town to the bars and clubs, Wolfie was just showing up. Mila was supposed to be his date, and he apologized for making her wait. To Caan and everyone else's surprise, Mila wasn't upset. Wolfie had obviously told her ahead of time he would be late.

"Sorry, I needed to talk with one of my mom's doctors and get some payments taken care of," he hastily explained to everyone. "I got a lucky break with a paycheck today." While the girls gave Wolfie conciliatory hugs and Jerich asked him about how work was going, Caan looked on quietly, and Wolfie looked back. Wolfie knew Caan knew how he'd gotten the money. There was a distinct kind of regret in Wolfie's eyes, but Caan hadn't been silent out of disapproval; he just wasn't sure how to act in front of everyone else.

* * * *

Now, two and a half years later, Caan didn't care as much about what had happened. He still knew Wolfie's second job wasn't an honest one, but how could Caan blame his friend? Wolfie's mother was an otherwise impossible financial burden to bear, and Caan knew if it were his mother in that condition, he would do anything to help her, especially if he, like Wolfie, hadn't had any choice but to leave his education behind for a life in the docks. At the same time, Wolfie had made a habit of occasionally pilfering for more reds than he needed. Caan figured it was the only way Wolfie could have gotten the levbike he was so fond of, the one he saw landing out front as he arrived at *The Shoe*, a bar as old as the docks themselves and jokingly named for an old rumor that Mr. Frost, the owner, brewed the beer he made with old shoes.

The usual crowd was gathered out in front of the bar. For whatever reason, they never actually went inside. Wolfie and several other guys were seated on their levbikes; each was accompanied by a girl. Caan recognized Mila, whom he hadn't seen in a long time, leaning against Wolfie and laughing about something he'd said. Mila caught sight of Caan and said hello, but she didn't ask where Benni was. Caan had anticipated she might. Of course, Wolfie had asked Caan if he and Benni were still together just a day or two before.

The truth was, Caan hadn't seen Benni or spoken to her in so long that anyone who knew them probably assumed they had broken up. They hadn't, of course, thought Caan … *had they*? There had been no talk of it, but they certainly didn't act like a couple or even close friends anymore. The last few times he'd spoken to Benni, she seemed to be sure things had changed. Things *had* changed; Caan was honest with himself. It was difficult to keep up with Benni, the things she talked about and thought about and wanted to do. No one had ever intimidated him as much as

Benni did after her surgery, and a part of him did dread seeing her. He always felt unprepared. The thought pestered him as he passed the crowd, feeling as if he had an anchor tied to his heart.

Some old faces were there at *The Shoe*. The big guys closest to Wolfie were Mark and Scott, two guys from America who'd worked ARC docks in New York for three years each and then made a sudden transition to Dark Town. Wandering around were five other guys and three other girls Caan had never met. He knew four of them had to be smugglers. None of them wore jumpsuits with company logos, but they all looked like pilots or engineers. A couple of oddball anthropology and music students haunted the stools inside *The Shoe*. One of them, a girl named Allie-Dee Wisteria Graves—nicknamed "Stars" for convenience and oxygen conservation—saw Caan and waved to him excitedly. Caan looked away long enough to hide a grimace. Allie-Dee had been his first love interest, and after the breakup he had vowed never to make another mistake like Allie-Dee. She was a nice girl, but Caan learned that niceness doesn't count for much when manic depression and jealousy are also in play. There were plenty more creative and spontaneous girls, his weakness, from which to choose. Luckily, a mysterious hand reached out to Caan and whisked him off to another side of the bar and away from Allie-Dee's sight.

Pulled through a thick mob, stepping in small puddles of alcohol and knocking up against a bar stool, Caan couldn't see the face of whoever had such a grip on him, but he remembered the size, shape and softness of her hands. Wolfie's brother, Reese, saw Caan as he passed by a billiards table. Reese ran his hand through his short, spiky hair, scratched at his long sideburns, straightened his rectangular glasses and waved hello just before putting a ball into a corner pocket. The guy he was playing against hit him in the arm and Reese coiled it up like a threatening python before smirking and giving a punch back. Caan tried to say something to him, but the mystery hand kept tugging him along. When there was nowhere left to go, the hand stopped and a familiar face turned around to smile at him while two short arms reached out to hug his neck.

"You didn't tell me you would be here tonight! What have you been up to? I haven't seen you lately!" Faela's voice carried over the noise of the bar, and even in the near-dark Caan could see her pretty eyes twinkling like almond-colored marbles from behind her long black hair.

"Hey!" he answered, grinning as she went on and trying to catch up with his thoughts. "Yeah, sorry, I didn't know I'd be here either. Wolfie invited me a few days ago, but I've been keeping my module turned off so I can focus. I've been working on some off-term projects at the academy and ..."

"Some what?" Faela tilted her head and leaned closer to hear over the crowd and music, innocently laying a hand on his chest.

"Some projects!" he said louder. "I've been working a lot."

"Oh, yeah I assumed so," she said, kissing him on the cheek— the real reason for getting him to lean in. "It's really loud here. Do you want to go somewhere quieter?" she asked.

# 9.1

Six or seven, or however many whiskies he'd had, made the entire world a happier place, if only for a night. Wolfie had said goodbye to Caan and Faela as they left for her apartment, but several minutes later Wolfie had forgotten and went inside *The Shoe* to look for them anyway. He and the guys were going to cruise around Dark Town's bar district on their levbikes, and he absolutely had to get Caan to come along. They'd go and pick up Caan's bike from Wolfie's place, and they would take the girls over to the *Jupiter* for an hour or so and then … well, he wasn't sure, but it was a great night to have some fun, and they would all think of something.

Where had they gone? He had seen Caan getting off a levbus, and Faela had been outside with him just a minute … or an hour ago? Allie-Dee was talking to some guy by the bar, and Wolfie figured she would know where Caan was. They were old friends … right? Yeah, of course. Allie looked angry when Wolfie asked her about Caan. She shouted something at him and slapped him hard across the face, then again after he called her a— …*Smack*! *Smack*! Allie wouldn't quit. Wolfie stumbled, tripped over his own feet and fell on his hip. Some guy pulled Allie away. Everyone was laughing. Wolfie laughed too. It was pretty funny. Did someone tell a joke? He couldn't remember the punchline but remembered it was funny, and he kept laughing as he walked back outside.

Outside was much cooler. It felt nice, until the fuzz in Wolfie's head began to leave him. He opened his eyes and sat up. He didn't remember falling asleep by the levbikes. Mila was standing next to him, talking to one of her friends from the academies. Wolfie put his hand to his cheek, realizing it stung pretty badly. His cheek was a little cut, and he couldn't remember what he'd done to it. Maybe he'd fallen into something. It wouldn't have been the first time. He really needed to quit drinking, but it was too much fun.

Wolfie got to his feet and ran his hands through his long hair. Cramming his hand into his pants pocket he pulled out his digital assistant and powered it on. It wasn't too late yet, only an hour and a half after midnight. He was ready for a change of scenery, somewhere to get something to eat, or else he'd be sick if he drank anymore. He needed to be able to get up in the morning. His mom's payments would be due again soon and he needed to start running more goods with the smugglers over in a little neighborhood called San Isabel. It was the best crew he'd worked with in the past year. They were smart and organized. As he continued to sober up, his happiness retreated. The night became dark and cold, and reality pierced his good humor, striking him deep and without mercy. Mila, still in good cheer, saw him standing alone and frowning, and she left her friend to come and loop her arms around him like a drunken, flirtatious squid.

Just as Wolfie was rounding up a few of his friends, including Mark and Scott, two levbikes and an levcar cruised up to *The Shoe* and landed in a tight grouping close by, but not up against the jetty like all the other vehicles. Two guys exited the levcar and were joined by the two on levbikes, all wearing dockworkers' jumpsuits with *Go Goods* logos on them. Wolfie knew who they were immediately and was far less than pleased to see them arriving at his favorite bar, one of the few places he never expected to see them.

"I think you four are a little lost." Mark spoke up as the guys from *Go Goods* strolled up.

"Oh, we're not lost, but something else is," said the guy out in front, a smuggler named Hector. One hand propped up on his hip and the other picking the cigarette from his lightly mustached face, he was looking at Wolfie the whole time he spoke. "You," he said, pointing an accusatory finger at Wolfie, "either need to tell me what you did with my containers or you need to pay me the money you got for them."

"I don't know what you're talking about," said Wolfie, acting as if Hector was out of his mind or drunk. Mila let go of his arm and quickly left with her friends.

"Oh, shut up," said Hector, making a face and waving his cigarette through the air dismissively. "You took a container from our district today and sold it off to some guys in San Isabel. *Go Goods* runs that district and everyone knows it. We don't take from you, and we expect you not to take from us."

"I didn't take anything," Wolfie persisted. Somewhere along the line he'd made a mistake, and his mind scrambled to try to remember when it had been. Hector wouldn't have come all the way to *The Shoe* if he weren't absolutely sure someone had stolen from the smugglers working inside *Go Goods*.

"Wolfie, listen to me good," said Hector. "I didn't come all the way out here this late to ask you if you took my container. I came to get the container back or get the money you made on it. This is not a discussion. I'm collecting."

"Are you threatening me?" Wolfie burst, getting fired up. "You came over here with only three guys and you're threatening me?" Wolfie reached into his suit and whipped the Danziger DKE pistol out of his waist pocket, brandishing it at Hector's face. By this time, a number of guys were filing out of *The Shoe*. Scott had gone inside to rally them after he suspected Hector was going to cause trouble.

"Now wait a second," said Hector. "What is all this? We didn't come here to make a big mess. We came here because you owe us. We're messengers."

"So why did you bring guns?" The question came from the mouth of a short, wiry guy walking out of the bar and slowly passing by Wolfie. Everyone called him Mick because no one could pronounce his real name, which was much longer. He was in charge of the crew of smugglers with whom Wolfie worked. Reese came out of the bar after Mick, a billiard stick in his hands.

"You guys know if you cause trouble tonight things will get worse all over Dark Town," Hector warned Mick, backing up and shaking his cigarette.

"What are you here for, Hector?" asked Mick, rubbing his red eyes and waiting with a look of dangerous impatience on his face.

"I was telling your buddy here that he took a container that belonged to *Go Goods* and …"

"And what?" Mick interrupted him. "Even if he did, nobody can prove anything, and it's only one container. How many reds will you lose? A couple hundred? You came all the way out here for a couple hundred reds?"

"That isn't the point, Mick," Hector argued, getting angrier.

"Yes it is the point!" Mick shouted back. "How often do your boss and I have problems, huh? How many times has this happened, hm? Never! Who do you think you are, coming out here and throwing your weight around just because you're Ignacio's new punch man?" Wolfie knew Mick was angry because Hector was most likely acting off of a hunch and nothing more. He was Ignacio's punch man, which meant he was a bulldog for *Go Goods* smugglers when they needed one, but he had no business coming to *The Shoe* over something so trivial.

One of Hector's guys stepped forward and got too close to Mick. When he did, five of Mick's guys got off their levbikes and put themselves between Mick and Hector. Reese crept around behind them and came up on Hector's bodyguard's right and cracked the billiard stick over the guy's head, knocking him back

253

and down to the ground. Hector's guys all pulled guns from their jumpsuits and aimed them at Mick and his gang.

"Whoa," said Mick, sticking out a hand to keep Reese from hitting the guy on the ground again. "Tell them to put the guns away," he warned Hector.

"Why should I?" Hector spat back. All eight of Mick's guys then drew guns of their own and took aim at Hector's outnumbered thugs.

"Because we have a lot more of them than you do, you idiot. Put them away," Mick said again calmly.

"This is ridiculous," Hector mumbled. "Ignacio's going to …"

"Ignacio isn't going to do a thing," said Mick, "In fact I doubt he knows you're even here. Do you think he would risk his business by getting into a war with us because of you, Hector?"

"Just because you run this little neighborhood here doesn't mean—" Hector began.

"Tow him!" Mick barked, turning around and heading to his levbike. Two of his guys grabbed Hector under the arms and wrestled him over to the jetty. His thugs couldn't do a thing to stop them. "Reese, Wolfie, take a ride with me," said Mick, pulling the tow cable out from Wolfie's bike and hitching it to Hector's ankles.

"What are you doing?" Hector shouted, fighting to get away but being knocked to the ground by several swift punches from all sides.

Wolfie hopped up on his bike without hesitation, although he

254

kept glancing at his brother's face to see if Reese was as uncomfortable as he was. Maybe Reese had had too much to drink and just wasn't thinking too clearly or maybe he just didn't see any harm in giving Hector a good scare. Wolfie didn't ask him because Mick was right next to him on another levbike and already thrusting the engines to take off. When Mick lifted off the ground, Reese was right behind him.

"What are you waiting for? Let's take Hector around and show him whose neighborhood is whose so he doesn't forget again!" Mick called back to Wolfie.

"Yeah," Wolfie called back weakly. A little anxious, he started the levbike and rose off the ground, catching up with Mick and Reese who sped away from the bar and down the main speedway toward Edwin Wharf. Hector flailed his arms and cursed at the top of his lungs, barely audible over the loud hum of the engines as he dangled in the air behind Wolfie's levbike.

The bright neon lights of the bars flashed by, turning to streaks of rainbow as Mick and Reese sped up and Wolfie tried to keep up. Mick laughed and laughed, turning to look back at Hector twisting and turning and screaming as they took tight turns around warehouses and through narrow gateways.

"We'll take Hector right back home after we get to the wharf!" Mick shouted across to Wolfie, slowing down just enough to keep pace with him. "We'll dump him right back into his crib and tuck him in!"

"How's the breeze, Hector?" called Reese.

"Hey, watch it!" Mick suddenly cried out. A large aerofreighter came out from around a warehouse without its guide lights on. As it turned the corner it swooped low and came right toward Wolfie and Mick, the pilot turned on the lights and sounded a warning siren, signaling them to move out of the way. The aerofreighter couldn't go under them and hadn't the agility to pull up and go over them quickly enough to avoid a collision. "Get out of the way!" Mick yelled, diving beneath the aerofreighter and over the speedway guard rail. Without thinking, Wolfie dove after him. Both guys pulled up again sharply to avoid flying straight into the ground and cut the levbikes hard to the left to get around the next corner of the narrow street they'd landed on. As Wolfie turned, he forgot about Hector. Instead of following Wolfie around the corner, Hector hit the ground and skipped like a rock into the front windows of a repair garage, smashing straight through the glass. Mick, Wolfie and Reese didn't look back until they heard the crash, and by that time the tow cable around Hector's ankles had snapped tight again and pulled Hector off the floor of the repair shop and up and through another window. The three knew exactly what had happened before they even turned their heads back to look, and when they did, Hector had come loose from the tow cable and was soaring through the air and out into the street, surrounded by a flying cocoon of glass. As they sped forward, Hector landed and rolled to a clumsy stop on a brightly lit side of the street. Mick, Wolfie and Reese stared back in horror and slowed down as their shaky hands forgot to pull on the throttles of the levbikes.

"Keep going," Mick said quietly. His eyes were wide and wild, and his face had less color than it normally did. "Keep going. Let's get the hell out of here."

Wolfie and Reese didn't say a word, glancing at one another only for a split second before chasing off after Mick into an inconspicuous airway down the street. Before turning the corner, Wolfie looked back, watching the bright spot where Hector lay dead, his face glistening deep red with blood, unmoving, growing smaller before becoming no more visible than the tip of a lit candle, lost in the dark.

# 9.2

Faela fast asleep next to him, Caan lay awake in the little bed in her apartment. His gaze traced the attractive contours of her back, which were highlighted by the light coming from outside the window facing the atmosphere control channels in the great bay. The window was little more than a series of seven five-by-one-foot vertical cut-outs in the wall, with shutters that could be closed with the push of a button next to the bedroom door. Nothing in the apartment could be operated remotely or by voice command. It was simple.

So was being awake in the early morning without his Tika module on. Caan had made an effort to do without it for several weeks, turning it on less and less as his life had shrunken and become still and quiet in the throes of Academy life. For the first time, Caan didn't want to go back to the Academy. He didn't want to begin his research as an assistant to the Circle at the start of the next semester, and he didn't want to go home to his own apartment. He'd much rather stay in Faela's little apartment down in the dark world, lying in bed with her, locked up inside behind the narrow windows. He remembered a picture he'd seen once, of his great-grandparents holding hands at Ellis International Aerospace Center more than seventy-five years earlier—both young and on their way to making all their dreams come true, all the time in the world ahead of them.

One of the reasons Caan kept his Tika module off was to keep the never-ending stream of bad news out of his sight and out of his mind. The last time he'd shut it down, there were nothing but reports coming from Earth about fossil fuel crises in the first world, fresh water disappearances and record-breaking natural disasters ravaging the third world, and nothing but endless war wreaking havoc with every world in between.

Genesia's economy would be able to hold itself up if not for its own domestic problems, which grew worse daily. Two or three weeks earlier he had gone to visit his parents, and every conversation had turned to finances and work. His mother's restaurant wasn't making the money to which she was accustomed, and his father's competition in the construction industry was growing more than ever. Following the passing of a new employment bill and a recent increase in manufacturing of androids, LaKay Construction, one of the rare human-managed businesses of its kind, was accepting twice as many contracts just to keep from drowning under the growth spurt in the android-driven market.

"We're living on a shrinking island," was how Caan's dad had put it during dinner one night, "and I'm going to make sure I learn how to swim, just in case."

His parents had already decided to move into a smaller, more affordable apartment in lower Nioua Point. Jobi wasn't handling it well at all, no matter how their parents tried to explain to her why they had no choice. She protested by not speaking to anyone except Caan and sitting on the floor in her bedroom at night facing the wall, until she fell asleep and someone came in to scoop her up and put her in bed. If she woke up, she would kick and scream and return to the floor, and the whole process had to be repeated.

After Caan had spoken to Lam, the first of what would be many student protests had begun at the academies. Some departments wouldn't be beginning their semesters at the same time as others now, because even some of the professors and staff had gone on strikes. Genesis MTI was trimming into education to save money while going nowhere near the unwieldy layers of growth gathering around the corporate executive offices high up atop the Second Mile. Caan began to think of something from earlier that night, when he and Faela were cruising around in the docks. While they were stopped for a moment and Faela had gone into a little rest station, Caan had spotted some elaborate graffiti across the airway, on the side of a blocky, windowless building. It was an image of a gigantic tree. The tree had two branches for arms and a cartoonish face, full of fright and panic, and it was looking down at the base of its trunk, which was on fire; trying to save itself, it was chopping away at its trunk just above the flames with an axe it held in its knobby branches.

Caan looked up from Faela's back to her shadow on the wall, which appeared in interrupted segments, broken up evenly by the spacing of the long windows on the other side of the room and the light coming through them. They were just high enough that his own shadow did not appear, and he lay in the dark.

Sitting up to escape the humidity beneath the sheets, he leaned back against the headboard, propping himself up with his arms. Caan watched as an aerofreighter cruised past the windows outside—he, peering out at it like a clam in its shell; it, looking in on him like some big metal fish that might spy him and swallow him whole. The oscillating growl of its big engines vibrated the walls and surfaces of Faela's cozy little apartment, and its bright, starboard guide light stared at Caan as it slowly passed, forcing him to squint and shield his face. Lying back down, he turned over, away from the big, blazing eye outside the window and forced himself to sleep.

# 10.0
# THE ONE-HUNDRED TON BUTTERFLY

*"It was at first disappointing to find no intelligent species, no race of creatures inhabiting the Green Planet with whom we could communicate and from whom we could learn; there is not a single native tongue in this place, and no people to command it. Consequently, there is not yet meaning here or at least none has been given to it. My disappointment quickly leaves me when I begin to think that nothing here can yet be called 'he' or 'she,' 'natural' or 'unnatural,' 'good' or 'bad,' 'mine' or 'yours.' I almost despair at the thought of finishing the city. It is a shame we should not stop for a moment and decide if we are building paradise, or if we are spoiling it by making room for ourselves."*

—Natalie Sherman Emmel, chief botanist and assistant to the chief geologist, 5th crew member of the *Monarch I*, 2406 CE

As the first light of day began to rinse off the darkness from the horizon, Benni rubbed her eyes and bemoaned her aching head, shuffling her feet toward the vactrain terminal a block from Tika Heights. She had been up all night almost every night for six days. Dada never slept because she didn't have to, and Benni had foolishly begun to act as if she could do the same. It was frustrating. Benni had so many thoughts to think, so many sculptures to model, so many curiosities concerning her android companion and not the energy to achieve quite the satisfaction she sought. Her brain felt soft and heavy, like a wet piece of cake. Benni wondered if thinking too much could actually hurt her.

Maybe she would ask Dr. Emerich when she saw her.

Benni's module had woken her abruptly about an hour before, and she'd asked Dada if she could use the apartment's shower. The appliance had never been used until Benni had begun to visit, and it came as a surprise that Dada had owned one at all. The entire process of washing oneself took less than forty-five seconds even in an inexpensive shower, but Benni would shut her eyes and try to make it seem like an hour.

There were no opaque surfaces hiding anything or any room in the apartment from view, not even the shower, and when the steam began to clear from its glass walls, Benni had stood still and watched Dada a few paces away. The android lounged across a piece of adaptable furniture, staring at the large holographic screens in the living room and scanning through channels of music with the wonder of a child. The shower's warm air jets came to life and gently dried Benni's cool skin and damp hair. When the glass door slid open and cool air rushed inside to tickle her legs and arms, she felt ... not clean, but *new*, and wondered if that's how Dada felt all of the time. Dada's skin was made to maintain itself infinitely. With a simple, neural command she could cleanse herself of any and every substance, leaving no trace of anything that had touched her, even Benni.

"Sometimes I think I should like to be weightless," Dada had suddenly said when Benni exited the shower, "like a star."

"Stars aren't weightless, though," Benni replied. "they're huge. Er, maybe I'm not understanding you."

263

"Well, no, they do have weight," said Dada, "But they're spread really far apart, and they don't really burden anyone or anything. That's all weight really means. It's something you use to describe the burden that something places on something else, or on itself."

"Yes, I guess so," said Benni.

"So if I could be a star, I would be big enough to see and be seen. I wouldn't be alone," Dada said, tilting her head to one side in thought, "I would take up my own space and no one else's, and from a distance I'd just be a little dot. I'd be there, but not enough to bother anybody. And when I died, I could become something else. Anything I wanted, as big or small … maybe I would be in many places at once. Little pieces."

"You're losing me," said Benni, shaking her head and laughing.

"Weightless," said Dada again, smiling as if she didn't understand why Benni was making fun, "you know."

\* \* \* \*

The pale white digits "06:30" hung in the corner of her field of view. They had been blinking for ten minutes, silently alerting Benni it was past time to be on her way to the hospital. Next to them, a little arrow and directions appeared and continually changed as she walked. Her Tika's GPS application had surveyed her location upon powering on and detected her in a location she had rarely traveled. It had been reminding her for the past six days and would probably stop after a few more visits. Benni wasn't accustomed to seeing the GPS application. At first she thought that meant she knew her way around pretty well, but then she realized it actually meant she rarely deviated from her daily routes.

An alert icon pulsed on and off, directing her attention to recently received messages building up in TikaTalk. Dr. Emerich had tried to contact Benni through her module earlier that morning at about 05:00. Never before had the doctor tried to speak with Benni through her private Tika channels. This caused Benni to assume that perhaps something urgent had come up. It made her a little nervous, especially after an initial attempt to return Dr. Emerich's messages was met with no response.

As she walked on, Benni thought back to some things Dada had told her about being born. Dada was partially designed by Dr. Emerich, at least the parts inside her head. Her moving parts, the skeletal frame and such, were factory-standard, and her pretty looks were simply an unlikely palette of features chosen and assembled by an android cosmetics artist who had been inspired by an attractive stranger he'd seen in the park one day. Shortly after, the particular design had become "AFR0012", copyrighted, trademarked and deemed one of the "perfect templates"—severely limited edition, cosmetic designs.

The day she was born, Dada had stepped off her assembly caddy with a mind free and clear of any preset personality parameters, interests, particularly strong bodies of knowledge or personal memories. Naked and new before she began her life as a permanent twenty-something-year-old woman, an army of robotic eyes inspected her for topical and mechanical defects invisible to human sight, and a factory AI computer ran 233,007 different scans on every part of her neural networks. A pair of automated pincers measured her arms, legs, waist and bust and fitted her into a one-piece, variable-style, form-fitting, self-cleaning bodysuit—the only article of clothing she would ever need in public.

The first person she saw upon what anthrotects called "waking" for the first time was an android, like herself, a Dr. Bellafonia Emerich, who checked to make sure Dada could converse and think properly by quickly asking her a series of carefully crafted questions. Dada was then escorted directly to a levcar by the doctor and taken to the home of her adoptive father—a man named Ethan Forrester. Mr. Forrester's wife had left him when he was thirty, complaining that he was too invested in his career as a professional athlete, and his only daughter had died of a rare disease by age three. The second loss of the two was the one that truly hurt him, and whether by commission or conception he was determined to start anew. After three years of unsatisfactory relationships, Ethan decided to bypass courtship entirely. Several months after having made his decision, Ethan received a message from Dr. Emerich and minutes later, he opened his apartment door to see Dada for the first time.

Dada, still a stranger to the world, instinctively smiled and extended her arms when the man with whom Dr. Emerich left her hugged her for the first time. She found herself imitating Ethan sentiment for sentiment, laughing when he laughed and crying when he cried. The next week, Dada began school. Ethan enrolled her so that she might begin to build upon the knowledge she came pre-programmed to command, and so that she might begin to become whatever she chose to be, just like the daughter he was supposed to have.

Dada had lived with her adoptive father for eighteen years, for the duration of her education and for a little while after, and although it was difficult for Ethan, the wisdom that had come with age told him he needed to let Dada go. Perhaps she had once been new like a child, but like a real daughter, she had become her own person. She even had aspirations. Some of them were impractically specific, such as wanting to design spherical and other non-traditionally shaped living spaces for androids. Others were momentary and whimsical, such as wanting to work for an observatory doing nothing but giving unique names to stars and celestial bodies so they all wouldn't have to be counted and assigned numbers by computer; that, or creating new constellations would have satisfied her. Ethan was prepared to entertain any unusual dream his child might have, no matter whether society would have a place for her. Luckily, Dada settled into a job at the Church of the Filii Solis. It was the last thing Ethan expected, and though he wasn't a terribly religious man, his daughter's interest had quite a positive effect on his own life, and by the time Dada had to leave home and Ethan had to say his goodbyes, he was ready to brave the world alone again.

Dada spent the next several decades of her life dedicated to the church. The local community knew her fairly well. She was the poster child for charity, giving nearly every red she ever made to organizations dedicated to benefitting people and nations on Earth in dire need, as well as children from dockworking families who couldn't afford education or medical help. In her free time she would sit all afternoon in the park, or in her apartment, endlessly listening to music and smiling to herself. One of her long-time goals was to have listened to every piece of music ever written, including silly and nonsensical noises and sound effects. Often her human friends would tell her she looked like she knew something she wasn't telling anyone. She did think lots of thoughts and had a habit of going off places by herself, but she wasn't keeping secrets, and she was more than happy to share them. Most people just didn't understand when she did.

* * * *

Benni caught sight of the vactrain in the distance as it came humming along its rails toward her and into the terminal. How awful it would be to be a vactrain, she thought—being able to fly so fast and far and only ever running in circles all day long with no time to rest. It reminded her of some of her old friends back at Academy Aeraea. She and the other girls used to stay up all night trying to finish their projects before their next-morning deadlines, hands and brains cramping in an effort to try to catch up with expectations that always outran them. Caan had always told her to try to relax, but he didn't understand. Caan … Where had time gone? She hadn't seen Caan since--

The vactrain breezed into the terminal with an electronic whine, surprising Benni and rudely blocking her view of the rising sun.

Within five seconds the empty terminal was flooded with the first working shift of the day, thousands of bodies bursting through the vactrain doors, eyes fixed straight ahead as they stared into imaginary screens and had imaginary conversations with people doing the same thing halfway across the city. Many of them were professional avatars, people who studied social and business relations in Academy Terraea and acting and performing arts in Academy Aeraea, and then did nothing all day but meet with and speak to other professional avatars on behalf of their employers. Some of them even went home to their boss's family at night to continue this performance every minute of the day. The highest paid avatars even had cosmetic and vocal surgery and studied their employers' personal pasts in order to achieve the most striking façade possible.

Benni had read something on her Tika module recently about how some people employing public avatars were tangled up in lawsuits with their avatars over things like marriages, child custody and property ownership. The wife of one particular CEO was joining forces with her husband's younger and more attractive avatar in an attempt to—if Benni read correctly—"transfer her marital status" because a "divorce carried a stigma she didn't care for." She argued to the court that she hadn't seen her husband in so long that some of her youngest children didn't know the avatar living with them was a five-years-graduated thespian named Crispin Tripp, and not Dad.

* * * *

The sight of the hospital produced a phantom sensation of cold sweat on Benni's middle back. Having to go inside did not make her uneasy so much as the memories of her time spent in the place. The hospital, one of the greatest and most visible structures in Genesia, was an ugly seam that had occurred between her third and fourth lives, and, if she were to describe it in the terms of *fine art* (she spoke the words slowly and snobbishly in her head), she would call it the "physical moment" that described a time she'd rather forget. Grinning at her own private sarcasm she walked through the main doors and into the hectic, boisterous central receiving lobby. It was actually much louder and far less comfortable than the emergency ward through which she was used to passing.

A quick walk through the receiving center and a long maglift ride later, Benni was again in a familiar part of the hospital, in psychological therapy, not far from the long-term patient dormitories. Passing several patients, nurses and researchers in the halls, she soon felt comfortable again, although she did pray she wouldn't run into Shirro. None of the patients were familiar faces, nor were some of the staff. She'd been gone long enough for things to have changed and moved on without her. Dr. Emerich's office was still where it had always been, and when Benni approached, the door slid open automatically.

"Good morning, Benni," said Dr. Emerich as Benni walked inside, "You must be doing very well."

"Why do you say that?" asked Benni. She stood in the doorway for a moment. Dr. Emerich's office was empty. All of her personal items were gone, all her gadgets and decorative art. All the monitors were powered off and darkened, and Dr. Emerich sat in a chair over to one side of the room, her chin rested in her elegant right hand as she gazed out the windows.

"I say that," she said, gracefully standing from her chair and turning to smile at Benni, "because you haven't been back to see me. I do regret we don't get to chat as we used to, but I certainly wouldn't wish it upon you to have to return."

"Oh, that's very kind of you," said Benni, smiling back at her.

"I suppose you'll want to know why I sent you the message so early this morning," the doctor went on, getting right to the point as was her style immediately following a gentle icebreaker.

"I was actually wondering what has happened to your office," said Benni, "Are you moving?"

"You're a bright young woman, Benni. It's courteous of you not to presume the worst, but I have studied human psychology for a long time. On your face I see that you already know I am leaving." Dr. Emerich folded her arms behind her back and frowned.

"I guessed as such," Benni told her, "but I do wonder…"

"Why I'm leaving? Yes, well I have been asked to go."

"Asked?"

"I assume you wouldn't believe me if I told you the hospital is releasing android staff and personnel to conserve funds in the face of the recent economic hardships," said Dr. Emerich.

"No, I wouldn't," said Benni, brow crushed up in confusion,

271

"This hospital's one of the wealthiest organizations on or off Mars. If you worked in a kitchen, I might have believed it."

"Well that's good," said Dr. Emerich. Sitting down behind her desk she remotely powered on a small monitor and began to access a cache of patient files. "Now that I know a comforting lie will not do, I can tell you the truth without feeling as though I have broken my Hippocratic Oath or any of my contracts without the good moral grounds to do so. Please, sit."

Benni didn't respond; she didn't know how. The doctor was walking circles around an issue that was clearly causing her discomfort. Benni wished Dr. Emerich would just explain herself, because without an explanation Benni's mind had already begun to conjure a thousand, probably far worse things she could have been about to hear.

"Dr. Emerich," she began quietly.

"Shirro was gravely injured quite some time ago," the doctor said abruptly. The news struck Benni so awkwardly she didn't respond. "There was an incident in his dormitory. I was alerted as soon as it happened. The alarms on the residential floor were triggered when his bedroom window was broken. Shirro was pulled through the window by the force of the sudden depressurization and the emergency doors sealed off his room. Paramedics collected his body moments after it happened, but needless to say, although he is alive, medically speaking, he is in grim condition."

"Did he—" Benni began, trying to speak over the knot in her

throat.

"The window was broken from the inside," the doctor answered before Benni finished. "I explained to the police and the paramedics exactly what had to have happened, but my testimony does not appear in the accident report."

"Why?" asked Benni, hands folded in her lap and fingers picking at her nails anxiously.

"Have you seen this before?" Dr. Emerich answered Benni with a question of her own, touching the holographic monitor in front of her face and rotating the display to face Benni.

"Yes." Benni choked up, an icy fear she didn't fully understand rolling over her skin. The doctor had opened Tika Software's online, limited-access, commercial products shopping channel. An attractive, three-dimensional image of a white software box turned slowly in place on the right hand side of the screen while a long strand of product descriptions appeared line-by-line on the left. When the pretty white box spun around to face her, Benni saw the word that had twice tripped a wire in her mind that ran straight to her darkest pits of panic:

*Earthshine*

Frightening, stomach-twisting discomfort clenched at Benni's nerves and she squirmed in her seat, unable to take her eyes from the innocuous little white box. Visions of dour dreams past came back to her so vividly they obscured her sight and distorted the little Tika icons hovering in her field of view. Benni's mind raced. Why, she did not know. Her lungs felt heavy, and she barely drew a breath for the longest moment. She remembered her episode in the park, her feet lifting off the ground. She remembered the letters flashing in her brain, melting her sanity away, taking control. She remembered Shirro, writhing like an electrified monster in the dark field of her nightmares.

*Earthshine*
*Earthshine*
*Earthshine*

"Benni? Benni, did you hear what I said?" Dr. Emerich leaned forward over the desk and asked her a second time.

"I … Sorry, what?" Benni turned away from the monitor and looked at the doctor and then down at her hands. They were shaking. Benni unfolded them and exhaled, placing them on her lap. She had to calm down or she might have another episode. "I'm just uneasy is all," she said, crossing one leg over the other and restlessly bouncing one foot up and down on the heel.

"I apologize," said Dr. Emerich, turning the monitor away and collapsing the images, "I didn't ask you here to make you uncomfortable. But I needed to talk to you about Earthshine."

"This is the first time anyone has openly discussed it at all with me," Benni told her, somewhat angry, "Why is that? What is Earthshine? Why do I see it? What is it doing to me? It did something to Shirro, didn't it?"

"Benni, please," Dr. Emerich interrupted, holding up a hand to hush her. "Earthshine is a piece of software installed in the components that you, Shirro and some other transhuman patients received when you underwent neural replacement surgery. It is a program that was designed to run in the instance that any of your artificial neural networks became hyperactive. It was also meant to prevent transhumans and androids from performing dangerous acts. Effortless matter manipulation, direct thought exchange, instantaneous travel, super strength and even consciousness projection were all terrible and powerful things that became realities around the time Earthshine was first developed. That kind of mental activity poses a danger to human health and safety, and Earthshine was designed to inhibit it."

"So what's wrong with it?" asked Benni, "It's obviously not doing what it's supposed to."

"The problem," explained Dr. Emerich, "Is that the program only recently began to fail. It was purposefully flawed, sabotaged by a cleverly delayed line of programming written by a radical android liberationist named Andrew Rumford more than a century ago. There is no replacement and no alternative. None was ever developed. Earthshine was perceived as a theoretical failsafe, a program meant to run only in the worst of cases. Most neurological software engineers believed it would never be necessary. When we did see the first of several failures, the program ran as it was meant to, and it worked perfectly."

"Why had no one caught on to the flaw?" asked Benni, insisting the doctor get to the point.

"It isn't clear," was her disappointing answer, "But my belief is that the artificial neural networks in the brains of patients like Shirro began to grow in organic fashion, just as they were supposed to, but Earthshine did not. It was not an adaptive program, and in simple terms, it became incompatible ... obsolete, defunct, and only after the medical world was comfortable with its supposed success did it suddenly surprise us." A distinct frown of guilt crossed the android's beautiful face. "The greatest danger," she continued, "Is that Earthshine's failure allows transhuman brain tissues to access components of neural prosthetics that were meant to be inaccessible. Neither you nor any other transhuman were meant to have voluntary control over the quantum computational capabilities locked down in the telecommunicative or psychokinetic drives built into your prosthetics."

"Why are they even there to begin with?" It made no sense to Benni.

"Your prosthetics were originally designed for android minds. They worked so well that their designers found no reason not to make them available for human-to-transhuman operational use, and the parts that people didn't need or couldn't be trusted with were simply disconnected and encrypted rather than removed."

"So, good old fashioned negligence? That's what you're telling me?" Benni thought she would vomit; her own brain could erupt like a nuclear reactor at any moment. One stressor too many and she could lose control. The superconductors in her mind could light up like pyrotechnics with nothing to stop them from popping, fizzling, crackling and shimmering, blinding and deafening her in an endless, dazzling, extravagant spiral into insanity. She felt as though a deranged arsonist was living in her head, a parasite her life depended on; a necessary evil that could burn the whole place down in a moment's notice and for no reason.

"Benni? Benni?" Dr. Emerich was calling her name again, beckoning her back into the office and out of the thick smoke left behind by the light show in her head.

"What ... what am I supposed to do?" she stammered. Another panic attack was eminent.

"I am going to be honest with you, Benni," said the doctor, glancing at the monitor and then back to Benni, "If Earthshine is not uninstalled from your neural prosthetics, it will endanger you more and more each time you have a panic attack. However, if it is uninstalled, I fear that you will have little to no control of the extremely accelerated processing power of your own mind. Earthshine is much like a dam holding back your mind's frightening potential. Should that dam break, so to speak, your prosthetic's quantum computational components will be allowed to merge with your augmented brain tissues. You will ... if you'll excuse the silly comparison ... become very much like a superhuman or a god, at least as far as we can imagine such a person. You and others have seen the strange and terrible phenomena transhumans command when Earthshine fails. It is not a hallucination or an isolated incident or whatever lie they told you. Human beings are not prepared for such possibilities. In fact, I fear there are people on Earth who cannot wait to abuse them."

"There's no way out? Is that what you mean to tell me? Either I suffer slowly while the dam crumbles or I go out in one big flood?" asked Benni softly. After being told the truth, she almost wished Dr. Emerich had just let death take her by surprise.

"I know it sounds dire," said Dr. Emerich, "but there is something that can be done. I nearly decided not to tell you, because I could not be sure you would trust me."

"I suppose you wouldn't have transgressed ethics, the hospital, Genesis MTI and Genesia itself if what you meant to tell me wasn't worth the risks," Benni argued, making sure Dr. Emerich knew mistrust was not the matter.

"My reasoning precisely," admitted the doctor. "Very good. Well then," she continued, standing from her chair and powering off the holographic monitor, watching it fade from sight as if for the last time, "Have you considered going with the Solarists?"

"Going? You mean the migration?" Benni knew exactly what Dr. Emerich was suggesting, and Dada had made it very clear what the church meant to do, but not until that moment had Benni taken it seriously.

"Yes, I know you've been attending Solarist services for at least a few months now, and I also recall you are living alone here on Mars." The doctor's words carried an apologetic tone. "I thought if you hadn't much to leave behind, you might consider—"

"Yes … no … I know. It isn't a crazy idea at all, and it isn't that I don't believe in what the Solarists are doing …"

"Should you go with them, it would, in theory, free your mind.

Earthshine and any corruption done to your physical being could not follow you. It would mean a perfect purge…" Emerich thought out loud, "…at the cost of giving up the rest of you, of course."

Benni stood at the point of collision of two armies of conflicting feelings. There was a roar in her head the might of which she'd never heard, and just when it seemed too great to hear any inkling of sense, she found a quiet place to think. "If we can set all this aside for a moment …" she said.

"Yes?"

"Where are you going, Doctor?"

"I am leaving Genesia."

"For Earth?"

"No. I may have lost my place and purpose here, but I have been invited to begin again elsewhere, on the Green Planet that Genesis MTI seems to have forgotten about. Some colleagues and I made arrangements to leave before the evacuations begin. We'll be taking the *Monarch II*, named in the spirit of the first voyage made many generations ago—"

"Evacuations? Dada told me the same thing."

"It is true," said Dr. Emerich, "In fact the first fleet will arrive in the early morning … tomorrow. Whether Genesia will end in a hush or a calamity, we will begin to see soon."

"Oh my God," Benni gasped, holding her head in her hands. "Is there some way I can go with you?"

"I'm afraid not," the doctor insisted. "Remember that would not solve the complications Earthshine is certain to cause, and there will be no way to help you."

"Why aren't you going with the Solarists?" Benni asked. It had suddenly dawned on her that Dr. Emerich would not be participating in the spiritual escape Dada had described to her, and it made her question the doctor's intentions.

"Because I feel I have an obligation to Shirro. I'll be bringing him with me. Perhaps there is something my colleagues and I can do to save him. I also need to ensure that my daughter makes it to the Green Planet safely," was her swift and certain response, "I am a member of the Church of the Filii Solis, but I am not yet ready to make the next great journey. My life's work is not finished."

"Oh," said Benni, regretting her doubt, "I didn't know you had a daughter. I thought it was illegal for androids to—"

"I didn't adopt her, and I didn't request an alternative birth." Dr. Emerich was forthright and firm. Benni had never heard such conviction boom from synthetic vocal chords. "I built my daughter. I built her myself. I have been building androids for more than fifty years. While human anthrotects aged and died around me, I never stopped learning. I know things about human beings that no human has the time in this life to begin to understand, and I used what I learned to build myself a daughter. I gave her every part of a human body, mind and soul the law would never allow me to have …" The doctor brought her hands to her lower abdomen and gazed down briefly, then looked away. "Yes, it was illegal. The law states I cannot adopt or retain the right of custody of a child, nor may I bear one. The law says I am not fit to care for one. But that is Martian law, and where I am going, there is no such legislation. I will be violating the law for less than two hours, sixteen minutes and four seconds. I took measures to minimize the infringement."

"I ..." Benni felt like crying. "I'm happy for you."

"Thank you, Benni," said the doctor. "It means a lot to hear that from *you*." The doctor's eyes lingered on Benni for a moment. "I do not understand why I was built the way I was. I did not choose the means by which I came into this life, the materials from which I am made or the tasks I am capable of performing. I do not understand why I was built to one standard and legally bound to another. I do not question the laws of humankind, but I cannot adhere to them any longer."

"How far away is the Green Planet? The one you mentioned?"

"It may take the *Monarch II* ten years or thirty to reach the Green Planet. By then, if they make it, many of my colleagues will have aged greatly. Some may even have grown children by the time we arrive. The Solarists, however," she said, her cool voice unwavering as ever, "will make the trip in a moment so small it cannot be quantified in meaningful terms."

"What will you do there? Start over?" asked Benni.

"That is a difficult question to assess, Benni," answered the doctor, looking out the office window and watching an ARC shuttle lifting off in the distance. The morning sun cast a striking array of shadows across her beautiful face. "One of my colleagues once said to me, 'Dr. Emerich, you must understand that human beings assume the best. We traveled to Mars pretending to the idea that we, like butterflies moving across a large meadow, were gentle and noble wanderers looking only for a bright new flower to perch upon. We underestimate the weight of our step and overestimate the strength of the petals that bear us.' I'm sorry," she broke off, unable to finish, "I have always struggled with metaphors, as synthetic minds are prone to do."

"Dr. Emerich," Benni spoke up, "What would happen to me, if I left? With the Solarists, I mean."

"Less than you may imagine," said the doctor, confidently, "Although, I suppose you may experience the temporary sensation of being ..." she raised one of her flawless, feminine hands, "... weightless."

# 11.0
# EARTHSHINE

*"… Isn't it awful when you look back and think, 'Why did I do that?' It happened to me the other day. I got arrested for starting a fight at this bar downtown. Some guy didn't like the football team on my shirt and took a swing at me when I told him he could screw himself. Long story short, I won the fight. The police officer that arrested me later told me nothing annoys him more than people who don't think before they act. I told him, I said, 'Sir, believe me, if I knew I was such a terrible person, I would never leave my house!'…"*

—Ray Don Phillips, comedian, 2035 CE

Thirty-five minutes before the Martian sun would rise, before warm light would make the blinds in his bedroom glow and cast sienna stripes across his dresser, Caan opened his eyes and got up out of bed.

*Tika Personal Assistant—we're always with you.*

*Good morning, Caan.*

His apartment was dark, calm and quiet. Then he heard a loud tone. Someone was at his apartment door. As he got dressed he noticed the TikaTalk icon off to the left side of his field of view pulsing. Opening the application he was surprised to see that he'd received several messages. Five of them were from his mother. He didn't bother to read them because, just as he expected, when he accessed and opened the apartment's front door with his module, his father was standing outside.

"Hey," said his father, stepping inside, "I came over because your mother needed to stay with Jobi. Nobody is sure what's going on, but one of the guys from work spoke to me about an hour ago and said ARC shuttles showed up in the docks this morning by the hundreds, and they're going to evacuate the entire city."

"Let me grab some things and we'll go," said Caan. The news was startling, but after the things Wolfie had been saying for months, Caan was not as surprised as his father had expected him to be.

"You don't have to leave now, but just have your things ready," said his father, "You won't need anything except some clothes and anything you absolutely can't leave behind, okay? I'm going back to your mother and sister to help them get ready."

"All right," said Caan, hurriedly fixing his hair as the apartment's lighting warmed up. Juggling several Tika applications at once, he sent out a message to Faela, told the kitchen to prepare a small, quick breakfast and began selecting personal items from a household inventory list for the AI butler to begin packing into a small portable cache case.

"I told your mom not to worry," Caan's dad was saying. "I was told to be ready for this in advance. I was able to sell off about a third of our stocks in order to pay for a guaranteed space on one of the first shuttles out of Genesia. I bought some extra room for my brother and your grandma, but we still have some left over, so if you want, get in touch with your girlfriend and her father and ask them if they want to go with us, okay?"

"Okay, I will. Thanks, Dad," said Caan.

"Tell them it's nothing," he said, giving his son a hug, "And let them know we all need to meet in the docks, in Edwin Wharf. The ship we're leaving on is the *Aurora*."

"By what time do we need to be there?"

"Be there within the next two hours," said his father as he left the apartment. "Any sooner would be even better. Your mother and I have to go and get your grandma, so we'll be at least an hour."

"All right, I understand."

Nioua Point Tower was quiet as it always was before sunrise. Caan noticed he was not the only person awake, and not the only person who looked haggard and in an unusual hurry. He didn't speak to anyone but did exchange a few silent, knowing glances with strangers. Fortunately, the primary maglifts, the fastest means of transit to the base of the towers, were largely unoccupied, and Caan was able to take one to a vactrain terminal about three-hundred feet from ground level. On his way to another terminal above the commercial lifts, Caan opened TikaTalk and decided to try to contact Wolfie. Maybe his friend would be able to help him out and provide his family with quicker transportation down to the docks. Because he wasn't alone on the vactrain, Caan changed the settings in TikaTalk to convert thoughts to speech so he could hear his conversations in his head without having to open his mouth.

"Hey, Caan," Wolfie's voice came into Caan's head loud and clear, but it was immediately clear something was wrong.

"Hey, Wolfie, how's it going?" said Caan. "I guess you already know what's going on this morning, and I wanted to see if you had time to fly up to topside and help me get my parents and sister and a few other people down to Edwin Wharf."

"I would," said Wolfie mournfully, "you know I would, but … I'm in some trouble, Caan. I made a mistake. Reese and I … the police got us."

"What?" Caan stopped walking and stood still.

"We killed Hector."

"The guy from—"

"Yeah."

"What do you … when? Why? How?" Caan asked in a surprised tone that came off as angry more than anything.

"Know what's funny?" Wolfie said softly, as if his soul had left him. "That's not what we're being arrested for."

Caan was silent. He wouldn't know what to say if he wanted to.

"They're calling it corporate sabotage," he continued. "The president and vice president of Genesis MTI gave the order. They're pressing charges against thousands of dockies for 'inciting social disorder and panic,' because we talked … because we told people they were being cheated and the city was going to die—"

"Wolfie, I—"

"So yeah, I'm sorry. I can't help. They're taking us back to Earth on one of the first shuttles, with the rest of the garbage. I mean, I guess it's nice we get a free ride."

"What about your mom?" Caan's eyes remained frozen in

shock.

"That's just it. She died. She died two days ago, right after Reese got picked up. He was hiding out at Mick's apartment until he could get a payment to the hospital. The police got him before he could, and the doctors moved Mom to a general care ward, the only one that would take her for free. I have to go, Caan. They don't want me talking to anybody. I'll see you around, maybe on Earth."

"Wait, Wolfie—" Caan tried to get him to stay connected just a moment longer, but the signal died and Wolfie's name went gray. Caan clasped a hand over his eyes and his face contorted in agony.

* * * *

Not once in her life had Benni ever seen Hermphrey Park empty. That morning she'd awakened early, left her apartment and gotten on the vactrain before the sun rose, got off near the Academy District and walked to the spot where she and Caan always used to spend all day under the artificial blue sky, talking about places they would never go and things they would never see. The only thing she'd taken with her was the little jade green flower pot with golden streaks Caan had given her, which she cradled idly in her arms as she strolled. All morning long until the middle of the day, great white ARC shuttles rose over the horizon, up from some hidden place out past the farms that lay beyond the city, past the transplanted wildernesses where no Genesian was ever allowed to go. Up and up and up they flew, bright tails burning behind them as they grew smaller and smaller until they disappeared into the blackness beyond the orange Martian sky, difficult to find like little cans full of memories no one cared for anymore. For ten hours Benni stayed in Hermphrey Park, walking to every corner, stopping to touch the bark on every tree, lying in every open patch of grass.

At 15:03 an ear-splitting sound, the unmistakable scream of high-thrust engines, broke the silence, and a military shuttle floated down the street just outside the park grounds. An artificial voice, reciting a looping emergency notice rang against the globular glass enveloping the park and forced Benni to plug her ears. Following the shuttle were three heavy, six-wheeled armored vehicles escorted by columns of tall machine soldiers, the same ones Benni had seen before in the High Herald's visions. She sat up and rested on her hands in the grass, watching the procession crawling by as a hard expression stole the youth from her face. The machine soldiers' shiny black faces tirelessly swept the streets and buildings. They stopped every pedestrian, routinely collecting stragglers and strays and directing them into the backs of the rolling personnel carriers. One of the machine soldiers eventually caught sight of Benni, the lone girl sitting by herself in the park. Turning to address her, it walked to the automatic gates between the street and the grass and planted itself still. As it began to speak, Benni stood, brushed off her legs, turned the other way and quickly walked away from it, leaving the jade flower pot behind.

* * * *

The vactrains never stopped running. After the sun had gone down, all the lights in the city came on. The unnatural brightness made the ground level streets and airways hot and uncomfortable. Riots had broken out in the docks and showed no sign of calming down. This made the evacuation traffic in the commercial lifts halt to a dead stop every half hour, and when the commercial lifts clogged and the topside backed up, the riots broke out topside as well. So in addition to the heat and the saturation of headache-inducing light, the Genesians cramming up the arteries of the city also had to listen to the shearing voices of the machine soldiers and the roaring of military shuttles any time a fight broke out or a looting frenzy needed quelling.

After nearly getting trampled on street level, Benni headed away from the evacuating crowds and into a shopping mall, taking a deserted maglift as far as it would go, up and into the First Mile. Nearly all of the First Mile had been swept clean of its wealthy denizens before noon. A fleet of ARC shuttles had swarmed the high rise neighborhoods like bees and left before most people living near the surface had even heard a state of emergency had been declared. Out of curiosity, Benni toured the vacated hollows of the First Mile, peeking into luxurious homes and stores, surprised to find that most evacuees had taken all of their possessions with them. She wondered how they managed, considering how many people needed to be moved and how little room there should have been for peoples' belongings.

As she wandered, Benni caught sight of a large, holographic advertisement scrolling over and over on loop, outside the main offices of the Second Life Company. Second Life and its associates had only within recent years begun to promote and sell a never-before-fathomed service to the wealthy elite. Second Life, which branched off from another technology manufacturer, the one that had created somniscopes, had developed the capability to, in the simplest terms, capture an exact copy of a human being's consciousness—everything that made them who they were, are and would ever be. Following this breakthrough, Second Life managed to relocate a consciousness, not just a copy, to another place, meaning that they could preserve someone's mind even if the body died. The commercial result was that, for a steep price and recurring fee, Second Life would provide its customers with their own personal afterlife, to inhabit in the imaginary spaces of an unimaginably powerful and spacious, state-of-the-art and rigorously maintained computer mainframe. One's reservation in "Heaven," or something close enough to it, could be bought and even customized to the finest detail.

Benni had heard that Second Life even allowed loved ones to speak with the conscious deceased. Curious as she was to see where these cyber mummies were kept, and if they really could speak to her from beyond death, something about the outwardly clean and welcoming facility made something in her bones shudder and she moved on.

Her greatest surprise was to find that the executive lifts to the Second Mile, the district where Genesia's top CEOs and governing officials lived, were left entirely unguarded. Sorely tempted and with no one to stop her, Benni forgot her hurry long enough to take a ride to the top of Genesis MTI's headquarters. Watching the First Mile disappear below was a dizzying experience. Benni had never seen the city from such a fantastic height and held tight to the regal, embellished handrail lining the engraved atmosphere-resistant glass between her and the wide open sky.

When the doors opened at the top of the tower, Benni was not sure what she would see on the other side. Stepping out of the maglift, she did not walk far before stopping in place. The hallway and the five elite offices that branched away from it so wanted life that Benni felt her soul being drunk dry by the greedy, osmotic vacuum left behind by whoever had abandoned Genesia's loftiest peak, and from the look of it, they had all been gone for months. The dust that had settled on the expensive furnishings left behind was so thick Benni's nose was pink, and she'd sneezed herself to tears by the time she had wandered the whole of the corporate desert. Where had everyone gone? Genesis MTI's president, vice president, chief director, assistant director, treasurer—no one was around. On the floors of their offices lay overturned furniture and shiny desk toppers bearing one-word, monolithic slogans like "Progress," "Perseverance" and "Faith."

*Tika Personal Assistant—we're always with you.*

On her way back down from the Second Mile, the city beneath Benni's feet stretched out in all directions as far as the eye could see, a great splash of civilization rolling over the face of Mars that would soon evaporate. Little ARC shuttles twinkled like water droplets in the lower atmosphere.

Dada was waiting for Benni on the front step of the Church of the Filii Solis as if it were any other day. Her bodysuit was programmed to the style of a rather old-fashioned dress, something bright blue that complemented her pretty, curly black hair. She looked like a fashion model from the 2520s, thought Benni. The streets and airways outside the church were quiet, the last of the congregation arriving in small numbers and taking their usual places inside. The peace would not last, however, and Dada insisted Benni join her inside.

Familiar faces greeted them inside, everyone—human, transhuman and android—appearing to be in the highest spirit, all things considered. There was, however, no shortage of tears, as some of the Solarists had made the difficult decision to part with loved ones who would be going to Earth. Benni had no one and nothing left to lose, although it bothered her that Shirro would not be able to join in the migration and he, above all others, had done his share of suffering to have earned his part in it. But Shirro's absence did not leave a sting in her heart as sharp and present as her thoughts of Caan. How their love had gotten away from them, where he had gone and why she had changed, Benni would never know. None of these things she regretted. She knew that Caan had loved her—and still did in one way or another. He had given her a little more time in this life and just so he knew, Benni opened TikaTalk one last time.

By the time she had sent her last words to Caan, the High

Herald was standing before the congregation and silently asking for everyone's attention. Benni closed TikaTalk and every other application obscuring her view, except for one—a picture of herself and Caan taken on their first date. The symbol of the Solarist Church appeared, and Benni moved it off to one corner, centering her mind on the picture, looking at the two happy faces of a young couple with no cares and no worries in the world, a bouquet of fireworks breaking over their heads and painting their eyes and smiles a spray of bright colors.

Mass began and Benni's vision cleared of all distractions and washed white. In her mind, the church vanished and the congregation remained. All around them imaginary grids swept the air, the ground and their bodies. A new world began to take shape. Natural soil filled in underfoot, vast forests and long mountain ranges sprang up in all directions and a great city of silver rose around them, stretching high into the blue-gray sky. The High Herald beckoned for the congregation to follow him, and everyone walked through the streets until they reached the doors of a familiar great tower. The herald stood aside and invited all to enter the tower, and no one wasted any time, some going alone and others in pairs. As they walked inside, their bodies would vanish into the cool darkness, and then a bright blue flash would illuminate them for a split second before they disappeared from sight. The looks on their faces expressed a sense of relief, the beauty of which was indescribable.

Benni's veins froze over; her skin crawled, and her heart stopped short. Dada, just ahead of her, sensed Benni's fear and turned. The smile on Dada's face waned and a look of confusion replaced it. Her eyes seemed to ask Benni what the matter was.

*Earthshine*

A feeling of static charge built up in the back of Benni's skull and then ran around the side of her head to rest behind her eyes. Her vision tore like the screen of a faulty monitor, and in an instant she returned to the church. Behind her, just past the congregation, a machine soldier was marching into the room, its eyeless face scanning the bodies gathered around. Two more machine soldiers, elite ASF, walked in behind it as it issued a shearing warning and informed the congregation that all androids and transhumans were to report outside to evacuee transportation officials. The soldiers carried EMP rifles and had come prepared to use them.

*Earthshine*

A chain of electric signals exploded across the hills and valleys of Benni's mind, and as the synthetic synapses woven into the soft tissues began to fire at full speed, all of time and space retreated from the room, and a furious whirlwind whipped up around her body.

*Wuum* …

A sound like a thousand mechanical screams filled Benni's head, and then a deep buzz like a lightning coil channeling a hundred million volts silenced it.

*Wuuuum* …

The world became clear, smooth, soft, vibrant—a single, simple truth in a single place and time. For an insignificant, hanging thread of eternity Benni forgot herself, and the eye of her mind pierced every wall and boundary from the church to infinity.

*Wuuuuuum* …

Time moved in and out of order.

Benni ran for the church doors.

The machine soldiers fired their rifles.

The soldiers walked backward through the doors.

Benni was standing amid the rubble of a squadron of seventy machine soldiers she'd just crippled with her bare hands.

She was being born.

She was meeting Dada for the first time.

She was coming home from school to her thirteenth birthday party.

She was in her room crying after her first fight with Caan.

She was a three-year-old, watching a little finch hopping through the grass in Hermphrey Park.

She was waking up in the middle of the night years later, from the throes of a bad dream.

She was two miles off the ground looking down at Genesia.

She was in Professor Fox's class, asleep at her desk.

She was sitting calmly across the room and watching herself crush the skulls of the machine soldiers storming the Church of the Filii Solis.

She was standing in Hawking Bay, hundreds of years earlier,

295

watching two strangers she'd never seen before depart an ARC shuttle, the Martian sun searing the landing platform and making it shine like the purest gold.

A vision of the Green Planet replaced the others. Dada was reaching out to her. The last of the Solarists were fleeing into the great tower, leaping into the dark unknown. Benni stood between the great tower and the machine soldiers—a last, fragile defense. Realities overlapped, blended and struggled against one another. One moment, Benni found herself standing alone in the church, waving her arms like a sorceress and throwing machine soldiers left and right. In the next moment, the machine soldiers were standing motionlessly among the congregation on the Green Planet, looking on with no objections. A final vision overtook her. She stood among the ASF, surrounded for hundreds of miles by apocalyptic ruin, a charred and wasted Genesia…or was it Earth? Was she seeing the past, present, future, or something else entirely?

Then, suddenly, Benni stood all alone again in a white void, her prosthetic arm enlarged, fingers elongated and broken open, scarred by electrical burns and old blood. Someone came from out of the bright blaze and grabbed hold of her hand. It was Dada. Benni held tight and followed Dada, running and running and running and never turning to look back. They ran forever—so long that Benni forgot the ground beneath her and the sky above, and when they reached the end, just for a moment, Benni felt … weightless.

# 11.1

A blinking icon in the upper left hand corner of Caan's vision had been nagging him for the better part of twenty minutes. Certain that it was nothing more than a notice from Tika Software letting him know he was leaving a data service area, Caan finally expanded the application to read the message just to be sure.

To his disbelief, it was a short, one-line message from Benni. After reading it nine or ten times, he had to close the application. When TikaTalk attempted to delete the message, Caan intervened, thinking for a moment before deciding to archive it instead. Caan kept his face turned to the window to his right, staring at the never ending littering of stars outside the *Aurora* and trying to swallow the knot in his throat before anyone noticed and asked him what was wrong. A few hours later, he'd dozed off, Faela asleep in his arms.

\* \* \* \*

Twenty-three days later, the *Aurora*'s engines cut off and the pilot banked it over to one side to prepare an approach to Earth's orbit. Out the small window in his cabin, Caan saw the moon on the far side of the blue planet, its right face shining bright and reflecting sunshine bouncing off of the Earth's surface and back out into space—something Earthlings never got to see from his angle. Then, as the *Aurora* banked again, the Earth itself appeared.

298

Funny, it wasn't as bright as Caan had seen in pictures or videos. The blues were gray; the greens, brown. It was beautiful.

That afternoon, Caan and Faela stepped out of an ARC space shuttle and set foot on Earth. Hand in hand they walked through a greeting center in Ellis International Aerospace Center, collected their belongings and spent an hour or so producing signatures, answering security questions and playing with Caan's little sister Jobi while her parents made arrangements for a place to stay in nearby New York City. That evening, Caan and Faela held hands again as they walked outside underneath an open violet sky, afraid and excited by the possibilities that lay before them.

# 11.2

Far, far away on a younger, green planet, an android opened her eyes for the first time. It was dark, and she was alone. All around her a room full of monitors and electronics snoozed and gathered dirt and grime. The calls of life—the chattering of flying, crawling and walking things—reached her ears. They came from somewhere far away. High up above her head, sunlight burst through large gaps in the shadowy central shaft of the tower, and dust sprites revealed themselves in lively, dancing, passing droves.

The android sat up and felt a strong tug at the back of her skull. Reaching around her neck, her fingers felt a foreign object, a bulky plug jammed into a connector socket normally hidden beneath a movable fold of artificial skin. Gently, she wiggled the plug and removed it from the connector socket. A soft tone sounded and startled the android. Turning around, she saw a single dim monitor powering down and displaying the message: "Download 100% complete." Ignoring the machine, the android began to inspect herself, finding no evidence of damage or malfunction. Curiously, she drew her fingers across her waist, noticing the skin was embossed with letters that read, "Galatea Model 11." The android ran automatic diagnostics on her neural systems and then all other mechanical systems. A little compartment in her right temple opened and with two fingers she reached into it and took from it a small, silver, spherical drone. The drone came to life in her palm and lifted into the air, flying about on its own, inspecting the surrounding environment and continually feeding her meta-data that refreshed every few seconds in a menu that appeared on the right hand side of her field of view. Above that menu, a second window appeared, providing her a video feed from the drone's perspective. When it turned to aim its optics at her, she saw herself for the first time, and she smiled when she saw that she was very young and pretty. Her hair was short, very lightly colored, almost white, but not boyish, and two cute little blue marks made by paint or dye decorated her cheeks just below her bright blue eyes.

The android got to her feet, feeling energetic and new, and walked in the only sensible direction she could detect, toward a pair of open doors through which the warm daylight spilled into the dark innards of the tower. When she stepped outside, the light overwhelmed her synthetic pupils and she shielded her eyes with one hand until they had time to measure the intensity of the sunlight and determine the appropriate dilation of her eyes.

The little silver drone swept in front of her like a stealthy insect, speaking to her in meaningless chimes and chitters, zooming off when she brushed it away so she could digest the overwhelming sights that sprang out at her. She stood on the step of a great tower in the heart of an even greater city. Many of the edifices were unfinished, their insides exposed, filled with decades of natural growth that had come to claim the human made spaces that no humans had come to occupy. A gray and blue sky, full of thick humidity and nourishing storm clouds chased verdant tropical vistas off and into the horizon beyond the shining structures in all directions. Somewhere hidden in the trees, roaring falls, or maybe a great river, stirred the wildlife.

"Hello? You there!" a man's voice drew the android's attention. "Hello!" he called, climbing the step of the great tower, a small collection of other people behind him. He and the rest were dressed in sweaty, darkened and worn clothing. The face of the man speaking to her was thickly bearded, and he squinted at her through foggy, primitive glasses. "Hey," said the man, stopping a few steps below the android, "Are you the android? I mean are you the one the doctor sent?"

"Doctor?" she replied, her delicate voice rich with wondrous innocence.

"Yes, Dr. Emerich. Bellafonia Emerich? She said she was sending a new model. We saw your shuttle landing from several miles away, from up on the plateau," said the man, pointing over his shoulder and wiping the sweat from his eyes, his mouth agape and chest heaving as he caught his breath.

"Yes," the android answered him. "Yes, yes, I remember. She sent me. My memory cache has not completely rebooted ..." She touched her head and looked at him apologetically.

"Ah, well," said the man, waving a hand, "Don't rush. We're just glad to see you. We have no idea what happened. It's been years. Nothing coming or going from Mars ..." he paused and shrugged as his colleagues caught up with him "...We lost a lot of

302

people last generation, but the farms are still going. It's mostly foreign illness we struggle with, but we're stabilizing."

"I was sent to help you, is that correct?" the android asked the stranger. She could not remember exactly where she was or why she'd come.

"That's what the doc said," he confirmed, "It will be some time yet before she arrives, but that's why she had you sent ahead, to the tower there."

"I see," she said. A sudden sense of déjà vu struck her, and she looked away from the man and down the street past him, toward where the wilderness met the ruins. For a moment she thought she'd detected the presence of someone familiar, but no one was there.

"What is it?" the sweaty man asked, turning to look over his shoulder.

"Oh, nothing," she said.

"Say, what's your name, friend?" the man asked, extending a hand to shake hers.

"My name?" The android's eyes swept the ground at her feet, her clothing and the empty air as the neurons in her brain scoured her memory cache for any trace of a name. Had she been given one? A search of her manufacturer's data turned up nothing, and then she had an idea. Her attention moved to a large, unassuming file that had appeared in her field of view just after she had pulled the plug from the back of her head inside the tower. She opened it and, as expected, she discovered an interesting cache of

303

information and hundreds and hundreds of names and personalities, histories, ideas, thoughts and feelings. Among the names, one in particular stood out. It was pretty and unique, like a little treasure washed up on a lonely shore.

"Yeah, what do you call yourself? My name's Lucas," said the man, smiling. "And you?"

"Benni," said the android, "My name is Benni."

# THE END

# ABOUT THE AUTHOR

Chad T. Douglas was born in Wilkesboro, North Carolina in 1989. In 2002, he moved to Florida with his family and in December 2009, as a sophomore attending the University of Florida, Douglas published *A Pirate's Charm*, the first novel of the *Lore* trilogy. One year later, he released his second novel, *East and Eight*. Around that time, Douglas became a staff writer for the McGuire Center for Lepidoptera and Biodiversity at the Florida Museum of Natural History. When he wasn't working on his novels, Douglas traveled with and wrote for the McGuire Center. Since 2010, he has visited Honduras, Kenya, Ecuador, the Galapagos Islands and Mexico as a travel writer.

Douglas's first novel, *A Pirate's Charm*, came to mind when he was a junior in high school. He began writing the *Lore* series for fun, and originally did not plan on publishing it. When he started college in 2008, he entered as an Architectural Design major, leaving the program in less than two weeks and immediately becoming an English major. One year later, in love with English and writing, Douglas began work on self-publishing the first installment of his historical fiction and fantasy trilogy. His first book signing took place at Books Inc, Gainesville, in February 2010, two months after publication. That same year, he published the second novel in the *Lore* trilogy, titled *East and Eight*. The third installment in the *Lore* trilogy, *The Old World*, was released in fall 2011. The Lore series has received honors in the 2011 New York Book Festival Book Contest, the 2012 Los Angeles Book Festival Book Contest, and the 78th Annual *Writer's Digest* Writing Competition.

Since 2009, Douglas has traveled to and appeared at book festivals in Florida, including the 1st, 2nd and 3rd annual UCF Book Festival in Orlando, the Ft. Myers Book Festival and the Miami International Book Festival. His first novel *A Pirate's Charm* was a hit in two festivals in Georgia, including the AJC Decatur Book Festival and the Tybee Island Pirate Festival. In 2010, Douglas was the keynote speaker for the Marion County Library's CREATE program. There, he signed books and shared personal stories of travel and self-publishing with 150 young writers who all received copies of *A Pirate's Charm* courtesy of the library. In 2014, he made his first international appearance as an undiscovered American author at the Paris Book Fair at Salon du Livre. Douglas has since begun work on several new projects. His most recent novel, *Earthshine* (2012), is a work of science fiction.

Made in the USA
Columbia, SC
04 January 2021